Praise for Carolyn Haines and

Greedy Bones

"The cast is in fine form (including the helpful ghost, Jitty), and it's good to be back in Mississippi . . . One of the more entertaining episodes in the series."

—*Booklist*

"Captivating—readers will enjoy *Greedy Bones* from cranium to phalanges."

—Don Noble, Alabama Public Radio

"Jitty, Dahlia House's wonderfully wise 'haint,' [is] one of the best features of this light paranormal mystery series infused with Southern charm."

—*Publishers Weekly*

"Never undone by a ghostly spirit, a handsome movie star, or even the oddball small town Southern folks most of us will easily recognize, Delaney is at her best when unraveling multiple puzzles. Ramp up the excitement and tension, add the often chuckle-out-loud humor, and they add up to one of the best of the Sarah Booth Delaney mysteries."   —*Delta* magazine

"As usual in Haines' 'Bones' series, the latest entry is charming light entertainment; a few serious notes about biological terror and family ties add interesting depth."

—*Times-Picayune*

"An excellent 5-star read."   —Armchairreviews.com

ALSO BY CAROLYN HAINES

Wishbones

Revenant

Ham Bones

Fever Moon

Bones to Pick

Penumbra

Hallowed Bones

Crossed Bones

Splintered Bones

Buried Bones

Them Bones

My Mother's Witness

Summer of the Redeemers

Touched

Judas Burning

Greedy Bones

CAROLYN HAINES

St. Martin's Paperbacks

This is a work of fiction. All of the characters, organizations, and events portrayed in this novel are either products of the author's imagination or are used fictitiously.

GREEDY BONES

Copyright © 2009 by Carolyn Haines.
Excerpt from *Bone Appétit* copyright © 2010 by Carolyn Haines.

For information address St. Martin's Press, 175 Fifth Avenue, New York, NY 10010.

Library of Congress Catalog Card Number: 2009007913

EAN: 978-0-312-37711-3

Printed in the United States of America

Minotaur hardcover edition / July 2009
St. Martin's Paperbacks edition / July 2010

St. Martin's Paperbacks are published by St. Martin's Press, 175 Fifth Avenue, New York, NY 10010.

10 9 8 7 6 5 4 3 2 1

For Jordan Nocon and Justice Williamson,
the best of the lot

Acknowledgments

The germ of an idea for this book came during a visit to my dear friends in West Point and Starkville, Mississippi, during a book tour. Because of my deep love for and work with animals, I've always had a high regard for Mississippi State University in Starkville, where the Mississippi veterinary school is located. Amanda Lawrence, a Research Associate III at MSU who loves "sick" bugs and frisky cats, especially two named Fingers and Abby, sent me an e-mail about the potential for mayhem in the insect world.

In the twisted coils of my fevered brain, a plot was conceived. The resulting book has more to do with fantasy than reality, and Amanda has no responsibility for the liberties I took with science.

Many thanks are due to Suzann Ledbetter Ellingsworth, a good friend and a great reader. When my notion of a plague grew too biblical, she reined me in. Also many thanks to Vicki Hinze, who offered her reading skills and comments.

While writing is a solitary endeavor, a good book always reflects the intelligence and care of a great editor. Kelley Ragland fits that bill. From Jessica Rotondi in the public relations office to assistant editor Matt Martz and artist Hiro Kimura and the marketing and sales representatives, the St. Martin's team has made this book, like *Wishbones, Penumbra,* and *Fever Moon,* a great publishing experience.

Marian Young is more than an agent; she's a trusted friend and accomplice in literary endeavors, equine conspiracies, and much more.

I have to thank Joe Downs, who made a generous donation to the Birmingham, Alabama, Hand-in-Paws organization, which is devoted to helping animals and humans. At a fund-raiser for Hand-in-Paws at the Alabama Booksmith, Downs won the drawing, which included using his name as a character in this book. Many people bought a "chance" to be a character with all proceeds going to Hand-in-Paws. The generous support for animals and good works by all who participated is greatly appreciated.

I also want to thank the booksellers who have hand-sold my novels. And the many, many readers who joyfully "hook" their friends and relatives on the first book in the series—and turn them into reading addicts. Without all of you, there would be no writers.

1

Dusk is a tricky time of day in the Mississippi Delta. Pinks, mauves, and lavenders illuminate the western sky while cobalt blue creeps forward in the east. Unlike dawn, dusk is a time of ending, and I've never done well with good-byes. Even with a lover at my side, or a friend, or my gallant horse and hound, the close of a day carries a twinge of sadness.

Today, I wonder if I can find the strength to climb the front steps of Dahlia House, home of the Delaney family for nearly two hundred years.

Things are worse than even I imagined. Oscar Richmond, the husband of my partner in the Delaney Detective Agency, is dying. There seems to be nothing medical experts can do. Now real-estate agents Regina Campbell and her assistant Luann Bigley are showing the same symptoms: a fever high enough to cook a brain, chills, a rash that spreads by the minute and then erupts in draining pustules, and, finally, coma.

There is no doubt that some terrible illness has settled upon the land and the people I love. I am heartsick and scared.

"Bad times a'comin' to Zinnia, Sarah Booth."

Jitty's voice was soft and distinctly black, and I knew Dahlia House's resident haint was with me.

"If I turn around and you're wearing a robe of many colors and you say something like you're going to lead your people out of Egypt, *I'm* going to figure a way to exorcise you from this house," I warned her.

Though I would never, ever dare to let her know, I was so damn glad to hear her voice, I wanted to jump up and kiss her.

"You might consider revisitin' Sunday school. You're mixing your Bible stories. Moses led the people out of Egypt, not Joseph."

"And the walls came tumbling down." I shifted so I could take a gander at my ancestral ghost. Jitty had a tendency to skip through the decades to find costumes that flattered her latte skin and calendar-girl figure. What I saw shook me.

"Brother, can you spare a dime?" She wore tattered rags and held out a cardboard cigar box that I recognized had once held my collection of toy cowboys and horses. Dirt smudged her face, and there was a new gauntness to her high cheekbones.

"Are you sick?" Even asking caused me to leap to my feet and stride toward her. As far as I knew, ghosts didn't get sick, but my last adventure in Costa Rica had taught me that I knew almost nothing about the rules and guidelines of the Great Beyond.

"Soul-sick," she answered.

She was barefoot, her naked legs dusted with a haze of dirt. I'd honestly never seen her in such a condition. If I wore sweatpants to the corner gas station, she chewed my butt. Any slip of appearance and I put the future of the Delaney womb at risk. In other words, a potential stud might see me unadorned and be thrown off his desire to breed me on the spot.

"They run out of soap and hot water in the non-corporeal realm?" I asked, striving for a lighter note.

"I remember when the Confederate soldiers came through here, marchin' toward home after the war. Starvin', wounded, carried on by desperation. Same thing happened after the Flood of 1927. Poor folks barely hangin' on. Then again, during the Great Depression. Hardship and hard times."

Hell, if I'd been depressed earlier, Jitty now had me two steps away from finding a cotton rope in the tack room.

"Stop it." I put my hands on my hips. "This isn't doing either of us any good. We're both worried about Oscar, Regina, and Luann. I'm terrified that if Oscar dies, Tinkie will give up, too. I can't have you out here looking like a ragamuffin from a Dickens novel, spouting doom and gloom." Tears blurred my vision, which only made me angry. "Stop it, damn it."

When I blinked away the tears, Jitty was staring at me. Though she was still dirty and wearing rags, her face was rounder. The corners of her full mouth slowly tilted upward. "You know, for one second, you looked exactly like your great-great granny. You got Alice's fightin' spirit. I knew it was under all that mopin' and self-pity. I just had to find the right button to push to rouse it up."

I had been played.

On the heels of my righteous anger, though, was relief.

Jitty may have used foul means, but she'd managed to rattle me out of my maudlin mood. I was fighting mad, and that's exactly what she meant to accomplish.

"Oscar is going to be fine. Everyone is going to be fine." I swept my arm out to include the entire county. "Anything else is unacceptable."

"May I make a suggestion?"

Whenever Jitty asked permission to do anything, it always meant trouble. "No."

She grinned. "You know 'no' don't mean 'no' when you say it like that."

I leveled my gaze into hers. "If you say one word about my empty womb—"

She waved me to silence. "It's about Tinkie."

"Go ahead."

"She looks to you, Sarah Booth. You hold strong for her. Through all the hard times, you stand steady. Folks got to have that strength when they can't see the next day."

"Sage advice. The problem is how to go about it when I'm as scared as she is."

"You might crack open some of those old magazines in the attic. Once upon a time there was a man with polio who taught a nation how to hold on." Her tone had softened, and I couldn't help but wonder what of her own memories she'd stirred.

"I'm not illiterate," I said. "I know about FDR." But my words were lost on a sudden breeze that swept across the newly planted cotton fields silhouetted black against the fiery gold-peach glory of a dying day. From behind me the sound of a car approached.

Graf! Somehow Graf Milieu, my handsome lover, had managed to escape his Hollywood duties and come to stand with me. But when I turned, it was to see the tan and brown colors of the Sunflower County sheriff's cruiser pulling up at the steps. In the front seat sat the tall figure of Sheriff Coleman Peters, the man who'd broken my heart—and falsely charged me with murder.

He got out and slowly came up the steps. In the near darkness I couldn't see his face, and I was glad he couldn't see mine. In the long and complicated years of our relationship—from high school adversaries, to the initial contentiousness of my first P.I. case and, finally, to the blossoming and acknowledgment of unrequited love—we fought a strong and powerful attraction that bound us. Only recently had we accepted that love wasn't enough to overcome the obstacles in our path. Through it all, I had never dreaded seeing Coleman. Now, I couldn't breathe. My lungs constricted. Because I knew that nothing less than tragic news would bring Coleman to Dahlia House. He'd come in person to tell me that Oscar was dead. I made a small sound, seal-like, and staggered.

"Oscar is still alive, Sarah Booth." Coleman was at my side, his familiar arms easing me into one of the rocking chairs on the front porch. "I didn't come to tell you anything bad. I tried to call, but no one answered. I left messages."

I held on to one fact—Oscar was alive. At last I drew in sweet oxygen. The strength returned to my limbs. "Thank you," I managed.

"I didn't mean to scare you."

I nodded. "I shouldn't jump to conclusions." Inhaling deeply again, I asked the logical question. "What are you doing here?"

"The illness is spreading."

A swallow worked down his throat, and again my

5

brain seized. "Not Tinkie!" She'd been at the hospital since we got in from Los Angeles. But Oscar, Regina, and Luann were isolated. Tinkie hadn't been near them.

"No, not Tinkie." His voice was tired. "It's Gordon."

Gordon Walters was one of Coleman's two deputies. "But—how is he?"

"He's in the isolation ward with the others. Doc Sawyer is worried." He lifted his chin a fraction, a signal I'd learned to read as meaning he'd made a tough decision. "Sarah Booth, this could be serious. I'm going to call in the CDC and ask them for help."

The Centers for Disease Control was headquartered in Atlanta. If asked, they'd send in specially trained agents to try to find the source of the illness. "That's smart, I guess. Doc doesn't know what this is, but he isn't sure it's contagious. The isolation ward is a precaution."

"We have to determine what this is. The CDC is our best bet, I think."

Five months ago, the use of "we" would have made my heart sing. Now, though, I felt pain and sadness. My brief stint in Hollywood had changed me. Success had shown me my strengths as well as my limitations.

"Will you help?" Coleman asked.

"Don't ever doubt it. I'll do anything I can." In the gloaming of an April evening, I caught the hint of a sad smile on his face.

"I knew you would."

"I feel responsible for this. Tinkie was with me in Costa Rica and Hollywood because of my film career." When a killer destroyed all the footage of Federico Marquez's remake of *Body Heat*, my fledgling career was pretty much tanked. Tinkie would have been home in Mississippi taking care of Oscar if she hadn't been so worried about me.

"She made her own choice. It's the sixty-forty rule of life." He gazed out over the long stretch of cotton fields that were part of my land.

"Is this a Daddy's Girl rule?" Coleman was far removed from the pampered world of the DGs, but he'd grown up surrounded by them.

"Nowhere close." He was amused by my wary tone. "This is one that even you can use."

"So tell me."

"When you're a child, you make decisions that are totally, absolutely, irrevocably correct. The best an adult can hope for is sixty-forty. Sixty percent good and forty percent bad. In an adult world, it can never be one hundred percent right. Statistically impossible."

I considered this. My mind ran through my most recent actions—playing Maggie the Cat last January, going to Hollywood, sleeping with Graf. Damned if Coleman wasn't right. While my choices had been good ones, they'd all cost me something. Some had come at a high price.

"Okay, I give you the sixty-forty rule."

"Hollywood and a film career was what you needed to do. The right thing. Sure, it had a downside. But 'mostly good' is the best any of us can hope for. Sixty percent. You have that in spades, Sarah Booth."

"Thank you, Coleman." I wondered how he rated his decision not to dump his crazy, lying, conniving bitch of a wife. Oddly enough, he told me.

"Connie was a one percent moment. I chose pride and honor over love. That was one of the worst mistakes of my life. I've filed for divorce, but that's not what I came to tell you. Tinkie is still up at the hospital. She looks like she's going to drop. Doc Sawyer wants to sedate her, but she won't let him. Maybe you could talk to her. Take your buddy Cece along for muscle."

"I'll go now." But I didn't move out of the rocking chair. My body was paralyzed by the revelation that Coleman fully understood the depth of his choices. He knew. Too late, but he knew.

"I'll call you tomorrow and fill you in on everything I've discovered," he said. "I do need your help with this. The CDC should be at the courthouse tomorrow morning."

"You can count on me." Funny how only ten minutes before, I was hoping that my white knight would ride up and I would be able to rely on him.

Coleman got in the patrol car, the window down. The sweet spring breeze, tainted now in the darkness with jasmine, that saddest of all fragrances, filled the air.

"Good night, Sarah Booth," he said.

"Good night."

Tinkie stood in the hospital corridor watching her sick husband. A clear glass window separated her from Oscar's bed as effectively as an ocean. The impulse to rush forward and catch her before she keeled over was hard on me.

Before I could act on my gut feeling, Cece Dee Falcon, journalist and friend, blew by me and grabbed Tinkie's elbow.

"Tinkie, dahling, you look like caramelized shit. That would be shit dressed in an exquisite sauce, but shit nonetheless." Cece gave Tinkie her sternest look.

I hurried forward and pinched Cece as hard as I could on her taut, firm derriere. She had the unfair advantage of male molecular structure that gave her lean hips and sleek muscles. Cece, who had once been Cecil, was the society editor of the local *Zinnia Dispatch*. Against the opinion of her family, the town, and most of her friends, she had become the woman she was destined to be. I adored her.

"Don't fuss at me, Cece," Tinkie said. "I can't help it."

Never one to yield to badgering, Tinkie was at the end of her tether. She was about to collapse. I gently took her other arm. "Let's get some coffee."

She pressed her palms to the glass. "I can't leave him. I'm afraid if I do, he'll give up."

I glanced beyond her at Oscar, and my heart contracted. He lay in a bed, a ventilator pumping oxygen into his lungs. Tubes fed fluids and medication into his veins while other tubes drained things away. Sores covered his mouth and eyelids. No telling what horrors were hidden beneath the sheet.

At a slight angle were the beds of Regina Campbell and Luann Bigley. They looked equally awful. Members of their families were camped farther down the hallway.

Doc had created an isolation ward out of what had been the neonatal unit. A federal grant had built a new facility for Sunflower County babies, and this space, equipped to quarantine patients, had been empty. Until now.

As I stood there, shocked into silence by Oscar's appearance, several nurses, each wearing protective clothing, wheeled in another bed. Deputy Gordon Walters lay upon it looking already dead. His condition, if it could be judged by appearance, was more dire than Oscar's.

Tinkie stumbled, and Cece and I held her up as we battled our fears.

"You need something to eat." Cece attempted to draw Tinkie away from the window. "We'll go to the hospital waiting room. That's not three minutes away."

Tinkie shook her head. "Oscar knows I'm here. He'll know if I'm gone."

I found my cell phone. "I'll call Millie and get her to fix a plate." Millie ran the local café where we often met to discuss cases or simply to gossip. She was a big part of our close-knit group. I placed an order for chicken-fried steak, mashed potatoes and gravy, fresh green beans, and dewberry cobbler.

"Hold her up," Cece said, waving me to take Tinkie's arm. "I'll be right back." She disappeared down the hallway, her high heels efficiently smacking the linoleum tile.

"Is there any change?" I asked Tinkie.

"No. I saw Doc about four hours ago, before they found Gordon. Doc doesn't know what it is or how to treat it, but it seems that all of the victims have visited one place. An old plantation. Coleman is checking that out."

"What treatment is Doc using?"

"Oscar's on the most powerful antibiotic I.V. they have. They've tried steroids." Her fingers brushed across the glass window of the isolation ward. "Doc has consulted with specialists at Johns Hopkins. They considered transferring him, but until they can figure out what this is and how it's transmitted . . ."

I rubbed her arms. She felt cold to my touch. "Where's Chablis?" Chablis was her dustmop of a dog that long ago was the source of our friendship—and partnership in the detective agency.

"At home. Can you keep her for a few days?"

"Sure. I'll get her when I pick up your food."

"Make way, dahlings." Cece returned carrying a chair and deposited it so that Tinkie could sit and monitor the window.

"Does anyone know what happened?" I asked.

Tinkie's blue eyes were glassy with fatigue and near shock. We'd been home twelve hours, and she hadn't left the hospital hallway.

"Oscar and the bank manage the lease on the Carlisle

estate," Tinkie explained. "It's a thousand-acre plantation Erin Carlisle and her brother, Luther, own. Luther called Oscar yesterday morning and told him he had a buyer. He wanted Oscar to make sure the house and property were in good order, so Oscar rode out there and looked around."

For a long moment there were only the sounds of two nurses talking at a nearby desk. At last Tinkie spoke again. "He went back to the bank, ate lunch, and about two o'clock, Margene went in to give him some papers. That's when she found him on the floor, moaning, with those ghastly sores breaking out all over him. Doc said when Oscar got to the hospital, his temperature was . . . a hundred and five." She covered her mouth with her hand to hold back an anguished rasp.

"When did Regina and Luann get sick?" Cece asked.

"That same day. Later in the evening."

"And Gordon?"

Tinkie looked so lost. "He went out to the Carlisle place around six o'clock. From what I understand he checked the house, walked the area, then went home to change clothes. He called in for medical help from there. He was nearly unconscious by the time the paramedics got to him. The only strange thing he said was that the cotton at the Carlisle place was extremely high, like a late-August crop instead of newly planted. Oscar had told Margene the same thing."

"And Regina and Luann? Were they at the Carlisle plantation?"

"Coleman has confirmed that. They went out, hoping to list the property." Tinkie rubbed at her eyes.

"High cotton," I mused. "That would seem to be a good thing. A farmer might get two crops a year instead of one if there was a variety that developed this fast."

Tinkie fumbled in her pocket and brought out a tissue. "As far as we know, neither Oscar nor Gordon saw anything unusual except the cotton. Of course, they're not talking now."

I relayed the news about the CDC to both of them. Cece met it with a frown. "Are we positive that it's the Carlisle place that Oscar, Gordon, and the realtors have in common?"

That was an excellent question, and one that needed an immediate answer.

Cece picked up Tinkie's hand. "You're going to have to help us with this, Tink. We can't do it without you."

The blank look she gave Cece concerned me. "It doesn't matter where he got it, Cece. The only thing that matters is that he gets over it."

That wasn't my partner talking. That was exhaustion and desperation and fear. Tinkie loved Zinnia and the people of Sunflower County. She hadn't yet projected this illness to other residents. In her mind, it was contained within the walls of the hospital, within the room where her husband and three others lay dying.

"I'll get the food and Chablis," I told them.

"I'll stay here," Cece told me. "Just hurry."

2

Photographs of the movie shoot of *Body Heat* plastered the walls of Millie's Café and took me by surprise. There were pictures of me, Graf, the cast, and a number of stars who'd dropped by for a visit when Millie was on location in Costa Rica with us. One shot of Graf and me, obviously in lust and playing our roles to the hilt, made me blush.

I must have looked stunned, because everyone in the place stopped eating and turned to stare at me. When the applause started, I burned with embarrassment.

"Sarah Booth!" Millie came out from behind the counter and grasped my hands. "Our own movie star!"

"Of a movie that no one will ever see," I reminded her. All of the footage of the film I'd starred in had been destroyed by a crazed killer.

"I saw it, Sarah Booth, or at least parts of it, and I'll

never forget how great you were." She gave me another squeeze. "How's Oscar?"

I shook my head, unwilling to verbalize his condition. "And Tinkie?"

"She can't go on much longer."

"I've fixed her some food." She went behind the counter. "She has to keep her strength up."

The plastic container she handed me must have weighed two pounds. "I'll stop by there as soon as the café closes and see if she'll let me sit with Oscar for an hour or so."

"Maybe she'll listen to you."

"Likely not. She resembles you in that regard, Sarah Booth. Stubborn as a rock." She took the sting out with a wry grin. "Does Coleman have any idea what's going on?"

"Not exactly." I wasn't comfortable talking about Coleman's plans in a place bustling with customers. The fear of a serious illness could spread, which was one headache Coleman didn't need.

"You two will figure this out. Once Doc knows what's wrong with Oscar, he'll fix him right up."

Whether Millie believed that or not, she was the kind of friend who said it with conviction.

"I'll relay that to Tinkie when I deliver the food."

Millie checked to see who might be overly interested in our conversation, then leaned closer. "Luther Carlisle was in here earlier, Sarah Booth. He was meeting with a fellow in an expensive suit. The conversation got sort of heated."

My interest was piqued. "What were they talking about?" I spoke softly.

"Every time I found a reason to go close to them, they shut up."

"Have you ever seen the other man before?"

Millie considered. "No. He's not from here. He looked like money, though, and I heard someone had made Luther an offer on the Carlisle place. Might have been him."

"If he comes back in, call me."

"Sure thing." She put a hand on my arm. "I know you need to get that to Tinkie while it's hot, but I thought I'd mention the stories about the Carlisle place. There're folks who think it's cursed."

There was cursed and then there was *cursed*. "Ghost, demon, Indian burial ground? What kind of curse?"

"Mrs. Carlisle tripped on the stairs and fell to her death. Mr. Carlisle hanged himself in the old barn. Left two kids behind. Their boy, Luther, moved off the property, and their daughter, Erin, disappeared from the Delta. She went off to college and never came back. Just dropped off the face of the earth. She didn't even show up for her parents' funerals. The property's been in a trust the bank manages for the past ten years."

I did a quick calculation. Erin Carlisle would be in her late twenties, six grades behind me. Luther, I vaguely remembered from school. He was at least seven years older than me, so our paths had crossed infrequently.

"Does Luther still live in Sunflower County?"

"He does, but I can't pin down Erin. She was always a pretty girl. If I remember rightly, she disappointed her family. Went off to some art school instead of Ole Miss. Wouldn't have a debut. Sounds like someone you might have run with, doesn't she?"

"Maybe. Thanks, Millie." I leaned over and kissed her cheek. "Even if you are awful hard on me, I still adore you."

She swatted my arm as I left. I had to pick up Chablis and get some nourishment into Tinkie, but the history of

15

the Carlisle estate snagged my interest. In the South a lot of old homes get reputations as haunted, but "cursed" is a notch up the ladder. Seeing if it was warranted would be worth taking a stroll through the library archives in the morning.

Though Cece convinced Tinkie to eat, neither of us could talk her into going home. There was a strict "no dogs allowed" hospital rule, but I smuggled Chablis in, tucked into one of Oscar's sweatshirts. When the little pup looked through the window into the isolation ward and saw her daddy there, her soft cries nearly broke my resolve to be strong for Tinkie.

Chablis, who was still delicate after the attack on her in Costa Rica, put her little paws to the window and moaned.

"He's going to get well," Tinkie told the dog, holding her gently. "He has to. And Gordon, too. And the real estate ladies."

Cece had managed to finagle a cot for Tinkie, and she'd set it up smack in the middle of the hall. The hospital had prepared a room with comfortable chairs for the families of the sick, but Tinkie refused to leave the hallway.

We did get her to lie down after she ate, but she never left the window and Oscar, only six feet away clinging to life.

I had my horse and hound to feed, and with Chablis stashed in my shirt, I left the hospital. Cece would stay for the night and I'd return in the morning to take up watch with Tinkie.

Doc had done everything possible, but when I got home I opted to try some Internet research, anyway. Sweetie Pie, my loyal hound, was curled at my feet. Beside her, Chablis rested on a silk cushion. The dogs were a comfort I sorely needed as I read with growing horror the medical Web sites that spoke of gruesome illnesses with symptoms matching some of the Sunflower County victims. Thank goodness Tinkie didn't have access to a computer.

When at last I signed out, I ached all over and felt a strange nausea. Hypochondria. Reading about all those horrible diseases had made me sick.

"You need to take better care of yourself." Jitty's warm voice came from the darkened landing of the hallway. There were times when Dahlia House seemed way too big for just me and my dog. This was one of them. Jitty's company was welcome.

"I'm fine."

"You better eat somethin'. No need to worry 'bout ever' pound now that you're home from Hollywood."

"I'm not hungry." The idea of food simply wasn't appealing. "I'm too tired to eat. I'll make up for it in the morning."

"What about a glass of milk?"

"The dairy association hire you to boost sales?" I couldn't see Jitty, and I only wanted to sleep. She could pick the darndest times to harangue me about things. Normally, she didn't want me to eat. A layer of belly fat might detract from the merits of the Delaney childbearing organs.

"You got to keep up your strength, Sarah Booth. Healthy immune system and all. Don't you watch any television?"

"I'll buy some orange juice tomorrow. Remember, I've been gone. The larder is bare." I trudged into my bedroom and sensed her behind me. When I turned, I saw why food might be her major obsession. She looked like a greyhound—lean and hungry. Again she wore clothes from a desperate era. "Could you please aim for the twenties or maybe even early this century? A time of opulence and greed might be nice."

"I show up the way you need to see me."

Now that was a revelation. Unfortunately I was too weary to plumb its real meaning. "I need to see you happy and healthy. Not starved and desperate."

"You need to take care of yourself."

I shed my clothes and crawled naked beneath the covers. "Can we talk about this tomorrow?"

Jitty tapped her foot. She disapproved, but I simply didn't care. I couldn't remember ever being so exhausted.

"You can't go gettin' sick, Sarah Booth. That would be the last straw for Tinkie."

"Not to mention that it would be bad for me." I could still toss out a zinger.

"Good health is not a jokin' matter."

"I'll never go hungry again." I pulled the covers over my head in case she threw something.

"Mockin' Scarlett O'Hara won't save you."

"Tomorrow is only a day away?" I tentatively offered the line from *Annie*.

"I love the smell of napalm in the morning," Jitty said, her distant voice echoing.

Either I'd driven her away or I was tunneling into sleep so fast, not even she could catch me.

Since I came home a year and a half ago, Mrs. Kepler at the library had mellowed. Initially, she'd been suspicious of my motives and aware that as a middle schooler I'd checked out *The Wind in the Willows* and lost it. Disregard for a book didn't sit well with her, but there were extenuating circumstances in the deaths of my parents, and so she'd finally forgiven me. In recent months she'd helped me with several cases. Though she believed that rules were the fabric that held a great town together, she could occasionally bend them for someone in great need.

Tinkie was that someone.

Mrs. Kepler met me at the library at 7:00 a.m. and showed me to the old newspapers and local history section.

"I'm going down to the Pig to get some coffee," she said. "Will you be okay?"

"Couldn't be better." I pulled some money from my pocket. "Could you get me a pack of—"

"I will not buy you cigarettes. As smart as you are, you should know better than to smoke. Think of what you're doing to your lungs, to your heart, to—"

"A pack of cheese crackers," I said solemnly. "My stomach is ready to digest my backbone and I haven't had a chance to shop for food."

"Of course." She took the money and left, and I was alone with the unlimited research abilities of the library.

The Carlisle plantation had a fascinating history, as did most of the Mississippi land. It was settled by Anglo-Irishmen who came to America to escape—famine, religious persecution, economic servitude—and what difference did it make? They were escaping an unacceptable life and were willing to undertake a huge risk coming here.

The Carlisles originally settled in the Carolinas, hoping to produce tobacco. Stories of the Delta land, topsoil eight feet deep, and a nation of Choctaw and Chickasaw Indians, who were a bit friendlier than the Cherokee, drew the family to the heart of Mississippi.

The War Between the States was not even a glimmer on

19

the horizon as the Carlisles, like many other landowners, cleared the land with slaves and convict labor from the state penitentiary not fifty miles away.

Smart, hardworking, and determined, the family saw their holdings grow from a hundred acres to more than two thousand. When Mississippi gained statehood in 1817, James Carlisle became one of the first senators, a position he held for two terms. Though he retired from office, the Carlisles never completely left politics. They merely moved behind the scenes, a power at the rear of the throne. And then the war came.

Carlisle roused the state legislature in a fiery speech, pointing out that secession was not a violation of federal law but a right of statehood. At his urging, Mississippi became the second state to secede from the Union on January 9, 1861.

I skimmed through the hardships and deprivations the family endured, the names of those wounded and killed at the various battlefronts that still evoke horror and loss among old Southern families.

I came out on the other side of the war with a story of Clayton Carlisle, one of the richest planters in the South. He'd held on to half the family land through war and Reconstruction, and he'd profited.

Moving on into current history, I read the news story of Lana Carlisle's tumble down a flight of stairs. Not a week later, Gregory Carlisle hanged himself in the equipment barn. Lana's death was ruled accidental, and Gregory's a suicide, presumable because he was so bereaved by the death of his wife.

But perhaps he died by his own hand—guilty of Lana's death. Call me a cynic, but I've come to understand that people are capable of great cruelty and meanness, especially where money is involved.

Certainly this family had had its share of tragedy, and it was no wonder rumors of a curse had spread.

In Gregory's obituary, his daughter, Erin, was listed as living in Jackson. I made a mental note to look her up. Gregory's son, Luther, had opened a trailer park on the south side of town. Happy Trails. Right. After seeing the nightmare of FEMA trailer encampments on the Mississippi Gulf Coast after Katrina, I didn't have high expectations of Happy Trails.

I'd stop by and talk to Luther. Maybe he could shed some light on chemicals used on his family property. Tinkie said the bank had leased the land to Mississippi Agri-Team, a farming consortium. Lester Ballard, the head honcho at MAT, was also on my visiting list. I was curious about this cotton he'd planted that was two feet tall when most cotton was just breaking the soil.

The front door rattled, unlocking, and Mrs. Kepler walked back in, her reusable grocery bag in hand. I had to admire her. She was nearly seventy and she was doing her share to keep the planet green.

"Thank you." I gathered my notes and crackers and prepared to leave.

"Please tell Mrs. Richmond that I'm so sorry about Oscar. You know they made a significant donation to the library last year."

I had no idea. Tinkie and Oscar didn't go around bragging about their good deeds. "I'll tell her you asked about her and Oscar."

She nodded. "I wish I could do more."

"We all do." I waved good-bye, then hurried to the car and my shift to sit with Oscar at the hospital.

3

On the drive to the hospital, I phoned Graf. He had an early call to read for a new movie, a Western written and directed by the Coen brothers. The part was perfect for him, and he would bring the cowboy/reluctant gunslinger to life. I wished him luck and told him that nothing had changed in Zinnia.

"Say the word and I'll come to you," he said. "No movie role is as important as you."

"Just hearing those words is enough." It was true, even though I wanted him beside me. I was always a bit startled to realize how much I'd come to rely on Graf for support. It was knowing that I could lean on him that made all the difference. Graf couldn't change what was happening to Oscar and Tinkie, though I had no doubt he would if he could. With Graf working in Hollywood,

I could focus totally on my friend and her requirements. "If I need you, I'll pick up the phone."

"I miss you, Sarah Booth. When Oscar is well, I want to set a date for our wedding."

"You haven't officially proposed," I reminded him, though his words had set my heart to thudding.

"I'm afraid you won't accept. If I just pretend it's a fait accompli, then maybe you'll go along with it." His voice was tense.

"You have to take the risk and ask me." A deep streak of traditionalism was a sudden discovery.

"What will you say?" He sounded nervous.

"I'm not sure." I wasn't stringing him along. I simply didn't know if I wanted to be married. I loved him. Far stronger and deeper than the way I'd loved him in New York when we'd first met and fallen in love—and broken up. In recent months, Graf had shown himself to be a man of complex emotions and to have a willingness to do the right thing.

"Haven't you ever dreamed of walking down the aisle in a wedding gown?"

"Maybe when I was eight. Right before I human-sacrificed my friend's Bridal Barbie."

He laughed hard and long, and it made me love him even more.

I owed him the truth, though. "Marriage isn't a legal state that appeals to me. I don't need an official document to tell me that I love you. There seems no point to it, unless we decide to have children. Then we should be married."

"That's something we need to work on."

I loved his enthusiasm. "I agree. As soon as Oscar is well, I'll be on a plane. You'll have to clear your whole schedule just so we can practice."

"Deal."

I pulled into a parking spot at the hospital. "If anything changes, I'll phone you."

"And I'll be in touch later, because I love the sound of your voice." He blew me a kiss and hung up.

It was just eight o'clock—an hour too early to be considered civilized by most DGs—when I walked into the hospital. I'd barely gotten my foot in the door when Doc Sawyer materialized from behind a soft drink machine and grabbed my arm.

"Holy shit!" I jumped at least eight inches. "Doc, don't you have enough work without trying to give me a heart attack?"

He drew me into his office beside the emergency room. "I want to talk to you, Sarah Booth."

His expression and tone immediately settled me down. "What is it?"

"Oscar isn't getting any better."

"Not any?"

"His temperature goes down slightly, but then it rises again. There doesn't seem to be anything we can do to help him." His eyes were bloodshot; his hair, always in the mode of Albert Einstein, was bedraggled.

"What are you saying?" I swallowed.

"His body can't sustain these spikes of high temperature. He's used the last of his reserves. And the truth is, there could be brain damage from the fever. The same applies to Gordon and the two women."

I heard Doc clearly, but my brain wouldn't process what he was saying. "What about ice packs? Can we do that?" I'd seen something like that once in a movie.

"They're all on insulated pads that run cold water beneath them constantly. It isn't really helping."

"Doc," my voice cracked, "what are you saying?"

He grasped both of my arms with his strong hands. "That Oscar and the others are probably dying. You need to make plans to stay in town long enough to get Tinkie through this."

I wanted to sit, but every chair in Doc's office was covered with a textbook or some kind of papers. They all pertained to the symptoms the patients were displaying.

"Isn't there anything we can do? Some expert?"

"I've spoken with medical men who've worked the worst countries rocked by famine. This is something no one has seen, Sarah Booth. This is new. Thank God it seems contained to only people who went to that damn plantation."

"We can't give up on them." My voice squeaked.

"I'm not quitting. I'll never stop as long as there's a breath in any of them. But I had to prepare you for the worst. Tinkie will need you. She's tough as nails, but Oscar is her Achilles' heel."

I knew that better than anyone. "What could this be?"

He cleared his throat. "Impossible to say without better information."

"You're sure it came from the Carlisle place?"

Doc hesitated. "All four were there within a twenty-four-hour span."

"Is there anything else that links all four victims?"

He shook his head. "They've been too sick to tell anyone anything. After Coleman meets with the CDC, he may have some answers. How are you feeling, Sarah Booth?" Doc asked.

"Fine."

"You're a bit thin for my taste."

"In Hollywood you can never be too thin."

He gave me a crooked smile. "I'm sorry about your movie."

I gave a one-shouldered shrug. "Sometimes it seems like it never happened, that it was all just a dream."

"That's the disappointment. It's how we humans protect ourselves from loss."

Doc had been my physician since I was a small child, and his wisdom was considerable. On occasion since my parents had died, he'd been a surrogate father. "How'd you get to be so smart?"

"It's all in the coffee." He motioned toward the pot in the corner of his office. It was a standing joke because he made it so strong, it could almost walk. "Try to get Tinkie to go home. We need to run some tests on Oscar this morning, so he won't be in the ward. It'll be hard on her, staring at his empty bed."

"I'll do my best."

The cotton fields—rich soil tipped with new growth—flashed past the window of my roadster as I drove Tinkie to Hilltop, the estate she shared with Oscar. She held Chablis in her arms, and Sweetie lounged in the backseat, occasionally slurping at Tinkie's cheek with a long tongue. As it turned out, it hadn't been too difficult to get Tinkie out of the hospital. Once they wheeled Oscar away for tests, the spell broke. Tinkie nearly collapsed.

"I'll take a shower and change. Then you'll drive me back, right?"

"Absolutely." I intended to drug her with one of my sleeping pills and see that she got some rest. Doc had okayed my plan and promised he'd call me once Oscar was returned to the isolation ward. While Tinkie slept, I would sit vigil at the hospital window. Tinkie desperately needed a break. Cece said she'd stayed awake all night.

"You won't trick me, will you, Sarah Booth?" Her blue eyes held trust.

"Nope." I'd never expected to use my acting skills in this manner.

"I think he's a little better, don't you?"

"We'll know more after the tests."

She stroked Chablis and looked out the window at a land as familiar as her own face. A rare pecan grove, the new leaves so bright, they were almost painful, flashed by us. "Where are we?"

"Nearly home," I said gently. She'd lost all bearings, geographical and emotional. Hilltop was visible in the distance.

"If Oscar dies—"

"Tinkie, don't even go there." She was breaking my heart. I thought Coleman had done sufficient damage that the old ticker was impervious to serious hurt. Tinkie had found a new place to crack.

"No, listen. If he dies, I want you to promise you'll go back to Hollywood and resume your career. I don't want you hanging around Zinnia because you're worried about me."

"I hadn't given it a thought."

She confronted me. "Liar."

It was all I had to give her. "Only for my best friend." At the front door Sweetie Pie and Chablis bounded out of the car, running around the house and exploring as if they'd been gone for half a century.

Even Tinkie's footsteps, usually so perky and authoritative, were subdued. She shuffled into the house and then into the bathroom while I brewed some coffee and whipped up her favorite breakfast, made from an old family recipe. Tinkie's maid had kept the house well stocked while she was out of town.

I crept upstairs until I heard the shower, then I crushed the sleeping pill in the batter for the French toast. By the time she came downstairs, a towel wrapped around her hair, I had breakfast ready.

I handed her a cup of coffee. She smiled and traded it for the one I was drinking out of. Tinkie was exhausted but she wasn't stupid. Of course, I was foxier than doping her coffee.

Ten minutes after she'd eaten, the drug kicked in. She had time for one accusatory look before I tumbled her onto the living room sofa, made a bed for Chablis beside her, and left Sweetie Pie to guard them both.

Tinkie would be out for at least eight hours, but I had only until Doc called to say Oscar was going back to the isolation ward. While I might drug my friend, I wouldn't leave her husband without a champion.

Happy Trails trailer park was ten minutes from the hospital down a narrow private road that in my childhood had been dirt. Now it was paved. Whatever I'd anticipated with a name like Happy Trails, the place was neatly located under budding pin oaks. Oleanders bloomed in profusion around a flagstone patio that held a huge barbecue pit. Trailers and lots were neatly maintained. There was a goofy golf course, a swimming pool, and what looked to be a common area for gathering and parties. I felt transported back to the 1940s.

A tall, slender man with sharp gray eyes, a straight, aristocratic nose, and thinning hair came out to meet me. Luther Carlisle. I had no high school memories of him.

"Can I help you?" he asked, pleasantly enough.

I introduced myself. When I told him I was a friend of

Tinkie and Oscar's, he nodded, inviting me into the trailer that served as his office.

"That's a tragedy," he said, settling me into a chair in front of his desk. He had a carafe of coffee, and he served me without asking. I took the cup, noting the delicate china that was obviously a family heirloom. Luther Carlisle was a strange blend of things.

"Oscar's been very good to the Carlisle family." He gracefully held his coffee cup and saucer. "He's made certain the plantation was well managed. Mississippi Agri-Team leases the land, and while the lease is a pittance of the value of the land, MAT pays on time."

"Do you mind if I ask who wants to buy it?"

Luther cleared his throat. "Janks Development. They got a big-time plan."

"They want to build what? A planned community?"

"A staged subdivision and a shopping center. Ultimately there'll be close to five thousands homes and all the stores necessary to support it. Jimmy Janks is certain this area's about to grow. Lots of foreign interests are rebuilding the downtowns of Clarksdale and Greenwood. There's talk of some big corporations moving industry here and training a workforce. The Delta's going to shine again."

"That's less than a fifth-acre per home." I wasn't a math whiz but I was good at figuring out the economics of land rape.

"Folks don't want a lawn to maintain." He jerked his head to indicate the trailer park behind him. "No one here has time to mow or tend a lawn. I figure all of that into the lot rental fee. Why should folks spend all that time and energy on a lawn? When was the last time you saw a kid outside playing?"

He had a point. Where I'd grown up blazing trails and concocting adventures in the woods and fields, kids

29

today were wired to computers and televisions. "Did your sister agree to the sale?"

"Erin won't agree to anything, but she's not here dealing with it. I filed in court, and when I get that document, the sale will go through and her share of the money will be banked."

Luther Carlisle was a bit on the defensive side. And well he should be if he intended to sell the land out from under his sister. From what I'd learned, Erin Carlisle hadn't been seen in Sunflower County in years, but to force a sale was extreme.

"Has Erin left the States?" I lobbed out a test.

Outside, a pickup truck, radio blaring, eased past. "No."

"Did you hire someone to look for her?"

"No."

"Do you have any idea where she might be?" He didn't want to find her.

"My lawyer's taking care of all these details. Far as I know, she may be dead."

"I need to speak with her. Where is she?"

He took a breath, and I could tell he was weighing his response. "She doesn't answer her mail or return my calls. My lawyer says I can file to move forward on the land sale. It'll be settled in the courts. I'm not doing anything illegal."

I crossed a leg. It wasn't the first time one sibling tried to roll over another where land or money was involved. But if Erin truly wanted to know what Luther was up to, she could easily find out. "How old was Erin when she left your parents' home?"

"She'd graduated high school. My parents were devastated by the whole ugly mess. Erin never thought of anyone but herself."

He was more than willing to talk about old family scandals—if it painted his sister in a bad light—and I was ready to listen. "What was the problem with Erin?"

"For one thing, she refused a full scholarship to Ole Miss. She was a heritage Zeta Zeta Phi, and she told Mother she'd rather live on the streets than pledge to that sorority. Or any sorority."

"That hardly sounds like a reason for a family split."

"It broke Mother's heart. She gave up her home and family to live here in Sunflower County. Zeta Zeta was her sisterhood, and Erin acted like it was some kind of cult."

I had personal experience in this area. "Maybe she simply wasn't a sorority girl. Surely that's not a reason to disown a daughter."

He watched me carefully. "Oh, the sorority thing was the proverbial straw. The real trouble came when she told Mother that Father was screwing the maid." His mouth compressed into a thin line, and anger sparked in his eyes. "She inflicted a lot of pain on the family. She destroyed us." He cleared his throat. "They both threw her out and told her never to come back."

"Was your father having an affair?"

He looked out the window as another vehicle passed. "I never asked. Wasn't my business to meddle in my parents' marriage. All I know is what Erin did hurt them both."

The story was odd six ways from Sunday. Although the rumors of murder and mishap were still floating around the Carlisle family years after the fact, Luther expressed disinterest in a possible love triangle, the accusation of which he said had destroyed his family. Tinkie, when she woke up, would be a better guide into the crazed conduct of high society. She could explain how a woman would toss out her daughter instead of her cheating husband.

"This developer you're working with. Jimmy Janks. He isn't local, is he?" I knew most of the builders around Sunflower County, but a project this big would require some high-dollar funding.

"Janks Development is an Alabama concern. Did a lot of building along the Gulf Coast. Condos, malls, that kind of thing. Jimmy Janks is highly qualified."

That remained to be seen. I changed directions, hoping to throw him off. "Why don't you live at the plantation, Luther?"

His face showed no emotion. "I prefer it here."

"Can you tell me why?"

"Too many hard memories, Miss Delaney. Imagine living in a place where your mother fell to her death and your father hanged himself." Whatever he felt, he didn't show any emotion. "Perhaps you were out of Sunflower County at the time of Mother's death. Some people thought my father pushed her down the stairs. They felt that guilt drove him to suicide. There's not a room in that house that doesn't hold some painful reminder of the way things used to be and how they ended up. Who wants to live with that?"

I could sympathize, but the whole thing didn't smell right. "Do you have sentimental attachment to the place?"

"I miss the house," he continued. "I miss those crisp mornings when Cook served us all breakfast together. Erin was young then. My parents were happy. I loved the farm and going out with Father to make sure the fields were in good shape and the crops coming along. I still dream about those days. But they're gone. Trying to cling to a fading memory won't change what's happening all around us, Miss Delaney. Progress can't be stopped. You can't run fast enough to stay ahead of it. Try, and you'll be crushed. This development deal is good for me and for Erin. Taxes are going up, the cost of farming is out the roof. It's time to let go of the past and step into the future. This is best for Erin, too, whether she agrees or not."

My cell phone rang, producing a ripple of relief. Luther was not a scary man, but his worldview was pessimistic to the extreme. I was about ready for a drink and it wasn't even ten o'clock in the morning.

"Oscar's headed back to the room," Doc said.

"Did you find anything?" A glimmer of hope would be welcomed.

"No." Doc's voice said it all.

"I'm on my way." I hung up and moved to my last question. "The cotton on your land is unusually mature. What do you know about that?"

"Nothing. As I said, Mississippi Agri-Team manages the crops on it. You got a question about that, take it up with them."

I thanked Luther for his time and lead-footed it to the hospital.

4

Tinkie and her father showed up late that afternoon. At first she was too angry to speak to me for sending the chemical sandman to visit, but when she realized that Oscar was no worse—and the nurses told her how I'd stood at the window, willing Oscar to heal—her anger broke.

"He's better, isn't he, Daddy?" Tinkie looked up at her father, and I could imagine her through the years of her childhood turning to him in that same way, asking for his reassurance. Tinkie loved her mom, but Mr. Bellcase was the end-all of her childhood universe.

"Oscar's a strong-willed man." Avery Bellcase patted Tinkie's hand. "He has every reason to live. He has you. No man in his right mind would leave that behind."

Tinkie at last included me in the conversation. "What did the tests show?"

"Doc hasn't said anything specific. He was waiting for you to return." For all that she'd gotten furious at me for tricking her, she looked better. The sleep had taken the gray tones out of her skin.

"Have you found out what this illness is?" She'd pinned her hopes on me and my investigative skills, and I felt the weight on my shoulders increase. Tinkie had saved me more times than I could count. I had to find an answer.

"A few things." I didn't want to mislead her. "We'll talk when I have a chance to check them out."

She grasped my shoulders. "Promise me you won't go to the Carlisle place. If that's the source of this illness, it's too dangerous."

"Someone has to look." I meant to be logical, not argumentative.

"The CDC will bring hazmat suits. Let them go, Sarah Booth. Promise me."

I couldn't imagine that stepping on a piece of property could bring personal destruction, but the Carlisle place did appear to be the epicenter of this disaster. "I won't take any unnecessary risks. I promise."

Mr. Bellcase watched the scene play out. With a tilt of his head, he indicated that he wanted to speak with me.

"I have to meet with Coleman and the CDC," I told her.

Mr. Bellcase kissed Tinkie's cheek. "And I'm needed at the bank. Your mother will take over for a few hours. Remember, you gave your word you'd leave."

Tinkie nodded, the façade of the obedient daughter perfectly in place. "I will, Daddy."

"I love you, Tinkie," he said.

"Me too."

I fell into step beside him as we walked down the sterile corridor.

"I've never approved of Tinkie's work with you," he said, "but she believes you can resolve this."

The problem was that I wasn't certain I could without Tinkie's help. We were truly partners—in the P.I. agency and in so many other ways. We worked as a team. Tinkie had a skill-set I didn't. Our cases often required both of our abilities.

"I'll do my best, sir."

"I know you walked away from a Hollywood career to be here with her." He faced me. "That won't be forgotten."

"Tinkie is my friend. She'd do the same for me, sir."

"If you need our help, the bank's resources are at your disposal."

"I need to find Erin Carlisle. The bank must have some address on her. It would be quicker than trying a computer search."

"Harold will get that information. Call him."

"Thank you."

We parted in the parking lot, and I watched Mr. Bellcase drive away. He was in the worst position possible—forced to watch his daughter suffer and unable to do a thing to stop it.

Coleman's office door was open, and a new dispatcher greeted me with a smile. "He's been waiting for you," she said, ushering me through the main office. It was strange not to see Gordon sitting at his desk.

"Sarah Booth."

Coleman's deep voice drew my attention to the far corner of his office, where he stood beside a man who was a twin for Omar Sharif in his younger days. "This is

Peyton Fidellas, an expert in airborne diseases and chemical reactions—"

"I've heard about your investigations and your film," Peyton said. "It's a pleasure to meet you."

Coleman motioned to a woman on the far side of the man. "And Bonnie Louise McRae, whose specialty is parasitic life-cycle development. They're with the Epidemic Intelligence Services of the Centers for Disease Control. Sarah Booth is—"

"I know Sarah Booth," the woman said. "She was always in trouble for skipping school and running wild."

I hadn't really noticed her, a serious oversight on my part. Where Peyton was darkly handsome, European exotic, and charming, Bonnie was California blond with a sharp arrogance and a body any starlet would kill to possess. She was walking va-va-voom. I looked her up and down. "Sorry, but I'm sure I'd recognize you if we'd met before."

"Try high school. Freshman year. I didn't graduate in Sunflower County. I decided an education was important."

I was beginning to think I'd forgotten Bonnie Louise McRae on purpose. "I'm sorry, Miss McRae, I don't remember you."

"Not a surprise. I wasn't in the popular set. My family farmed six hundred acres up in the north of the county." She stared at me as if I should instantly be able to conjure a map and pinpoint the axis of her birth, life, and departure.

Coleman cleared his throat. "Peyton and Ms. McRae will investigate the Carlisle place, which is ground zero for our investigation. Did you learn anything new from Tinkie?"

"No." I started to tell him about Luther, but for some reason I was reluctant to talk in front of the EIS agents.

Maybe it was because they were government and I had an inherent distrust of federal agencies. Maybe coming back to Sunflower County after a stint in Hollywood, I wanted to close the borders and exclude all outsiders. Or maybe it was because Bonnie Louise McRae came across as a bitch on wheels. Whatever the reason, I kept my lip zipped. I didn't have my partner to back me up if the situation deteriorated to a good old-fashioned hair-pulling.

"Is there an office we can use?" Bonnie asked Coleman.

"The county health department will let you have the back half of their building. It's beside the hospital, so that should prove convenient, I hope."

"Isn't there some place closer to the sheriff's office?" Bonnie asked.

"There's always the jail." Karo syrup had nothing on me. "That space would serve perfectly."

"Four people's lives are on the line here." Coleman cast me a warning glance. "Doc Sawyer is waiting at the hospital to talk with you," he told the EIS agents. "I'll be there in half an hour. I need to check on something."

As Coleman left the room, Bonnie Louise fell into step beside him. She linked her arm through his and simpered up at him, batting her eyelashes and swinging her butt like she'd broken a hitch in her get-along.

It was inevitable that Coleman would find another girl, especially in light of his impending divorce. But plainly put, Bonnie Louise McRae set my teeth on edge. Any involvement with her would be a repeat of his calamitous marriage to Connie.

My cell phone buzzed, and I answered it as I followed Peyton out.

"Sarah Booth, it's Harold Erkwell."

I would have recognized the banker's cultured voice,

but Harold didn't play telephone-guessing games. "How are you doing, Harold?"

"Worried. I've been at the bank a long time, and I don't ever recall Oscar missing a day of work. We're all in shock here."

"Me too."

"Mr. Bellcase is beside himself. He rushes into the bank, spins around, and runs out. Oscar's like a son to him, and he's terrified for Tinkie."

"I know." My mood sank a little lower.

"I have an address on Erin Carlisle. She's a photographer. A pretty good one, from all accounts. Does the carriage trade in portraits and photographs of important people."

"Was she difficult to locate?"

Harold laughed. "Not in the least. Luther knows exactly where she lives. Erin is opposed to selling the land for development. In fact, she's blocked a sale before. Luther is trying to slide this past her."

Goes to show that just because a man has bone china coffee cups in a trailer, he doesn't always have high morals.

Harold gave me her address and phone number. "Erin is . . . difficult. She's angry, and she takes it out on this county and the people who live here."

"How do you mean?"

"When her mom died, neither Luther nor her father let her know. Someone from the funeral home finally took pity and called her. She arrived just in time to see the casket going into the hearse for transport. She's never forgiven the people here. She felt, rightly so, that someone should have notified her."

"That's awful. Luther told me a lot of stuff, but he

acted like Erin's refusal to join a sorority was a big deal."

Harold hesitated. "Lana Entrekin Carlisle was a fifth-generation Zeta Zeta. Her ancestor was one of the founders. ZZ is *the* sorority at Ole Miss. Haven't you seen the billboards set up along the highways during rush?"

"I've seen them." I had indeed. Mortified described my reaction. The billboards listed a toll-free *suicide* hotline for girls who weren't offered bids for this sorority. "A tad extreme, wouldn't you say?"

"Erin was a heritage candidate. She was a shoo-in."

"Jesus, Harold, this is a sorority you're talking about, not membership to The Rapture."

"Social connections are often more important than any academic degree."

I couldn't argue that. Too often, life has nothing to do with merit and too much to do with contacts.

"Still and all, to cut her out of the family seems a bit extreme. I mean, she could have married a first cousin and produced a child with twelve fingers. That might have been a reason to kick her out. But a sorority?" I couldn't let it go.

Harold wisely ignored me. "Call her. She can fill you in on details I'm not privy to. The bank deals with Luther, but she gets a copy of everything."

"Thanks, but I have another question."

"No, my lust for you hasn't waned. Those photographs from Hollywood have only made me want you more."

Harold delighted me, even when he was being outrageous. He'd once proposed, but our friendship had recovered from that hurdle. "You know Jitty thinks I should marry—" I stopped dead. Jitty was Harold's strongest proponent. She viewed him as the perfect donor of sperm and the best potential partner for marriage. But I didn't need to tell him that.

"Who's Jitty?" he asked.

"Oh, a friend."

"From Zinnia?"

I was stumped for an answer. "Sort of."

"How are you 'sort of' from a place? Either you are or you aren't."

"She lived here once but doesn't now." I outdid myself with cleverness.

"Have I met her?"

"What is this? Sixty questions? She's a friend. Case closed. Saving Oscar is the focus."

"You're right. We can explore tomfoolery at another time."

"I'll contact Erin and let you know what I find out."

"Anything else?"

"Lana Carlisle. Did she trip and fall down the stairs, or did she have some help?"

Harold hesitated. "The death was ruled accidental. But there was gossip. A lot of it. Especially since the funeral was held so fast and Erin wasn't notified."

"Talk that Mr. Carlisle killed his wife?" I was remembering what Luther had said about Erin tattling about an affair. High emotions sometimes led to rash actions.

"That either Mr. Carlisle or Luther killed her."

Now that shocked me. "Luther was a suspect in his mother's death?"

"And his father's."

"Holy cow. Was there an investigation?"

"That was before Coleman became sheriff, so things weren't always done by the book. As you recall, there were some issues with our former sheriff."

"Thanks for the heads up, Harold."

"Glad to help. Call me if you need anything. I'm stopping by the hospital when I get off work."

"Cece and I will be by there as soon as we can. I think I'm going to make a quick trip to Jackson."

"Good luck, Sarah Booth." He dropped his voice a notch. "I can't wait to meet this Jitty person."

"Sure thing." Now I'd jumped on the gut wagon with a one-eyed dog. Before long, I just might have to feed him.

5

Image Photography was located on the north side of Jackson, Mississippi, in the Ridgeland area. I found the studio with ease and noted the parked Lexus and Mercedes crossovers and one vintage, baby-blue Nissan that obviously belonged to someone with excellent taste. I parked my antique Mercedes roadster that had been my mother's pride and joy next to it.

For fifteen minutes I watched the studio, taking the temperature of the clientele and what Erin Carlisle had given up an inheritance of land and comfort to pursue.

While I waited, I got the number for Mississippi Agri-Team in Yazoo City, Mississippi. My plan was to stop by there and speak with Lester Ballard, until a receptionist at the company told me he was out of the country.

"May I speak with someone about the cotton crop on the Carlisle plantation land?" I asked.

"I'm sorry, only Mr. Ballard can talk with you. He handles that property."

Across the parking lot, a mom came out of the photography studio with twin boys about five years old, dressed in suits and ties. The boys were miserable, tugging at their clothes. The woman looked like she'd stepped from a fashion magazine.

"When will Mr. Ballard return?" I asked, still watching the studio's front door.

"He should have been back yesterday, but there was a delay."

Another woman with a lovely young girl departed the photographer's. The child's white dress imitated a Victorian design. This girl was in hog heaven in her finery. She pirouetted on the sidewalk and then slipped into the passenger side of a Bentley.

"Where did you say Mr. Ballard had gone?" I asked.

"I didn't say. Shall I have him call when he returns?"

"Please." I gave her the contact information and got out of my car as another client exited the studio and got into a BMW convertible.

I strolled up to the storefront and examined some of the photographs on display. These were not graduation pictures or images of happy moments caught on film. These were portraits, as in the kind that brought to mind great painters. Art with a capital A. They had the quality of a painting in the use of light, texture, composition—a richness normally not captured by a camera.

Whatever else could be said, Image Photography had a clientele with taste. Erin had managed a career that blended art and commerce.

If I had a child, Image Photography is where I'd want her portrait taken.

Hoping the coast was clear and no additional clients lurked inside, I walked in and stopped at the reception desk. A young woman with dark-framed glasses angled stark against her pale skin looked up at me. "May I help you?"

"Erin Carlisle, please."

"She's in the darkroom and can't be disturbed."

"I'll wait." I took a seat in one of the chairs. Several magazines were spread on a coffee table and I selected one and began to read about vacations in the Eastern bloc and why they were such good bargains.

The receptionist watched me with discomfort but returned to her work.

Twenty minutes later, I'd skimmed through a series of articles on places to avoid in the way of restaurants, hotels, transportation, and travel guides. An itch of irritation, plus the sense that I should be back in Zinnia with Tinkie, made me snappish.

"Would you ask Ms. Carlisle when she'll be available to see me?" I asked.

"May I tell Erin why you're here?" the young woman countered.

I nodded agreeably, controlling my urge to point out that she could have asked that question half an hour sooner. "Certainly. I'm here to talk about her family estate in Sunflower County. I'm not going back to Zinnia until I do."

The girl's expression went blank. "I'll tell her." She got up immediately. She was gone about five minutes, returned to her desk without a word, and began phoning clients to set up appointments for the next week.

Footsteps sounded coming my way. I was looking at the door when Erin Carlisle stepped through it. She was striking, with honey-blond hair, blue eyes, and classic features. "What do you want?" she asked.

She wasn't friendly, but then I didn't need to be her BFF. "Can we talk privately?"

She waved me to follow her through a sitting area with several sets and into an office in the back. Leather sofa, plush carpeting, well appointed. Classy, just like Erin.

She put her hands on her hips. "What?"

"Four people who visited the Carlisle estate—your family property—have become seriously ill. They may die." I thought that would take the wind out of her sails, but her mouth only hardened.

"Over a decade ago, two people *did* die there," she said. "My mother and my father. And no one would do a damn thing about either of those murders. Why should I get worked up over the fate of some strangers who coincidentally got sick?"

"I don't believe it's coincidental."

"Are you suggesting someone on my property concocted an illness and is spreading it in the hopes of murdering your friends?"

" 'Murder' isn't a word to use carelessly," I warned her, but gauging her tight jaw, my advice held no weight.

"When someone deliberately takes another's life, premeditated, for personal gain, I'd say that's murder, wouldn't you?"

I nodded. "By definition, yes. Are you talking about your parents?"

"My mother was pushed down the stairs, and then my father was hanged. A murderer is roaming free and still trying to swindle me out of my share of the estate." She didn't mince her words.

"You think your brother is a murderer?"

46

"Perhaps a serial killer. Isn't that what you call someone who kills more than once?"

I didn't intend to banter psychopathic definitions with her. She was furious, and she was looking for revenge against her brother.

"Do you honestly believe Luther killed your mother and father? His own parents?"

She sat on the edge of the desk. "Luther is capable of almost anything."

I had the clearest memory of him sitting behind his desk in the trailer and sipping hot coffee from a delicate china cup. He'd been immaculately groomed, dressed in razor-creased Dockers and a crisp white shirt. He'd also been angry, though he'd covered it better than his sister. "Is he the reason you left Sunflower County and won't come back?"

She thought about it. "I loved that land and that farm with my whole heart. I had dreams for growing new crops, things that wouldn't deplete the land and would help the environment. I spoke out about something that made my parents so angry that with a bit of prodding from Luther, they threw me out. It was the best thing that ever happened to me. It forced me to work hard and build my business. I struggled and got better and better. I've built my future here."

She was talented, no doubt about it. But while she might avow the destruction of her roots, she was far from unattached to Sunflower County. "The official verdict on your mother's death was accidental."

Shaking her head, she stood. "I don't believe that. She was in perfect health. No bad heart or weakness or dizziness or anything. She didn't fall. She was pushed, and if the sheriff had been worth a damn, he would have found out who did it."

I couldn't defend Coleman's predecessors. "There were two people in the house. Not just one."

She cracked the knuckles of her long, elegant fingers. "My father and my brother."

"What if your father did it?" I asked. "Was there a big insurance policy?"

"Half a million dollars for accidental death. The policy was less than a year old. My father was the beneficiary. Trust me, he didn't kill Mom and then kill himself out of guilt and remorse." She laughed. "Not a chance. My father didn't know the meaning of the word 'remorse.' He would have spent that money and enjoyed every second doing it. Look, I'm sure my mother was murdered, but I'm doubly positive my dad was."

"Did you have Luther investigated?"

She looked at me as if a large zit had popped up in the center of my forehead. "Waste of time and money. Luther is smart. He fooled the coroner and the sheriff, but he can't fool me. You tell him that when you see him. And tell him that as executor of the estate, I'll tie it up as long as I want to. I know what he's up to, and I'll never sell to a developer. That land has been in the family since before Mississippi was a state, and he's not going to cover it in asphalt and shitty look-alike homes for soulless families who produce no-neck little brats."

Whew! Erin was passionate about the land. "Look, Ms. Carlisle, I'm not certain how your family plantation figures into all of this, but four people who went there are seriously sick. The CDC has been called in. There's something else very peculiar. The cotton there is two feet tall, much more developed than any other fields in the Delta. This leads me to believe something suspicious is going on."

"I wouldn't put it past Luther to do something to de-value my land for agricultural purposes. He wants to force a sell, and if no one would lease the land, I'd have to sell it to pay the taxes."

I noted again the use of the possessive, as if Luther had no share.

"Let me get something straight. Your father inherited your mother's insurance. Who inherited when your father died?"

Her only reaction was a deep inhalation. "I don't have time for this. Look, you have my permission to go inspect the land and house. There's a trust. Luther and I are equal partners in the land. If Luther says anything, tell him I know what he's been up to and I'm going to make him pay." She didn't hold back on threats.

"I've already spoken with Luther, and he seemed concerned about what's happening in Sunflower County."

She tapped a thick silver ring on her left hand against the fine wood of her desk. "I'll bet he cried huge ole crocodile tears, too. Pretended to be so concerned for his fellow citizens. Don't buy it. Luther cares about Luther. That's it."

"What did your brother get out of killing your parents?"

"Not what he expected, that's for sure." She pushed off the desk and paced across the room to a huge filing cabinet. Digging through a drawer, she kept talking. "He thought I was still estranged from Mom. He thought he'd permanently destroyed our relationship, but she and I had come to an understanding."

She pulled a large, heavy sheet of paper from the drawer and handed it to me. To my surprise, it was a lovely picture of a middle-aged woman who looked a lot like Erin. Lana

Entrekin Carlisle had retained her beauty, but there was no escaping the sadness she'd also endured. It was written in her eyes.

"This was taken only a week before she fell. And that bastard Luther didn't even call and tell me she was dead. I missed her funeral. When I finally got there, they were putting the casket in the hearse for transport to West Point."

"Your father could have called."

She made a sound of disgust. "Could have and didn't. He was furious that mother had changed the will, I'm sure. He thought he'd get the land back."

Now that was a point of curiosity. "How had the Carlisle land come into the hands of someone who married into the family?" I asked.

"Father made some really bad decisions in the seventies. He borrowed money at a high interest rate, then nearly defaulted on the loans. He'd put the land up as collateral."

Harold hadn't mentioned this to me, and it seemed that he would have. "The Bank of Zinnia held the mortgage?"

"My father did his business with a bank in Chicago. He liked going to the Windy City as a Southern plantation owner. I guess they saw him coming a mile away." She twisted the ring.

"So your mom bailed him out?"

"Exactly. And the land was transferred to her name. She was a far better businessman than my father ever dreamed of being."

"So when you breached the wall between the two of you, she changed her will."

"That's correct. She recognized how much I loved the place and I was returned as coexecutor of the trust." Erin was seemingly unaware that that action gave her and her brother equal motives for murder.

"Say Luther killed your mother before he found out about the new will, why would he kill your father?"

"Half a million in Mother's insurance policy. Had he not stopped my father, he would have run through it just as he squandered the Carlisle money. Luther wasn't about to let that happen."

"Do you know what your father spent money on?"

"Unfortunately not, nor do I care. Now you need to go. I have a sitting in two minutes."

She stood at the door waiting for me to exit her office. When I did, she followed me to the reception area.

"I've told you everything I know, Ms. Delaney. Everything. Don't waste your time or mine by coming back."

She left the room, and her office door closed. The young woman at the reception desk busied herself writing something down. She ignored me as I left.

Along with the cot, Cece had also managed to smuggle a recliner and a few other homey touches into the hospital for Tinkie. The families of the other sick people had left for a few hours, and I found my partner tilted back, her eyes closed, an OttLite reading lamp on beside her, and Mary Saum's latest book sprawled across her lap. Tinkie had aged in the last week.

I tiptoed to the window where I could view Oscar, Gordon, and the women. They were all four lined up, and it struck me that forty years ago, or less, they'd all been in a hospital nursery in tiny bassinets, arranged before another window for their parents to look on with pride. It just about broke my heart to think of the joy the earlier scene had provoked. Now, despair was the overriding emotion.

Gordon had no real family to watch over him, so I

concentrated on him for a while. His chest barely moved as the ventilator pushed oxygen into his lungs. The sores that covered his face and neck and arms—which was all I could see exposed above the sheet—had begun to scab over. Was the absence of fresh ones a good sign? I had to believe it.

Two hazmat-suited nurses entered the isolation ward and began a check of vitals and the administration of some clear fluid into the drips that ran into the arms of each patient. As I watched the process, I realized Regina and Luann had fewer sores and better color. They were on ventilators, but they seemed, somehow, more alive.

My attention turned to Oscar.

"Doc says he may not wake from the coma."

I spun around to find Tinkie in the same pose, but her eyes were wide open.

"Doc has never been accused of being an optimist. Tinkie, he has to tell you the worse-case scenario. He's like an older relative. He doesn't want to lead us to believe—" Where the hell was I going with this? No place Tinkie needed to follow.

"To believe in a miracle," she finished softly. "But I do, Sarah Booth. I've had my own miracle."

"You did indeed." Whatever happened to her breast lump—whether a piece of scar tissue, a bruise, a fibroid, or a cancer—it was gone. That was miracle enough for me to cling to for now.

"Have you found anything?"

"A lot of drama in the Carlisle family, but nothing solid enough to report."

"You will."

Her faith in me was humbling. "I'll try. That's for sure. Tinkie, can I take you home for a bit?" I knew the answer already.

She shook her head. "Mother will relieve me in a while. You hunt for clues. I'm fine. I want to be here when Oscar wakes up."

"Chablis and Sweetie are having a blast, but your baby misses the two of you."

"We'll be home soon." She picked up her book. "I think I'll read for a while longer. This keeps me from thinking about Oscar too much."

I bent and kissed her forehead. "I'm going to check with Coleman and see if the EIS agents found anything at the Carlisle estate."

"You'll call me?"

"You don't even have to ask."

6

When I pulled up beneath one of the budding white oaks that lined the courthouse square, I realized that news of the strange illness had broken with the media. Cece had honored her word and kept mum about it, but news vans from regional television stations in Memphis, Jackson, and Atlanta cluttered the public parking spaces.

The source of the leak could have been anyone in the hospital or the bank, and it was bound to happen. It was incongruous, though, to see the gathering storm of media on a day that had been gifted by the gods. The courthouse lawn was a riot of color, from the fuchsia-hued azaleas to the yellow, purple, and red flower beds that local gardening clubs tended.

Johnny Reb stood guard over the growing crowd, a bronzed soldier walking from the past into the present. As I passed the statue, I thought with a pang of the wonderful days I'd spent with my father in the courthouse. Protected and adored, I'd never considered that an accident or illness could steal the ones I loved. Now I knew how vulnerable we all were.

"Ms. Delaney, may I speak with you?" Peyton Fidellas emerged from behind one of the huge white pillars that supported the second-floor balcony.

"Have you discovered something?" I asked.

He looked past me at the crowd gathering on the steps. "The sheriff and Bonnie Louise are holding a press conference here in five minutes. Could we find a more private place?"

"Sure." I was curious why Peyton wasn't participating in the news orgy. Most people loved their fifteen minutes of glory in front of a television camera.

We went to the back vault of the chancery clerk's office, a place of old records and a few research tables—all vacant—because the courthouse offices had emptied to hear the press conference.

Certain that we were alone, I asked, "Did Bonnie Louise cut you out of the limelight?"

He shook his head. "I'm a scientist far happier running lab tests. I'm not interested in television interviews. Truthfully, she didn't want to do it, either, but I pulled rank on her. She's a good-looking woman, so she'll play well on the screen. When she realized she'd be standing beside the sheriff, she didn't object too much. She's taken more than a passing fancy to him. Beaucoup has noted that the sheriff's wife is AWOL."

"Beaucoup?" I couldn't help myself. Normally slang for "lots of," what did it mean in Bonnie's case?

"I gave her the nickname," he said, his smile charming. "Bonnie comes across a bit sour, but she's loaded with talent and smarts. I'm surprised, though, that she's interested in a married man. Beaucoup is normally by the book."

It wasn't my business to tell Peyton that Coleman had filed for divorce. "Did you want to tell me what you found?"

"I've spoken to the sheriff, and he made it clear that I should share this information with you."

My heart thudded. "What is it?"

"First of all, there's an issue with the cotton. It's a genetically engineered strand that allows for two growing seasons. The rapid growth is phenomenal. The cotton at the Carlisle place is nearing maturity."

Faster growing cotton wasn't so awful. Or was it? "You said genetically engineered—is that the problem? Were you able to reach Lester Ballard, the guy who manages the agricultural lease on the land?" The CDC might accomplish what I could not.

"Ballard is out of the country, and I've turned the search for him over to the sheriff. As to the genetically altered cotton, it's experimental but not dangerous, as far as I can tell. Were it not for the other problems at the Carlisle estate, the cotton could be harvested in a month, six weeks at most. But that's moot because of what's happening now."

"And that is?" I asked. Peyton's demeanor let me know this was serious.

"Boll weevils."

I thought he was joking. Boll weevils were a type of beetle that devastated the cotton crop from Texas to the Atlantic Ocean in the 1920s. The insect had been brought under control by effective methods of sterilization, improved species of cotton, cyclical planting, and some use of pesticides.

"Come on, Peyton, boll weevils?"

"In two days they've eaten the cotton plants at the Carlisle estate. Whole sections are stripped bare of leaves, Sarah Booth. This is devastating. The weevils are gnawing it to the ground. It's like a scourge."

I wasn't an authority on farming, but I did lease out the land around Dahlia House. Last time I'd looked, there was no sign of weevils on my property.

But every Delta child knew horror stories of the vermin that had destroyed an industry, an economy, and a way of life until they were brought under control.

"Weevils don't show until later on in the summer. If they eat the plants now, there's no place to hatch their young and . . ." I wasn't telling him anything he didn't know.

"Trust me. I'm as puzzled as you. These weevils aren't typical. They have a strange green color to them, almost like a pine beetle."

"How does this fit into what's wrong with Oscar and the others? Doc would have noticed if any of them were bitten by insects." I was having trouble connecting the dots.

"I'm not sure the weevils play a role in what's happening with Mr. Richmond and the other patients, but I am concerned. Times are tough enough for farmers. This could mean economic devastation for some of the last large landowners."

Clearly I could see why. But a cotton crop could be replanted. Oscar and Gordon and the women might die. There would be no replacing them in the hearts of their families.

"What will you do?"

"We've collected some samples. Beaucoup is the authority on weevils. She'll take them up to Mississippi State University at Starkville. It's the best facility in the nation for this kind of study and she also has a contact with one of the world authorities on insects that affect farm crops."

"What about Oscar and Gordon and—"

"We're still working on that. We'll begin testing the water tomorrow. There's a chance they drank from a tainted well."

Waterborne microbes fell under Peyton's expertise. He was new to the CDC, but Coleman had been impressed by Peyton's research background. "If that were the case, you guys wouldn't be in Sunflower County," I pointed out to him.

"I don't have the answers you want."

"That's not going to reassure anyone. If people perceive this as something that could spread, a panic will result."

"That's why we're holding a press conference. Sheriff Peters will give the facts, and Beaucoup will explain the basic science. This problem is contained to that single plantation. While it is potentially serious, we're on top of it."

"Would it be possible for me to go to the estate myself?"

His dark eyebrows arched in amusement. "You don't trust us to do our job?"

"My best friend's husband may die. I can't leave anything to chance. I would never forgive myself."

He shook his head. "Until we're certain that whatever is out there isn't airborne, I can't let you go. We've quietly quarantined the plantation. Several local farmers are helping us turn people away from the area. Luckily, the land is on a private road."

"What about the other landowners? You're sure there're no problems?"

"Sarah Booth, it's my belief that somehow this is all connected to that particular cotton crop. So far, the only cases of illness have come from people who've set foot there."

"And two of those people are my friends."

"Sarah Booth, your dedication to your friends is admirable, but you have a reputation for taking matters into your own hands. Don't do that here. We don't need another sick person. The CDC is on-site, and we should be able to reassure the people. Another new case would break the public's confidence in us."

He checked his watch, reminding me it was time for the press conference. I eased toward the door. "I'll check back with you. I want to watch the press conference."

I left the chancery clerk's office and walked down the empty hallway to the stairs. While I didn't care to be seen, I wanted to hear what Coleman and Bonnie Louise had to say. The simplest way to accomplish this was to slip out onto the small balcony that fed off the second-floor landing. I would be right above the action. While I couldn't see Coleman and Bonnie Louise—I simply could not bring myself to call her Beaucoup—I could hear them.

Surprised that no one else had thought of listening from above, I found myself alone. Coleman was already talking.

"I want to assure everyone that this is under control. We have four reported cases of an unspecified illness. But there have been no new cases."

"Is this an epidemic?" a male reporter asked.

" 'Epidemic' is not a word that applies here," Coleman answered. "Our medical staff in Sunflower County is on top of this. Experts have been consulted. We have the sick people isolated, and this is under control, but there is no indication that this is a problem with the potential of spreading. It is contained."

"What does the CDC have to say?" another reporter called out.

Bonnie Louise's tone was crisp and authoritative, but it still contained a trace of drawl. "We have full faith that in a matter of hours we'll have an explanation for the illness, which I point out has not spread. Sheriff Peters and his men, the county medical staff, everyone is working with us. We have four very sick people, but this is not an epidemic and there is no reason to panic."

"Will Sunflower County be quarantined?" a female reporter asked.

"There are no plans to impose a countywide quarantine. Things are under control." Bonnie Louise answered each question head-on, and I had to admire her for that.

"My office will issue a daily statement updating the media on any new information," Coleman said. "Thank you for coming."

The press conference was over. Leaning over the balcony, I caught a glimpse of him stepping back from the microphone. Bonnie Louise had her hand on his arm and a carnivorous smile on her face.

A cool spring dusk fell over the land as I drove home toward a sky glowing with peaches and lavenders. The sycamore trees that lined the drive of Dahlia House had budded into green. This time of year, every living thing seemed to jump into life. I pulled up to the front, where I was greeted by Sweetie Pie and Chablis. The little dustmop looked fine, but her near death in Costa Rica had left me anxious. Tinkie was counting on me to keep Chablis safe.

The dogs followed me to the barn, where I fed Reveler, my Connemara cross, and Miss Scrapiron, a beautiful mahogany Thoroughbred mare. Lee, my childhood friend who ran a breeding farm, had brought both horses back to Dahlia House. Had darkness not been upon me, I would have saddled up for a ride.

The dogs led me to the house. Inside, a huge chicken potpie sat on the kitchen counter. Millie had stopped by and left food. I dished up three bowls and settled in for dinner with my companions.

We were finishing when the phone rang. To my delight, it was Graf. I needed a dose of surrealism from Hollywood to put my day in perspective.

"Sarah Booth, I have four scripts here for you. Everyone wants you on a project."

"Really?" My stomach tightened and I felt a pang of nausea. Hollywood was far from conquered in my opinion. I'd barely nicked the surface of that tough city.

"Two of them look great. Want me to send them down to you?"

"Sure." Graf made me smile. "Thank you."

"For sending the scripts?"

"For being you." I gripped the phone so tightly, my hand cramped. "I miss you, Graf." I felt empty without him. The idea of going up to my old childhood bedroom, alone, was almost unbearable. The term was old-fashioned, but I "longed" for him.

"You sound pitiful," he said. "Say the word and I'll be there."

"No." I couldn't allow my weakness to spoil his shot at a film. "How's it going for you?"

"I took a meeting this morning with Ethan and Joel and they are so smart. I can't wait for this film to start shooting. It's the best role I've ever been offered."

Excitement rippled in his voice, and I closed my eyes and imagined that he was in the room talking with me instead of a continent away. "Tell me about your part."

He spoke for ten minutes about the role he'd accepted and the shooting schedule. I loved listening to him, the sense of being included in a special and very private world. I missed Graf and the movie business.

"You'll be fabulous," I assured him. "That part was written for you."

"So you think I'm gunslinger material?"

"You have the flair for it, and the looks, and the smile. You could steal a herd of cows and the lady rancher's heart."

He laughed, pleased at my blatant flattery. "They wanted you, too."

I almost asked him not to make it any harder on me, but I couldn't. "I'll find the perfect role once Oscar is well."

"Absolutely."

I heard the beep of his other line. It was still business hours in Hollywood.

"I love you," he said.

"Words to sleep by," I answered before we hung up, and I was alone in Dahlia House with two dogs and a potpie.

"You got a roof over your head, food to eat, and money in your pocket. Why so down?" Jitty stepped over Sweetie Pie, who'd fallen into a food coma beside the table.

She still looked like a refugee from a hunger camp. Her clothes were worn and torn, her face lined with worry.

"For goodness' sake, have some chicken potpie." I pushed the pan toward her.

"It isn't food I need," she said, "but you have some more. You're lookin' too thin."

"Do you realize that you're impossible to please? I'm too heavy, too thin, too busy, too lazy, too here or too gone."

"What's got you in such a fractious mood?" she asked.

"I miss Graf. I miss making movies."

She sat down at the table, her silver bracelets jingling softly as they slid down her arm. "You gave up a lot for friendship." For once she wasn't deviling me.

"And I don't regret it at all. It's just that I feel useless. I haven't accomplished anything. Oscar is still at death's door, and Tinkie is suffering. I don't know a single thing more today than I did three days ago."

"The fact that Oscar, Gordon, Regina, and Luann are hangin' on is a good thing. And no one else has come down with this epizootis. Now that's got to count for somethin'."

"It does?"

"You're on the trail of figurin' it out."

"I wouldn't go that far." I twirled my spoon in the chicken potpie. "I want to fix this."

"Back during the Great Depression, folks got caught up in a lot of things they couldn't stop or control. Hard times touched most ever'body."

"I don't know if I can stand to hear about this." I looked around the kitchen. Outside, night had almost fallen. I heard Reveler's soft whicker and Miss Scrapiron's answer.

"You can leave this and go to Graf, you know."

"I can't—"

"Sure, you can," she interrupted. "You can put a 'For Sale' sign out front and head to Hollywood anytime you want."

"It's not that easy."

She studied me in that frank way of hers. "You can't hold on to two different dreams, Sarah Booth. Not ones that are so far apart. But life has a way of showin' you the path you need to take."

"I'm not very good at listening," I said.

Her laughter was rich and soft, almost a touch. "You sure down in the dumps for a big-time movie star."

I got up and gave Sweetie the last of my potpie. She woke long enough to wolf it down in one quick whisk of her tongue. "I hate being helpless."

"Lots of folks are feelin' that same way. Times are tough. Not just here in Sunflower County, but all over. This ain't the Great Depression, but it sure ain't Camelot, either."

Jitty had the benefit of nearly two hundred years and those times she hadn't physically lived through, I believe she visited as a specter. I'd learned never to argue history with her.

"I could stand a dose of Camelot."

"You got a home here, friends here, a man in Los Angeles who loves you. You got riches that most people never see."

Oh, swell, a case of shame was exactly what I needed. "Thanks, Jitty. I feel worlds better now."

Her laughter filled the kitchen. "Now that sounds like my Sarah Booth. Sarcastic and sassy."

I headed out of the kitchen knowing she would follow me. "I'm going out to the Carlisle plantation. I want to look around myself."

"No, you are not!"

I faced her. "You can't stop me."

"Use your head, Sarah Booth. All Tinkie needs is to have to keep vigil over you *and* Oscar. Stay away from

64

that place. You got other people beside yourself to worry about."

I hadn't seen Jitty so worked up in a while. "I need to look for clues myself."

She sniffed. "Can't see no clues at night. Might as well wait until tomorrow."

On that note, I had to concede. Besides, I was weary. I'd had a busy and hectic day, but not enough to warrant the bone-deep fatigue that had seeped into me. I was barely able to keep my eyelids up.

"Tomorrow then," I countered.

"Get yourself in bed and take care of that body you treat so shabbily. I'd make you some hot chocolate if I could."

Chocolate laced with a shot of Kahlúa—that was a great idea. I turned to the kitchen to heat some milk and whistle the dogs inside. In the morning I'd investigate the place where all of this madness had started. When the sun was shining, I'd use the skills as a private investigator that I'd acquired over the past year and a half.

Tomorrow, I would move mountains.

But tonight, I wasn't even able to stay awake long enough to heat milk. I put the saucepan, unheated, on the floor for the dogs, dragged myself upstairs, and fell into bed.

7

I woke up to the sounds of Sweetie and Chablis racing up and down the stairs. It took me a moment to realize it was after nine. I'd overslept. The bed was so wonderfully comfortable that even though I had much to do, I hated to peel back the covers.

The thought of Tinkie, pale, exhausted, and standing at a hospital window guarding Oscar, was like a Hot-Shot against my thigh. Guilt-ridden, I bolted out of bed and padded downstairs to the kitchen to put on some coffee. I was ravenous.

Rummaging through the refrigerator to see what I might eat, I found only unidentifiable food items. I threw them in the trash. Thoughts of breakfast at Millie's made my mouth water. I'd grab some eggs and something for Tinkie and then begin my investigation of the Carlisle place.

The brewing coffee smelled delicious, and I stood with my cup in hand waiting for it to finish. The first wave of nausea hit me without warning. I made it to the bathroom off the kitchen before I threw up.

Hanging on to the toilet, fear traveled through my marrow. I fought against it. Since I hadn't gone near the Carlisle place, I couldn't be seriously sick. It wasn't possible.

The nausea passed as quickly as it had come, and I wiped my face and went upstairs to brush my teeth. By the time I got to the second floor, I felt fine. The idea of coffee was once again tantalizing.

Since I was already upstairs, I showered and polished off my morning routine in under ten minutes. Dressed in my favorite black jeans and a red shirt with black geometric designs that I'd picked up in a Los Angeles boutique, I was ready to start my day.

I made sure Sweetie and Chablis had gone out to whiz and were back in, poured a go-cup of black coffee, and hit the road.

Millie's was bustling, and I was unprepared for the wave of oohs and aahs that erupted when I walked in the door. The attention was heavenly. Two teenage girls actually asked for my autograph. When I explained that the movie had been destroyed and wouldn't be released, they didn't care. They'd heard about me, and in their books, I was celebrity enough.

Millie plopped a plate heaping enough for a farmworker down in front of me with a cup of hot coffee and a glass of milk.

"The potpie was delicious, Millie. But why are you feeding me like I'm a starving indigent?"

"You don't look good, Sarah Booth. You need sleep or food. I'm not selling sleep, so I'm piling on food."

Her logic was infallible. "Thanks." I tucked into the eggs and grits. "I got plenty of sleep last night. And I'm eating a lot of food."

She lifted my chin so that my face was better illuminated. "Your color isn't good."

A stab of fear zinged through me. I couldn't be sick. Not me. "I'm fine."

She nodded. "Worried about Tinkie, I'm sure."

That had to be it. Worry did strange things to the Delaney women. Stories abounded of tilted uteruses, snarled Fallopian tubes, ectopic pregnancies, and hydra-like endometriosis, not to mention the dreaded "fallen" uterus, as if the organ itself had committed a sin worthy of being cast down. All of these much-discussed ailments were laid at the feet of anxiety and worry. Genetics might dictate eye color or refined hands or the handsome arch of a foot, but worry and anxiety wrecked the breeding potential of Delaney women.

Millie put a glass of water on the table, and I snapped out of my mental family medical album. "I am worried about Tinkie. I'll take her some breakfast when I leave."

"Sure thing. I'll be back." Millie swung through the café, refilling coffee cups and dropping a smile or an "I'll get that, sugar" on her regulars.

I was looking straight at the door when Bonnie Louise walked in, her shapely legs tan and perfect in a pair of shorts and hiking boots. The Colorado fashion statement caught the attention of every man and woman in the café. Bonnie made a beeline toward me.

"Mind if I join you?" she asked.

What could I say? "Have a seat." I focused on the eggs and grits.

"Coleman says this is the best place to eat in the Southeast."

"He would be right." I aimed at pleasant. Surely by now someone had told her Coleman and I had a history, but she could only goad me if I let her.

"I'm glad I ran into you, Sarah Booth. I wanted to ask you something."

I stopped eating and waited.

"Word is that you broke things off with Coleman before you went out to L.A. Is that right?"

"That's really not your concern." A curl of nausea started in my upper stomach.

"I'm interested in him, and I wanted to be upfront about it. He told me he'd filed for divorce. He should be a free man in a matter of months."

I considered my response as carefully as I could under the circumstances. "Coleman feels an obligation for Connie. Married or not, he's always going to care for her."

"Not a problem for me." She waved at Millie as if she were in a fancy eatery ordering a minion around. "Coffee, and make it fresh." She dismissed Millie and zeroed in on me. "I gather that was a problem for you."

"What is the point of this conversation?"

"I like what I see when I look at the sheriff. I want him. But I don't like stepping on someone to get what I want. I'm asking because I want to be sure the field is clear."

I had no intention of explaining my complicated relationship. "Good luck," I said.

She nodded. "That's what I wanted to be sure of. I didn't want to move in on your territory."

So she wasn't a poacher; she was still a barracuda. But Coleman was a grown man. "I have no claim on the sheriff."

"I heard you were all hooked up with some handsome

Hollywood guy and would be going back out there as soon as this illness is cleared up."

"I haven't made any plans and don't intend to until Oscar is well."

"Not my business." She held up a hand like some teenager.

That really annoyed me. Bonnie Louise got under my skin. I sipped my coffee. The nausea I'd been battling surged forward, and I thought for a moment I might throw up. I looked down at her boots to see how much damage I might be able to inflict. The sensation passed, and I took a breath. "Are you planning a hiking expedition? I guess you've forgotten the Delta is flat."

She laughed. "I remember the land and the soil you call 'gumbo.' Down in the bogs it used to pull my shoes right off my feet. I used to ride with Daddy on the combine and the cotton pickers. I loved that."

For a split second the edge left her voice and I thought I heard true sadness. "Does your family still farm?" I asked.

"No." She picked up the cup that Millie put in front of her. "Good and fresh," she said to no one in particular.

My appetite had evaporated, and my stomach, while fine now, wasn't totally trustworthy. If the spastic gut didn't stop, I'd talk with Doc.

"What made you go into research?" I asked.

"I like science, and I like puzzles. Research has both. What made you decide to be a private investigator?"

"I sort of stumbled into it." No point fibbing about that.

"Well, stay out of this investigation, okay? Let me rephrase. *Stay* out of this investigation."

"Let me rephrase for you, Ms. McRae. Oscar is a friend. I'll do whatever it takes to help him."

"Get in my way, Sarah Booth, and I'll roll over you. I'm not some *localite* you can intimidate." Her face brightened and she began signaling.

When I looked over my shoulder, I saw Coleman walk through the door and head toward our table.

"Coleman, I hope this table is okay?" She looked around. "Sarah Booth was just leaving."

"Sarah Booth," Coleman said. "How are you?"

"Perfect. Any change in Gordon?" I asked.

He took off his hat, revealing a fresh haircut. "They're all still holding their own. Doc figures that's not as dismal as it might sound. They could be going downhill."

"Has he found the cause?"

He put his hat on the table. "They're still not sure if it's bacterial or viral or what. The tests so far are inconclusive."

"I'll catch up with you later," I said. "I've got to get some food to Tinkie."

"Give her my best," Coleman said.

"Yes, give her our best," Bonnie added.

I left the table without another word. Suddenly her nickname was perfect. Beaucoup Bitch.

Tinkie accepted the food and ate without comment. I don't think she tasted a single bite, but she knew she had to keep up her strength.

Standing at the window, I watched Oscar and Gordon. The nurses came in and hung new bags of fluids and left. Doc entered with two strangers in tow. They read the charts at the foot of each bed, examined the patients carefully, and then walked out in a huddle.

"Go find out what they think?" It was the first thing Tinkie had said in ten minutes.

"They won't talk to me."

"Since when did that stop you?"

"Got it." I ambled down the hallway, setting up position outside the swinging door that led to ICU. This was the only exit from the isolation ward.

Sure enough, less than a minute later, the door opened and the three men emerged. Doc saw me and paused. "Sarah Booth, this is Dr. Franklin and Dr. Formicello. They're here from the World Health Organization. I was hoping they might have seen something like this."

Both men were nearing fifty, and their faces showed lives lived out of doors. I glanced between them, picking up on the tension.

"We don't have any answers," Dr. Franklin said. "To be honest, I've never seen an illness like this."

"Nor I," Formicello agreed. "I hope this is truly contained."

"Can you guess as to whether it's bacterial or viral?" I asked. From the little I knew about medicine, it would make a tremendous difference. Bacterial would respond to antibiotics. Viral—probably not. So far, though Doc had tried at least four major types of antibiotics on the patients, none had shown improvement. Lab cultures had come back inconclusive.

They shared a look. "We don't know," Franklin said.

"Do the sores indicate some kind of contact with a poison?"

Again, they looked at each other and Doc. "Miss Delaney, we simply can't, and won't, speculate."

"Oscar's wife is near emotional and physical collapse. Don't you have anything you can tell her? Any tiny word of hope."

"The longer the patients survive, the better the odds. Mr. Richmond has been here for four days. He's survived

72

the high temperatures and the buildup of fluid around his heart and lungs—take that as a positive sign. In fact, all the patients have good health and physical strength on their sides. Older patients would be dead by now."

That wasn't exactly the glad tidings I wanted to take to Tinkie, but it was better than a death sentence.

When I reported back in, she handed me the half-eaten container of food.

"Will you take me home for a little while?"

She was so tired, she sounded drunk. "Sure. I'll come back and stay with Oscar."

"Mother's coming. I told her you'd take me home."

I sat on the edge of the cot beside her and put my arm around her. "He's going to pull through this."

"Why can't they figure it out?" she asked. "They've run tests for four days."

"I don't know." I told her about my conversation with Peyton, the genetically altered cotton, and the strange boll weevils he'd discovered in the fields.

"Do you think the gods are punishing Sunflower County?" she asked.

"Like biblical plagues?" I was astounded. Tinkie was the voice of reason, the optimist, the one who championed true love and goodness. Here she was talking Armageddon of biblical proportions, all focused on Sunflower County.

"Insects, disease, a shift in the climate." She looked at me. "I'm worried."

"Me too, but not about End Times. I'm not buying that stuff, Tink. There have been predictions about the end of the world from the Dark Ages on. People used to believe an eclipse was a sign of Armageddon. We'll figure this out. You have to believe that."

Her smile was weary but amused. "You're a good friend."

"You're a better friend."

Her smile widened. "You're the best friend."

"You're the bestest friend." I lifted her to her feet. "I'll track down Jimmy Janks, a developer who showed some interest in the Carlisle land. Might be illuminating to dig around in his background, especially in light of the fact that Erin Carlisle says she won't sell the land to be developed."

Tinkie's eyes lit. "If the land is overrun with weevils, and the crop is ruined, and there's talk that the place has some kind of agricultural problems, then no one will lease it to farm and—"

"And Erin might yield and sell to a developer."

"Good thinking, Sarah Booth."

"The problem with that train of thought is if someone thinks the land is diseased, they may not want to build a subdivision on it," I said.

Her expression disagreed. "Some developers build on top of swamps and wetlands and landfills and chemical dumps. A few illnesses and some boll weevils wouldn't stop them. You know they aren't going to tell the home buyers about the history of the land."

"Good point."

Tinkie stretched and stifled a yawn. "Stop by the bank and talk to Harold. He may know Janks. A lot of the developers do business at the bank."

I kissed her forehead. The food had helped her color a little. "Let me get you home. A hot bath, a few hours in your own bed. The world will look better after that."

"Can we pick up Chablis?"

"For you, we can even pick up wandering leprechauns with gnarled toes and knobby canes."

"Sarah Booth, are you on drugs?"

I propelled her down the hall. "I'm mainlining friendship. For the first time since we got back from Hollywood, I have this sense that things will be okay." I had no idea where the euphoria had come from, or how long it would stay. But for the moment I clung to it. And Tinkie did, too.

She linked her arm through mine. "I think you're unstable, but I need a bit of hope right now."

"You need your pup and some sleep. Let's make that happen."

8

Jimmy Janks had set up shop in a strip mall on the outskirts of Zinnia. The fake-stucco front was designed to look like the Alamo. For what reason, I couldn't begin to fathom, unless Janks had some Fess Parker/coonskin hat fetish that I didn't want to explore.

The strip mall contained a Tae Kwon Do studio, a smoothie place, the Janks Development Company, and a nail salon. Not a single parking space was occupied when I pulled in. Even though the brutal summer temperatures were still a month away, the black asphalt radiated heat devils. Beyond the borders of the strip mall was a lush field of new corn.

The martial arts studio wasn't open until three, when school students would be available for classes. I'd considered taking up karate but convinced myself it would be smarter to take shooting lessons. Which I needed to sign up for. I'd promised both Graf and Tinkie I would become proficient with a weapon. Something else on my to-do list.

I entered Janks's office and was greeted by a pretty receptionist who took me straight back to see "the man."

Jimmy Janks, wearing khakis, a button-down shirt, deck shoes, and a diamond Rolex, came from money somewhere up the line. His posture, his boyish haircut, his manicured nails, and perfect smile told me a lot about his background.

"Ms. Delaney," he said, extending a hand. "I've heard all about your exploits in Hollywood. Are you selling your family plantation? It would be a perfect location for—"

"Dahlia House isn't for sale," I said with a cold edge that froze him in mid-sentence.

"So many of the older land parcels are on the market, I just assumed . . . well, farming is becoming too expensive. Folks want to sell off the land and get out of a business that relies on the vagaries of weather."

As much as I wanted to launch into a tirade about paving the best farmland in the nation, I stopped myself. "Actually, I'm interested in your plans for the Carlisle land. Luther said you see development potential there."

He settled behind his desk, punched something into his iPhone, and gave me his full attention. "Luther desperately wants to sell, but the sister, Erin, won't even discuss it." He shrugged. "There's nothing I can do until the family comes to terms."

"You've spoken with Erin?"

"Not a chance. She ships my letters back marked 'Return to Sender.' Like that old Elvis song." He laughed. "She won't even hear me out. Luther said he's filed a petition in court. That's where it stands with him. Once it clears the court, he's agreed to my generous offer, which includes shares in the development. We'll both make a killing. The sister, too."

"When was the last time you were at the Carlisle place?"

He retrieved his iPhone, punched some more buttons, and said, "Two weeks ago. I went out there with Luther. We checked a couple of low places for a lake. Waterfront is where the money is in development. We found a couple of potential places, did some soil samples, then we left."

"Did you see anything unusual?"

"Tallest stand of cotton I've ever seen for this time of year, and an empty house that's going to have to be bull-dozed."

"Why?" I asked. "The Carlisle House is historic. Surely someone would want to live there." I hadn't been there in years, but I remembered it as a beautiful, raised plantation house with a curved, double set of steps used for many a Zinnia High School annual photograph.

"Historic, haunted, and out of style. Folks want glass, more width and less height, and modern conveniences. Those old houses, heck, by the time you repair the central air and heat, the electrical systems, the plumbing, it's just easier to raze them and start from scratch. Cheaper, too."

My opinions weren't important, so I tamped them down. I kept a calm face and listened to a man who had no sense of history. "Where are you from, Mr. Janks?"

"Call me Jimmy. We're an old Mobile family. Born under an azalea bush and all of that." He waved it away with disdain.

Child of privilege, a notch above the "entitled" gener-ation. "How'd you end up in the Delta?"

"Made some friends in college. Toke Lambert, Haney

Thompson." His grin was boyish. "Those guys know how to party. Anyway, I came up here to dove hunt with them on some of their family land, and I realized this area was perfect to develop."

I knew the men. Sons of Buddy Clubbers, who'd inherited their land and never struggled a day to claim it or work it.

"When you were at the Carlisle place, you didn't see anything out of the ordinary?"

"Nice stand of cotton. Nothing else."

Janks wasn't a farmer, so he wouldn't appreciate the extraordinary maturity of the cotton. "And you didn't feel sick?"

He laughed. "I don't have time to feel sick. I've got irons in the fire."

"There's some thought that the illness that struck down Oscar Richmond and the others came from the Carlisle place."

He leaned back in his chair. "That's a troubling idea."

"Would it affect your plans for the land?"

"I don't think so. I mean, the development we've mapped out will take at least a year to initiate. At least three to finish. By then, all of this will be cleared up."

"Has anyone else shown an interest in the land?"

"Not to my knowledge, but Luther would be the one to ask about that. When you do, tell him he'd better not be plotting a double-cross." He laughed, but there was a glint in his eyes.

"Thank you for your time, Mr. Janks."

"Not a problem. Ms. Delaney, this area is growing. Like it or not, the human animal demands forward progress. We're like sharks. If we aren't swimming forward, we'll die. Keep in mind, I'm not as bad as some developers."

"I'll take that into consideration." I walked out. Janks

might not be worse than others, but the end result was still the death of a way of life and a land I loved.

When I settled into the driver's seat, the car was hot and I was overcome with a lethargy that made me want to close my eyes and rest a moment.

I knew what was happening—I was trying to hide from the events unfolding around me. Illness, development, worry for my friends. The hot sun and the smell of clean leather were lulling. If I could just close my eyes for fifteen minutes . . .

A car horn tooted beside me. Cece sat behind the wheel of her sexy new hybrid. Her window went down, and she signaled for me to do the same. "Taking up martial arts?" she asked.

"Interviewing Jimmy Janks."

His office door opened, and Janks walked out and around the building to the side.

"Is that Janks?" Cece asked.

I recognized the predatory tone in her voice and reconsidered Janks. He was tall, well built, and good-looking in a deliberate kind of way. Not someone I would normally think of as fitting Cece's taste, but what did I know?

"That's him." In a moment he drove around the building in a big Tahoe with "Janks Development" written on its side.

"He might be an interesting subject for a profile in the paper," Cece said. "I'll find out what his plans are really all about."

"Just an excuse for you to find out about him." I wasn't fooled by Cece's sudden journalistic ambitions.

"One of the perks of my job, dahling."

Cece made me smile, and that was certainly welcome. "Where are you headed?" I asked.

"Back to the newspaper. I saw your car and wanted to be sure you were okay. It looked like you'd fallen asleep behind the wheel."

"Resting my eyes. Mind if I join you at the paper?"

"Not at all. Research?"

She knew me too well. "I want to dig up the story of the Carlisles."

"I'll help." She backed up and took off, and I followed. For a hybrid, her little car had pep.

The newspaper office was contained bedlam. Most Delta papers had been bought by large chains, but the *Zinnia Dispatch* was still locally owned. The news stories focused squarely on Sunflower County, with minimal regional and national copy coming off the wire. With all the emphasis on local reporting, the paper, through the decades, was an invaluable source of history.

While Cece busied herself setting up an interview with Jimmy Janks, I went to the stacks and began pulling newspapers. I had a general idea of when Mrs. Carlisle died, based on Erin's age and my years in high school.

I found the front-page story without difficulty, then sat down on a stool to read.

Lana Carlisle, the former Lana Entrekin, of West Point, Mississippi, was considered one of the state's outstanding beauties. West Point isn't part of the Delta but is situated in the northeast part of the state in what's known as the Black Prairie, another area with exceptional soil. The prairie lent itself to ranching more than cotton. Lana served the region well, capturing the title of Miss Mississippi during a time of strife for the nation and the South.

Though she didn't win the title of Miss America, Lana had been first runner-up. In 1974, she put beauty pageants

81

and the possibility of becoming a concert pianist behind her to marry Gregory Carlisle. The wedding, which united the powerful Carlisle family with talent and beauty, was big society news.

I leafed through page after page of fêtes, soirées, showers, luncheons, shopping trips to New Orleans and Memphis, menus, details on dress designs and lace, and charming moments of a "royal" courtship. Reading the stories, I thought of the fairy tale wedding of Princess Diana and Prince Charles. In 1974 Mississippi, this was as close to the Cinderella story as one could get—Delta royalty finding a princess.

After the wedding, which made headlines in Memphis and Atlanta, Lana settled into the Carlisle estate.

Had she found the lull of farming in a flat, fertile landscape boring, or had her roots hit the black soil called "gumbo" and taken a firm grip?

There were stories of her chairing the hospital charity drive and the garden club. She organized the Friends of the Library and other civic groups.

Through the 80s she was active, but in 1990, she announced her resignation from all civic clubs. There was a photograph of her at a farewell party at Tavia's Salon, a monthly gathering of intellectuals.

I studied the picture. She looked worn and . . . desperate. That was exactly the right word. As if something terrible hung over her head and she knew she couldn't avoid it forever.

Ten months later, she was dead.

"Beloved Delta Beauty Falls to Death" was the headline on the front page of the paper. Lana's death was ruled accidental by the coroner.

Gregory and Luther were quoted in the story and depicted as men devastated by grief.

"Lana was the light of my life. She was everything," Gregory said.

"My only regret is that Mother and Erin were at odds," Luther said.

A telling quote. Why air the family's dirty laundry in the newspaper at such a tragic time? And also untrue, if what Erin had told me was accurate. Whether Luther knew it or not Erin and her mother had patched up their breach.

Luther and Gregory had compounded the tragedy of Lana's death by failing to let Erin know that her mother was dead.

I pondered the implications of all this as I read the funeral arrangements. Burial for Lana Carlisle was in West Point, not Zinnia. Not in the Carlisle family cemetery, which would have been proper. Lana had gone home to West Point.

Gathering my notes, I returned the bound newspapers to their slots. There was no way to tell from the articles who'd arranged to send Lana's body to West Point—or why. But Sunflower County and the Delta had adopted the Black Prairie beauty as one of their own. It was almost unheard of for a woman who married into a wealthy family not to lie beside her husband in death.

If Lana had made the arrangements before her death—that was one story. Gregory and Luther shipping her off to West Point was something else again.

Shuffling the huge, bound editions of the paper, I found the one that contained details of Luther's death.

This story was also played on front page, but below the fold, which befitted the double tragedy of death by suicide. The exact coroner's ruling was "death by accidental hanging," a nice way to phrase it. The obvious facts were accepted. It appeared that no one considered the possibility of foul play.

Gregory Carlisle was buried in the family cemetery located on the estate.

Dusting my hands, I left the newspaper morgue and went to find Cece. As I drew near her office, I heard her on the phone.

"Well, Jimmy, I'd love to meet for dinner, and steak sounds wonderful. Carnivore would be a good description of me. Seven is perfect."

She was almost purring. I leaned against the door frame and listened without apology.

When she hung up, she flashed me a grin. "I'll find out whatever you want to know."

"And a whole lot more than that," I said. "I'm heading over to the sheriff's office to check the reports filed on the Carlisle deaths."

"Have you heard from Tinkie?"

My cell phone, that troubling implement, had remained silent. "No calls from anyone."

"I'm on deadline, but I'll meet you later."

"Sure thing."

As I left the newspaper, I had the strangest sense that everything that had happened in Hollywood was only a dream. The movie world seemed a million miles away, and I couldn't be certain if it was a good thing or a bad.

Coleman wasn't in the sheriff's office, and the new dispatcher showed me to the cubbyhole where old reports were kept. Since I had the dates of death for Lana and Gregory, it didn't take me long to locate the paperwork.

Nothing in the reports offered any insight into what had really happened at the Carlisle home.

In fact, the reports were nonexistent. There were no

diagrams of body placement, no interviews, no real information at all.

Since I was going to the hospital to see Tinkie, anyway, I stopped first at the health department to check out the CDC facilities. Beaucoup and Peyton had taken over the back office of the clinic, and I was pleased to see what looked like high-tech microscopes and other equipment. A hint of relief whispered along my neck. Maybe Peyton and Bonnie would come up with a solution that would save the lives of the four sick people.

"Hello, Peyton!" I called out as I stood around in the main office. The door hadn't caught properly, so the lock hadn't engaged. My first thought was to make sure everything was okay.

"Peyton! Bonnie Louise!"

The place was empty.

My second thought was to make sure the CDC team was sharing information. I went to the back room, where two desks had been set up. Beaucoup's was easy to spot— it was the one with everything neatly stacked and arranged. Peyton's desk was buried in paperwork.

Since he was the senior CDC official, I plowed through the stuff on his desk first. There were reports filled with language I didn't understand. I saw a notation regarding Mississippi Agri-Team and a phone number for Lester Ballard. Peyton was following the same leads that Coleman and I were pursuing.

My assumption—which was correct—was that the computers in the office were linked with the CDC network. Firing up the one on Peyton's desk, I did a bit of basic background work: I pulled Bonnie Louise's work record. She'd been with the CDC two years, and her service was filled with laudatory comments from her supervisors.

Before the CDC, she worked with the World Health Organization. She'd been around plague, famine, and disease plenty.

I brought up Peyton's file. He'd only been with the CDC for six months, but his private research credentials read like a blue-chip portfolio. He must have been earning in the high six figures in private industry, but the bad economy had sent a lot of folks scurrying for government jobs. There was nothing else noteworthy.

I shifted to Beaucoup's chair and began to read through the papers on her desk. Reports had flown between the field office in Zinnia and the main office in Atlanta. Beaucoup was a meticulous note-taker and she made it a point to keep her superiors in Atlanta abreast of everything.

She was also thorough. And detailed. And organized.

On the negative side, she didn't have a lick of taste. A tacky keychain, all pink cubic zirconium-emblazoned alphabet letters BLM, served as a paperweight. But I hit the mother lode when I opened her desk drawers. One contained clothes—tight jeans, a slinky pullover, flimsy underwear, and nice shoes. She was a woman with dating on her mind, and I knew whom she intended to wear those clothes for. I closed the drawer.

I didn't know what I'd hoped to find, but it appeared from the reports I read that Peyton and Beaucoup were shooting straight.

I reached for the last bundle of papers when the small note torn from a yellow legal pad fell into my lap. Coleman used such a pad.

"Dinner tonight?" were the only two words written.

Rising slowly, I replaced everything and left the office, taking care to latch the door firmly. The bright sunlight gave me a sudden headache, which resulted in a churning stomach.

While I was a snoop, I wasn't the kind of person who threw up in public. After a few moments, the urge to hurl passed. I wiped my clammy face and tried to find that mindset where I could sincerely wish happiness for Coleman and Beaucoup.

9

After a depressing two hours at the hospital, Tinkie refused to leave, and I finally went home. I wanted to do some research on the Internet, and I couldn't bear watching Oscar and Gordon and the two women who suffered in their glassed-in sick ward. My head was still pounding, and I saw no improvement in any of the patients. As Doc had pointed out, though, the longer they hung on, the better the chances they would outlast the illness.

I'd just sat down at the computer when the telephone rang. I answered it without even checking caller I.D.

"Sarah Booth?"

I recognized the cultured tones of Avery Bellcase. "Yes, sir."

"Have you made any headway?"

I had nothing solid to report. "Sir, I'm trying."

"If you can find the cause for Oscar's illness, I'll forgive the mortgage on Dahlia House. I'll pay it off myself."

"That's a very generous offer, Mr. Bellcase, but unnecessary. I'll do whatever I can to help Tinkie and Oscar. Tinkie is like a sister to me. Even Oscar has grown on me over the past year." Money couldn't motivate me like friendship did.

"Tinkie is my only child. To see her suffer . . ." His voice broke and he faltered into silence.

"She's my best friend. I know exactly how you feel."

There was a pause before he spoke again. "Doc Sawyer is worried about her. He's urged me to entice her from the hospital, even for short breaks. She won't listen to me."

"She's headstrong." I couldn't help a tiny smile as I said the words that Tinkie so often applied to me. "I'll talk to her tomorrow."

"She'll do things for you that she'd never consider if I asked."

"That's not true, Mr. Bellcase. Tinkie adores you. In all things, you're the person she relies on for wisdom and advice and the right action to take. You'd be surprised how often she quotes you."

"I knew your mother and father, Sarah Booth. Elizabeth was like a wild wind blowing through this town. She stirred things up and unsettled folks. James Franklin, well, he never felt a need to try to bridle her. He fell in love with her outspoken wildness, and he honored it. I so admired that about him. He let Libby be who she was. And they let you grow in that same way."

Even though he'd called my mother Libby, a nickname few people used, I thought he was getting ready to lower the boom on me. I dropped into defensive mode as he continued.

"In recent years, I've tried to give that same type of freedom and support to Tinkie. Her mother and I, we made her conform when she was younger. Her marriage to Oscar was appropriate and fiscally sound. Love grows in soil well fertilized and tended. It's the way things are done in families like ours. Until recently, I'd begun to wonder if perhaps we'd pushed Tinkie into a loveless union."

"Tinkie dotes on Oscar." I swallowed the emotion that had lodged in my throat. "They truly love each other."

"Not at first. Tinkie did what she was told. Oscar was a good match for her, a man who provided security, good judgment, a family history that excluded mental illness, alcoholism, and deviancy. Those things were all important when I thought of my daughter marrying and beginning a family."

I couldn't believe Mr. Bellcase was confessing this arranged marriage to me. I wasn't sure I wanted to hear it. "Tinkie would be lost without Oscar, and vice versa."

"Why are they still childless?" he asked.

Holy moly. I wasn't going near that topic. "When Oscar is well, perhaps you should ask them."

There was another hesitation. "You're a good friend to my daughter, Sarah Booth. Just don't get her hurt working on your cases."

"I'll do my best, but the truth is, I can't protect her from the things that hurt the worst. Nor can you."

He sighed. "That much I've learned. Have a safe night, and try to get my baby out in the sunshine tomorrow. Take her for a ride through the cotton fields and over to the river. Let her see the land. It may help her."

"Yes, sir. I'll do my best." I put the phone down. The conversation had exhausted me. Instead of surfing the Net, I unplugged and went to bed.

I awoke to the strains of a sprightly tune sung in a sultry contralto. I didn't recognize the song, but I sure as hell knew who the singer was. Jitty! And Sweetie Pie was howling along with her. A duet designed to drive me mad. I checked the clock beside my bed. Three a.m.

Throwing back the covers, I padded downstairs. The piano, an old baby grand, was in the music room, a place I hadn't even dusted since I'd been home. When I pushed open the door, I stopped in my tracks.

Jitty sat at the piano wearing an exquisite ball gown of midnight blue cut like a 1930s movie star's: sweetheart neckline, tight torso, and all. With her hair piled on her head and diamonds glittering around her neck and hanging from her ears, she was stunning. Believe me, I was stunned.

"What the hell are you doing?" I walked to the piano. "You can't play. You're noncorporeal. You can't press the keys."

She swiveled on the bench and stood up. Sweetie gave one last, mournful howl and settled down to sleep. Seemed everyone in the house could fall asleep on command except me. I was the poor schmuck who'd sail forth into the new day with bags under my eyes.

"You're exhausted," Jitty said.

She looked magnificent, and it only added fuel to my fury. "I might look better if I could sleep through the night. Why the serenade at three a.m.?"

"That was one of your mama's favorite songs," she said. "She and your father used to sing it together. James Franklin sang the part Sweetie Pie had."

Jitty knew good and well that any reference to my parents would pull me out of a bad mood. "Why now? Why three in the morning? Why are you so dressed up? When did you learn to play the piano?"

Jitty's chuckle was as soft as a butterfly kiss. "You're

the one havin' this dream, missy. Don't go askin' me the answers to things curled up and writhin' around inside your head. Man alive, Freud could have a field day with what's goin' on between your ears."

Sweetie Pie's low moaning howl—much like a blues singer telling about the pain of life—kicked in about then. I realized the music room was dusted and alight with candles. I *was* dreaming. I'd set the scene with Jitty dressed as a torch singer from the thirties, the piano, and my hound. I'd heard my parents sing that song, my mother's lovely voice and my father's untuned baritone.

"This is a dream, but what does it mean?" I asked Jitty.

"Only you can answer that, Sarah Booth. It's your subconscious at work."

I remembered the name of the song. "My Blue Heaven." My mother had loved it. The lyrics came back to me.

"When whippoorwills call, and evening is nigh, I hurry to my . . . blue . . . heaven." I sang the words softly. "A turn to the right, a little white light, will lead me to my . . . blue . . . heaven." I could almost see my parents laughing as they fox-trotted around the room deftly avoiding sofas and chairs.

My attention was drawn to the sheers pulled across French doors that led to a small, secluded patio. Long ago, when the music room was where young folks gathered to sing popular tunes, the patio had been a trysting place for couples to spoon, as Aunt Loulane had called it. Even into the 1960s, when a phonograph and records were the music to love by, Dahlia House's music room had been a gathering place for high schoolers to spin the latest discs, dance, and smooch on the patio.

My parents had shared more than one passionate embrace out there in the falling twilight. As the memories and sensations flooded over me, I thought I heard my mother's soft whisper.

"Mama?" Framed against the sheers was a silhouette of a man and a woman. "Daddy?" My feet were held in thick concrete. I could barely struggle toward the door.

I turned to Jitty for help, but the piano bench was empty, the piano closed and covered with dust.

The more I tried to move, the more I became stuck. My parents were just outside, and I couldn't get to them. For twenty-two years I'd hoped for this moment—for a word or an embrace—and I couldn't reach them.

"Mama!"

I felt something warm and wet on my face, and I fought to consciousness with Sweetie Pie licking me.

The bedroom was empty, except for my hound. My body was wrapped in the sheet like a shroud, so tight I couldn't wiggle an arm or a leg. For a long moment I simply lay there, panting and exhausted by my nocturnal struggles.

"Jitty!" I called. "Jitty!"

There was the slightest shimmer of air and she appeared at the foot of the bed. Her attire was a far contrast to the glamour of my dream. She was still wearing her Depression Garb, her face worn and tired.

"You'd best have a reason for givin' me double-duty tonight," she said. "Torch singer is a million miles from the place I'm in right now."

"Mama and Daddy were there."

She started to say something and stopped.

"They were. You know it."

"Sarah Booth, I tole you before, they're watchin' over you. Have been since the day they died."

"What did the dream mean?"

"I'm only a ghost. I don't have answers like that."

I freed a leg from the sheets and sat up. It was three-thirty, and there wasn't any point in going back to bed: I wouldn't sleep. I couldn't call Graf, because it was 1:30 in the land of celluloid. While working as a P.I., I could get by looking like a run-over sack of suet, but Graf had to look great.

I stood up and stretched.

"Where you think you're goin'?" Jitty asked.

"Maybe for a moonlight horseback ride." It was the best idea I'd had in ages. I thought of the rides I'd shared with Graf in Costa Rica. "I wish Graf was here. I miss him a lot." More than I'd anticipated.

"Call that man and tell him to hop the next plane home. He needs to be with you."

I laughed. "That's provincial. I'm a full-grown woman. To have a relationship with Graf and still help my friends, I can't call him every time I have a bad dream."

"Don't you dare go ridin' off into those cotton fields."

Jitty was seriously troubled, and I found it hard to accept. "I've ridden at night for the past year. What's the problem?"

"Folks weren't keelin' over from some strange sickness until just a week ago. You don't know what's in those fields."

"If it's something bad, Jitty, it can walk right in the front door. In case you haven't noticed, cotton is growing not a hundred yards from Dahlia House."

She turned away. "I noticed. And for the first time I can remember, I'm hopin' the crop fails. I don't want that stuff near you, Sarah Booth."

"Jitty!" I was appalled. No Mississippian would ever wish a cotton failure. Never more than an adequate student of history and economics, even I knew the devastation of such a thing. Jitty had lived through the Civil War and the boll weevil—she should know better.

"You've got to take care of yourself, Sarah Booth."

"I do, Jitty, but I have to live."

She kept her back to me. "The stakes are higher than you know."

I found a pair of jeans and slipped into them, along with socks and my boots. "It's a good thing I don't know how high these stakes are, because I almost can't hold up to the burden I'm carrying now."

I whistled up my hound and clattered down the stairs into the soft glow of a nearly full moon. Reveler and Miss Scrapiron were at the fence. Both whickered softly when they saw me. Again I felt the pain of missing Graf, but I refused to let it ruin what promised to be a wonderful ride. If I'd learned anything in the thirty-four years of my life, it was that happiness came from living each moment to the fullest. If I could manage that difficult task, I could be the partner for a dynamic man like Graf.

It took only a few moments to saddle Reveler. Miss Scrapiron trotted beside us until we reached the end of the pasture fence. She returned to her grazing while Reveler and I set out across the moonlit fields at a trot.

The night was cool, and the tiny cotton plants shivered silver in a light breeze. The moon gave plenty of light, and I knew the land, each dip and contour. This was Delaney land, much of it cleared by mules and sweat.

I'd seen the ghosts of slaves in these fields on foggy nights, heard the singing and the row calls that were so much a part of the tradition of the blues songs that I loved.

On hot days I'd watched the huge machines crawl across the acres harvesting the cotton. While my father had earned his living as a lawyer, he'd also farmed.

Sometimes he'd let me ride in the cab of the pickers with him. Sometimes he'd even let me steer.

The rows, loaded with white bolls, would fall to the picker. Behind us we left brown stalks and a few tufts of white that the machine had missed. Cotton was the lifeblood of the Delta. What would happen if an infestation of boll weevils destroyed the crop? With a country already teetering on economic crisis, such a catastrophe could put Mississippi back into a time warp of poverty and hunger.

When I finally came out of my dire thoughts of economic ruin, I found I'd ridden miles from home. Across a big field was the cottage that a handsome young bluesman had rented. Another page of my past rose up to haunt me on this strange night.

This was also the location where Coleman and I had first kissed.

The house he rented wasn't far. I checked my watch. It was nearly five in the morning. He'd be up in another half hour. I'd surprise him by riding up and having a cup of breakfast coffee. I needed to ask him a few things about the case.

Fifteen minutes later, Reveler and I walked down Coleman's dirt driveway. I wondered what happened to the house he'd shared with Connie. Knowing Coleman, he'd signed it over to Connie without a backward look.

Just as I slid out of the saddle, Coleman stepped onto the front porch of the wooden cottage. He wore jeans and a T-shirt, and he held a mug of steaming coffee. When he saw me, a smile spread across his face before he reined his expression in.

My stomach fluttered, and a delicate curl of nausea teased me, but I walked to the porch leading Reveler.

"Are you investigating on horseback now?" he asked.

"I couldn't sleep, so I went for a ride. I guess Reveler and I rode a little farther than I anticipated."

"Coffee?"

"I'd love some." I removed the bridle and let Reveler graze in Coleman's front yard while we sat on the porch and drank our java.

"Have you made any progress in the case?" I asked.

Coleman gazed to the east, where day was breaking. "Bonnie Louise believes someone deliberately loosed some kind of bacteria at the Carlisle plantation."

"Does she have any evidence of that?" I kept my voice neutral.

"She's examined some of the weevils at the Carlisle place. They're a mutant strain. Something she's never seen, and boll weevils are her specialty. She and Peyton believe the weevils and genetically altered cotton are connected. I've been trying to reach Lester Ballard for days. I gather he's so deep in the South American jungle no one can contact him."

"Have you talked to Luther?"

"I have. He doesn't have a clue. Or if he does, he isn't saying."

I brought him up-to-date with Erin Carlisle and the research I'd done into her family's past.

"So she thinks Luther may have done something to destroy the value of the land agriculturally."

"Maybe."

"Bonnie took some weevils to Starkville to the university. There's a scientist affiliated with the school who specializes in insects and he's agreed to help. Her concern is that these weevils have such a short gestation period." He rubbed his jaw and I saw he hadn't shaved. "It could be a serious problem for the farmers here. Everywhere cotton is grown. The good news is that this is confined to the altered cotton. The weevils, the destruction of the cotton, even the illness."

"Has she pinpointed whether the weevils are related to what's wrong with Oscar and Gordon?"

He shook his head. "No one can make that link."

"You said Bonnie Louise believed the infection was bacterial. Surely it can be treated with antibiotics?"

"Doc has used every antibiotic available. He's trying for some experimental medicine now. Nothing has touched this."

If antibiotics weren't working, in my mind, that meant viral. "Maybe some of those new bird flu drugs, something to attack a virus instead of bacteria."

"Sarah Booth, Doc's tried everything. Bacterial *and* viral."

We sat side by side in two old cowhide rockers. "That cotton didn't get there by accident. We have to figure out who and what is behind this."

"If Erin is correct, Luther Carlisle stands to gain financially if the land is contaminated for agricultural purposes," Coleman said.

I nodded. "And his sister, too. While she says she doesn't want to sell the land for development, she'd make a lot of money."

"I can't believe either of them would be stupid enough to infest a field with boll weevils." Frustration was evident in Coleman's voice.

I told him about Erin's suspicions that her brother was behind the death of her parents.

"I'll check into it." He didn't sound real enthused, and I knew he doubted that events so far in the past could help unravel what was happening now. But I'd come to understand that the past was the soil that sprouted the seed of the present. While I *clung* to my personal past, everyone carried a bit of theirs around with them.

The sun warmed the night from the front porch and for a moment I sat in the glow, glancing from Coleman to Reveler. I considered warning Coleman about Bonnie Louise's predatory nature, but I couldn't risk that he would misconstrue my interest. A breeze kicked in from the west and ruffled Reveler's mane and tail. Draining the last of my coffee, I stood.

"I'd better head home," I said. "I'm going to do some more digging into the Carlisle past. Cece's working on Jimmy Janks. If she finds anything, I'll let you know."

"Bonnie Louise may give us some answers."

"Yeah." I handed him my cup and turned to walk down the steps when I felt my knees weaken. Dizzy, I grabbed at the porch railing and missed. Before I could even yelp, I was tumbling down the steps. I slid into the cool grass still damp from the night's dew.

"Sarah Booth!" Coleman knelt beside me, his hands moving over my arms and legs, checking quickly for breaks. "Can you talk?"

"I haven't stroked out." I hid my embarrassment with gruffness. I wanted to sit up, but he held me down with one hand against my breastbone.

"Hold on a minute and give your blood pressure time to adjust. Unless you like kissing the ground."

I wiped the dew and dirt from the side of my face. "I'm okay. For a moment I was a little dizzy."

"Dizzy enough to fall and break your neck." He held out a hand and helped me to my feet. He half-assisted, half-propelled me into his house and sat me on a leather sofa. "What's going on with you?"

"I didn't get much sleep. I haven't eaten since . . ." I couldn't remember the last time I really ate a meal. "And I rode horseback for miles."

"I'll make you some toast."

A protest wouldn't do any good. If I wanted to ride my horse home, I'd have to eat something before Coleman would release me.

As the bread toasted, my stomach grumbled with hunger. That was all it was. I was light-headed because I'd failed to feed the furnace.

When he handed me the saucer, I ate like I'd been starved for weeks. Four bites—toast gone.

He made another two slices. "Want some jam?"

"Got any scuppernong jelly?"

He laughed. "It just so happens Mabel Donovan dropped some by a few weeks ago. Her teenage son ran away and Gordon and I tracked him to Memphis and brought him home."

While he loaded the toast with butter and jelly, I studied his bachelor digs. Clean, orderly, some nice furniture, but sparse.

He brought the toast, and we munched in companionable silence.

At last I stood, confident that I wouldn't topple over again. "I'd better get back. There's work to be done."

He walked behind me to the door. "I'm glad you came by, Sarah Booth. I've been worried that we might not be able to maintain our friendship."

"Me too," I said. "If I find anything, I'll let you know."

I rebridled Reveler, mounted, and turned south for home. Reveler wanted to canter, and I didn't see a reason in the world not to let him.

10

Probated wills are recorded in the chancery clerk's office, and I wanted a peek at Lana and Gregory's. Erin's story was interesting—and at conflict with what Luther had implied. The truth might be found in the terms of inheritance.

Clean, dressed, and ready for action, I hurried inside the courthouse. Chancery Clerk Attila Lambert, a man who'd overcome the nearly insurmountable political handicap of his name, greeted me with a smile.

"Miss Sarah Booth," he said, "how can I help you?" With his white hair, blue eyes, and pink cheeks, he had nothing of the demeanor of his namesake. Instead of rape, pillage, and burn, he played Santa each year in the Christmas parade.

He led me back to the records, where I could look up wills. "The books should be out on the table," he said helpfully. "There's been a run of interest in the recorded documents of the Carlisle family."

"Was Luther here?"

"Oh, goodness, no." He held a chair for me at one of the long tables where lawyers frequently did research. Once I was seated, he put the book in front of me. "It was the CDC person."

"Peyton?"

"Not him, the pretty woman, Miss Bonnie Louise. She's smart as a whip and such a pleasure."

"She wanted to look at the wills?"

"In-deed." He laughed aloud at his own pun. "Sorry, working with land titles and all." He cleared his throat. "Yes, she was very interested."

"Did she say why she was interested?"

"Something to do with land usage and inheritance. She didn't talk a lot." He stood in front of the table. "Is there anything else?"

"Why did your parents name you Attila?" I asked him.

His laughter was genuine. "It's not such a strange name, once you know the story. I was a preemie. My mother was nearly forty when she got pregnant after years of believing she was infertile. The pregnancy was difficult, and when I was born, there wasn't much chance I'd live. My dad came up with the toughest name he could find. He wasn't a student of history, but somehow Attila the Hun stuck in his imagination. He said the name would give me strength."

"There must have been some magic in that name."

"Maybe so, Miss Sarah Booth. Names are powerful things. At any rate, I wasn't much of a conqueror or warrior, but I seem to have excellent health."

"Thanks for the help. When I finish, what should I do with the books?"

"Leave them on the table. I'll put them away."

I found Lana's will first, and just as Erin had stated, Lana controlled the Carlisle land and left her daughter and son in dual charge of a trust. One could not move without the other's consent. Gregory, for all intents and purposes, was disinherited—except for the insurance policy he'd had on his wife and which wasn't part of the will.

When Attila poked his head around the corner to check on me, I had a question. "The Carlisle land is leased now. Who determines the terms of the lease?"

"I don't know. Luther seems to handle most of the business related to the plantation. From all I've heard, that girl never comes home," he said. "I assumed Luther had the majority interest."

Deciding that silence was the better part of valor, I didn't comment on Luther. I flipped the pages looking for the last will and testament of Gregory Carlisle.

The document was brief and to the point—all proceeds of his estate would go to his son, Luther. Erin wasn't mentioned. But there was an unexpected codicil—the sum of one hundred thousand dollars was bequeathed to Sonja Kessler of 2424 Parkside Drive in Chicago.

"How do I find out what was included in Gregory's estate?" I asked. "There's no list of property."

Attila shrugged. "We only record the probated will. His lawyer may know the details. Often those details are handled by a law firm to keep them private."

Harold might know, and he was a far more direct route to knowledge than any lawyer I'd ever met.

"Thanks, Mr. Lambert."

"Please, call me Attila."

I would try, but I couldn't make any promises. I gathered my notes and legged it over to the bank.

Harold met with me instantly. I'd barely sat down when his secretary brought in the coffee service complete with cheese Danish.

"You look hungry, Sarah Booth," he said. "Help yourself."

What was it with all the men in my life wanting to feed me? My mouth watered at the sight of the pastries, and I helped myself to one and a steaming cup of black coffee.

"Delicious," I mumbled with my mouth stuffed.

Harold laughed out loud. "You can be so childlike, Sarah Booth."

"I'm ravenous all the time," I answered, eyeing another Danish.

He pushed the plate closer to me. "When you come up for air, tell me what's on your mind."

I told him what I needed, which was confidential bank records for Luther, Lana, Gregory, and, if possible, Erin Carlisle.

He tapped his fingers together gently as he thought. "This is absolutely necessary to help Oscar?"

"I believe Oscar picked up some bacteria or something at the Carlisle place. Now the bacteria or whatever had to get there one of three ways—natural occurrence, deliberately put there, or accidentally put there. I'm voting for deliberate. If there's one thing I've learned from Tinkie, it's to look for the financial gain. That's what I'm trying to do."

Harold studied my face for a brief few seconds. "Okay. For you, I'll get this personally." He rose and left the office.

He was taking a risk. A big one. Violation of confidentiality and all of that. I had no legal authority to ask for such information. While he was gone I ate two more Danishes and downed another cup of coffee. I was just beginning to regret my pastry orgy when he returned with a sheaf of papers.

"Please destroy these once you've found what you need."

"I will."

He glanced from the empty Danish plate to me. "Are you okay?"

I nodded. Of course I wasn't okay. The Michelin Tire Man and I were about to claim kinship. I'd always had a healthy appetite, but my hunger for the pastries had been insatiable.

"There are no records for Erin. She moved her account from Zinnia years ago."

That was interesting, but not unusual. Why would she bank in a town where she didn't live? I took the documents he handed me. In one glance I knew I needed Tinkie's help. She was the financial genius in the Delaney Detective Agency. "As soon as I figure out if any of this is pertinent, I'll shred them."

"If this helps you uncover what's wrong with Oscar, I'll take any fallout that comes my way."

"Coleman could have gotten this with a court order." I was trying to make him feel better about violation of his personal ethics. Harold took his job seriously.

"Yes, he could have."

"But it would have taken time. By then . . ."

"Yes, by then, Oscar may be dead."

I rose. "Thank you, Harold.

"Good luck, Sarah Booth." His pale eyes were bloodshot, and he was tired and worried.

I put my hand on his shoulder and felt a weak pulse in my thumb. Harold worked on me in a strange way. My throbbing thumb let me know that our mutual attraction would never completely die. "Coleman and the CDC and I will leave no stone unturned. We'll find out what's wrong."

"Has there been any improvement in any of the patients?" he asked.

I thought about it. "I'm no medical expert, but I think the two women are a little better. Doc hasn't confirmed this."

"And Gordon?"

The deputy was worse. Sores covered his nose and mouth. Doc had applied ointment and pads and taped his eyes shut. "He's hanging in there."

"Tell Tinkie I'm available to do whatever she needs."

"I'll pass that along."

Clutching the documents, I left the bank and drove to the hospital where Tinkie sat guard, her father at her side.

The documents sprawled across a small table in the hospital cafeteria. Tinkie had commandeered a pad from the nurses' station, and she was making notes and calculations. The meticulous lines of figures meant nothing to me. I put two fresh cups of coffee on the table and a plate of toasted bagels and cream cheese. Unbelievably, my mouth watered at the smell of the bagels.

Absently, Tinkie began to eat, her total concentration on the numbers.

When she lifted her gaze, there was defeat in her face. "The figures all track, according to what you said was in the wills. There's no hint of misappropriation of funds."

"Well, damn." I'd hoped to pin something on Luther.

"Gregory didn't have a lot of time to blow through the insurance money after Lana's death. The check for half a million from the insurance company went into his account. Gregory made biannual payments to this Sonja Kessler prior to his death, and Luther continued them. There must have been an agreement between father and son."

"Sonja Kessler is next on my to-do list."

"She may be a good lead." Tinkie glanced at the snack machines and small food court as if aware for the first time of her surroundings.

Worry and fear, which had abated for the few moments she puzzled out the financial statements, settled back onto her features. "I have to go." She stood up as if she'd been given an electric jolt. "Oscar's all alone."

"No, your father is with him," I reminded her. "Mr. Bellcase is watching over Oscar and the others, too." Tinkie was convinced that if Oscar was left alone for even a minute, the Angel of Death would slip down the corridor and snatch him away.

"I need to be with Oscar."

I gently circled her wrist with my hand and held her. "Eat a little more. For me."

She sat on the edge of her chair and picked up another piece of bagel. "For you, Sarah Booth." She stuffed it into her mouth, chewed, swallowed, and stood. Oscar was all she had on her mind.

"I'm going to Chicago," I told her. "I'll be back as soon as I can."

"Sarah Booth, you may just be chasing your tail." Tinkie pointed at the papers still scattered on the table. "What if this illness has nothing to do with the Carlisle family?"

"Do you know something, Tinkie?" Oscar hadn't regained consciousness, hadn't spoken to anyone, but I'd learned the hard way not to discount the things that Tinkie could discern by listening to her heart.

She chewed the tip of her thumb, hesitating. "It's occurred to me that someone may have followed Oscar out there. Someone he was meeting. Someone who might have hurt him."

The words were like blows of a hammer. "I don't believe that." If Tinkie was accusing Oscar of a tête-à-tête with another woman, I didn't believe it at all.

"I've neglected him lately." Tears welled and slipped down her cheeks.

"Bullshit." I could not let her believe this.

"I've focused on myself, my dreams, my wants."

Guilt is an invasive virus. Once it breaks into a person's mind, it spreads and infects everything. "That's total crap, Tinkie. Don't do this to yourself."

"What if it's true?"

"Both Harold and Margene told you that Luther called and asked Oscar to sell the plantation. A legitimate business call sent him to that land. It wasn't some chance to have a fling in an abandoned house."

The silent tears let me know I wasn't making any progress.

"Oscar is totally in love with you, Tinkie. He was proud of your accomplishments as a private investigator. Even your father said so."

Her head tilted slightly as if her hearing was bad. "Daddy said that?"

Oh, thank goodness I remembered. "Mr. Bellcase has spoken to me twice. Both times he warned me against getting you hurt, and both times he told me how proud of you he is. And how proud Oscar is."

Tinkie's tiny hands swiped at the tears. "You don't think he was meeting a woman at the Carlisle place?"

"I'd bet my life he wasn't." My heart was hammering so hard, my stomach felt upset. The Danishes I'd gobbled in Harold's office had turned to lead.

The tears were gone and Tinkie's blue eyes were sharp and clear. "Do you think he could have been meeting someone else, a buyer?"

"From all accounts, he went alone, examined the property, and returned to the bank without incident. There's no indication anyone else was near."

She stood up. "Keep searching, Sarah Booth. I know Coleman and the CDC are working hard, but you're my best hope."

Lucky for me there were several direct flights to Chicago from Memphis, and I caught an afternoon plane that put me in the Windy City before sunset. Before I'd driven to Memphis, I'd called Graf to update him, and simply to hear his voice. I'd also let Cece and Millie know my destination. Sonja Kessler sounded like a paramour, but that didn't mean she wasn't a dangerous person.

I'd booked a room at a downtown hotel near the Parkside Drive address. Best I could tell by a bit of Internet research, Parkside Drive was in an older, established neighborhood.

One of the hardest winters on record had buried Chicago in snow after snow, but spring was everywhere I looked as I entered the downtown.

The Atria Hotel was old-world charm mixed with modern conveniences. My room was lovely and serene—and terribly empty. I thought of Graf and how much I missed him. My fingers circled my cell phone, and the temptation to call was almost irresistible. But I didn't. He'd told me his shooting schedule, and he was probably in the middle of his horseback chase.

I left my small bag on the bed and hurried back downstairs, where the doorman flagged a taxi.

"2424 Parkside Drive," I told the young woman behind the wheel. Her dark gaze caught mine in the rearview mirror, but she didn't comment. The cab eased into busy traffic.

While newer neighborhoods suffer from the McMansion Syndrome—huge homes set side by side on tiny lots—Parkside was a paradise of gracious homes, each nestled among ancient trees and hedges on several acres.

"Do you know anything about this neighborhood?" I asked the driver.

"Chicago businessmen built these homes in the early 1900s. During the school year the families lived here, then moved to the lake for the summers."

"Who owns them now?" I asked.

"People who want to preserve the historic downtown, people with that sort of consciousness. And money. It takes a lot of cash to keep up an old house. Maintenance . . ." She made a motion of doling out money. "And heating."

"It's so beautiful here."

"Yeah, money can generally buy a nice view and good neighbors."

The address we sought had a circular driveway lined with towering plants, maybe rhododendron. The cabby stopped at the door. "Shall I wait?" she asked.

"I don't look like the type who'll stay long?"

"No bag, don't know the neighborhood—those things tell me you're looking for something. Either you'll find it quickly and leave, or you'll just leave."

I liked her spunk. "Wait for me," I said.

She pulled a paperback from the front seat and settled back to read.

I walked to the leaded-glass entry and rang the bell. Instead of a butler, a tall, slender woman opened the door.

"Can I help you?" she asked.

"Sonja Kessler?"

"Yes." She looked beyond me at the taxi in the drive. "Who are you?"

"Sarah Booth Delaney, private investigator. I'm here about your interest in the Carlisle family."

I thought at first she'd stopped breathing. Her blue gaze, as large and clear as Tinkie's, held on my face but registered no emotion.

"I can't talk with you," she said at last. "I have plans for this evening." She began to shut the door.

I wedged my foot in the crack, wincing as the heavy door pressed against it. "Talk to me now, or Sheriff Coleman Peters will be here tomorrow."

That shook her up. She viewed me through the three-inch gap. "Why are you doing this?" she asked. "The past is dead and gone. There's no changing it. Just let it lie."

"I don't think so."

She stepped back, and I pressed my advantage by pushing the door open, revealing a beautifully decorated foyer. I followed her down a hallway into a small library where she'd obviously been working on some papers.

She was younger than I'd assumed. Much younger. A beautiful woman who must have begun her affair with Gregory Carlisle during her teens. Perhaps that was reason enough to pay her. A Delta planter and a teenage lover—the stories would have gotten ugly.

"Why have you come here?" She gathered the papers.

"The Carlisle estate has made payments to you for years. Why?"

She paused. "It's not what you think."

"Really?"

"Gregory was my father. He paid me not to come to Mississippi." She stacked the papers into a neat bundle. "Would you like a soda or some tea?"

11

The tea was strong and not sweet, just the way I liked it. Sonja was direct. "Once Gregory accepted that I was his daughter, he offered a yearly sum of money. Not a fortune, but enough. On his death I received a hundred thousand additional." Sonja's smile was pensive and she distractedly rattled the ice in her tea glass. "Hush money, some people would call it. Since I never knew Gregory, I took the money and let the rest go. I viewed it as a windfall."

The library's mahogany shelves were filled with books, sculptures, and other artwork. Persian carpets covered the oak floor. It was a room of expensive comfort. Sonja may not have had the family name, but she'd acquired the Carlisle lifestyle, or as close as she could come in a city instead of on a plantation.

"My mother was a singer," she said. From the mantel she picked up a photograph in a heavy silver frame and handed it to me. The woman at the piano was a classic Nordic type. Sonja, with her peaches-and-cream complexion, favored her mom.

"She's lovely."

"Mother didn't have good judgment when it came to men." She hesitated. "She fell in love easily and always with someone inaccessible. Then again, it's worked out for me." She put the picture back. "So you've tracked me down and discovered that I'm the bastard daughter of Gregory and a Chicago torch singer." Her chin lifted. "So what? Luther knows. The only person this will harm is Erin."

She knew her siblings' names, though she claimed no interest in them. "And you care about Erin?"

Pacing the room, she settled in front of the fireplace. "I don't know her. We're the same age. I've always found that to be ironic."

Irony was one way of describing it. "What's your contact with the Carlisle family?"

"I receive the money. I've invested wisely." She crossed the room again and I was struck by her confident carriage. She found a remote control on a side table and ignited a gas log in the fireplace. "I won't ask you to keep what you've found a secret. You'll do whatever you feel you must. It'll only hurt Erin."

Again, she expressed concern for Erin, a woman she'd never met—a half sister who'd grown up in the family from which Sonja had been excluded. "I'm not interested in dredging up the Carlisle history, Ms. Kessler."

"What did you hope to gain by coming here? Blackmail?"

"I'm searching for some link to the plantation that might explain a serious illness in Sunflower County. Best indications are that it's confined to the Carlisle land."

"I've never been there. I know nothing of the estate except for a few remarks Mother made when I was a child."

"Do you remember them?"

She looked out the curtained French doors of the library. Dusk was fading and night falling fast. "Mother said my father was wealthy, that he owned a large tract of land where it was like stepping into the past."

"And you were never tempted to go?"

"Never. I focus on things I can attain, not those beyond my reach."

A healthy philosophy, if it was true. "Before you were acknowledged by Gregory as an heir—"

"I made a good living as a retail buyer. Unlike my father, I'm very good at managing money."

"And you've had no contact with Luther Carlisle about the land? He wants to sell it. You haven't attempted to claim any portion of it?"

"I wasn't named in the will. Luther has made it clear that I have no interests in Mississippi."

"You might have legal standing." I wasn't certain about paternity and inheritance laws, but a sharp lawyer could have made a case for her. "Why didn't you come forward?"

"Once Gregory acknowledged me, I didn't try to make contact with him. I didn't want to cause trouble. I don't now. I'm more than comfortable, and arguing can't change a childhood of growing up without a father or siblings."

"True." But it was also true of human nature that most people wanted all they could get. "Do you have DNA proof?"

"Gregory insisted."

"And you've been perfectly happy not to know your father's family or any of your Carlisle relatives?"

"I didn't miss out on anything, Ms. Delaney. I had a mother who loved me."

Outside the French doors the lawn's perfect lighting showed the exceptional landscaping. Sonja had security and beauty at her fingertips, but in that one moment, I understood the loss that had touched her. "In that regard, you're luckier than a lot of people. When did your mother die?"

"I was seventeen. She was accidentally struck by a car while crossing a street." If she felt pity for herself, she didn't show it. She glanced at her wristwatch and frowned. "I'm sorry, but I'm meeting a friend and I'm running late."

"Thank you, Ms. Kessler. I'll be in touch if I need more information."

"There's nothing to add, Ms. Delaney. My connection to the Mississippi Delta is a cash flow from a bank. That's all."

Night had blanketed the street when I walked to the waiting cab. My cell phone rang as the driver took off for the hotel.

"Hello, dahling," Cece said. "I wanted to give you an update. Jimmy Baby is taking me to Memphis for dinner."

"How's Oscar?" I'd been away less than a day, but in my absence anything could have happened.

"The same. Oscar and Gordon have stabilized, but there's no improvement. The two realtor ladies have improved, but only marginally."

Thoughts of Tinkie made my head throb. "I'll be home tomorrow on the first flight out."

"Find anything of value?"

"Sonja Kessler is getting a nice cut of the Carlisle pie, which Luther is doling out per Gregory's dictates. She claims she doesn't want any more than she's getting."

"And when will she be canonized?" Cece's tone was dry.

"My sentiments exactly. But so far, there's nothing to contradict what she said. She says she hasn't filed any claim."

"Well, you may have chased that rabbit into a hole, but I've got a lead."

"What?"

"Jimmy Janks is not who he pretends to be. And don't say what you're thinking—that neither am I."

"I wasn't thinking that at all. But what did you find out?"

"He's not from Mobile, and he doesn't come from old money." She laughed. "In fact, dahling, he's about the worst imposter in the world. He knows enough about Mobile to get himself into trouble talking about it."

Cece had spent several summers visiting relatives in the oak-shaded lanes of Spring Hill, the zip code destination of that port city.

In the 1800s, Spring Hill was the place to survive yellow fever epidemics that raged along Southern waterfront towns like Mobile and New Orleans. The wealthy moved out of town and into the higher elevations, while the poor died of mosquito bites down in the flatlands along the Mobile River and Mobile Bay.

"I'm sorry, Cece, I know he struck your fancy."

"I'm a journalist first and a burning love machine second," Cece said. "The first time I went out with Jimmy, I realized he was a pretender to the throne of Junior League date material."

"Tell me." Chicago whisked past the cab window.

"Dahling," Cece continued, "he held his fork like a savage. I sat there thinking, has he adopted the Continental style for some reason? Then I realized he had no style at all. He clutched his flatware as if readying to attack his plate."

I couldn't help but laugh. There were more important things than proper table etiquette in Cece's life, but not many. "I'm surprised you didn't rap his knuckles with your bread knife."

"I considered it, but I knew if I chastised him for lack of upbringing, I'd never extract any information."

"And did you?"

"Enough to know he bears further research. In fact, that's why I'm calling. While you're in Chicago maybe you can track down his background."

"Here? In Chicago?"

"Yes, that would be the Windy City located in Illinois. Look around you."

"Save your sarcasm for your witty newspaper articles. I'm just shocked. Did he say he was from here?"

"He's not quite that dumb. The give-away was the fifteen-minute dissertation on the glories of the Chicago Bears, not to mention his intimate knowledge of the places Jimmy Hoffa might be buried. He knows Chicago and he doesn't know Mobile. Ergo, he might be from Chicago."

"Did you find anything on him? Something to help me get started?" Hunting down the background of someone in Zinnia was a different case than in Chicago. In Zinnia, I could most often turn up someone who knew everything, or most everything. In a city like Chicago, it was impersonal. While facts were concrete, they seldom told the whole truth.

"Preliminary Internet research showed nothing. The only thing I could find on Jimmy was his company and a list of the development projects he's done."

"College degree?"

"He never attended Ole Miss. I checked that out but didn't get any further. I would say Jimmy is definitely public school. That doesn't help much, I know."

"Could it be coincidence that he's from the same place as Gregory's illegitimate daughter?" How bizarre was that?

"You know what they say about coincidence, Sarah Booth. Look, I've got to go. He'll be here any minute."

The cab driver took a corner sharply, and my stomach lurched. The sensation did nothing to alleviate my concerns for my reporter friend. "Be careful with him, Cece. He may simply be a liar and con man or he could be dangerous."

"I'm on the double-alert. And I'll pump him as much as I can, and I don't mean in a sexual way."

"Behave, and don't put yourself in danger," I said. "Promise me you'll call Coleman and fill him in." We'd pulled up in front of my hotel and I rummaged through my purse for the fare. The minute my feet touched the pavement, my stomach settled.

"Will do. By the way, Sarah Booth, you're a damn determined investigator and a better friend," she said. "Tinkie should count herself lucky."

"No, I'm the lucky one. Don't take any risks," I warned her. "When I get home, we can tackle Jimmy together."

"Tackle . . . humm. That's an image I like. Ciao, baby."

"Cece!" But she was gone. It wasn't a good sign when she started using Italian phrases.

I paid the driver and gave her a fat tip. "Where are the public school records kept in Chicago?" I asked.

"It's a central location, not too far from here."

I asked her to meet me outside the hotel at eight in the morning. Before I left town, I wanted to pursue Jimmy Janks and his upbringing.

The night had grown downright cold, and I hurried into the lobby. The elevator lifted me twenty-two floors to my room. As tired and worried as I'd been, I still noticed the hotel décor, the strategic lighting, and the plush carpeting. There was even a spa service, if it wasn't too late for a facial or massage. A stay in a luxury hotel could do wonders for a girl's weary spirits.

When I unlocked the door, I froze. Something was wrong. The fresh, masculine scent of aftershave teased my senses. Someone had dimmed the lights, and a room service cart with a single red rose and covered platters for two commanded the center of the room.

A tall, dark stranger, a shadow in the minimal illumination, came out of the bathroom. "Your wish is my desire." His accent was vaguely Eastern European. Like Count Dracula. In the dimness, I couldn't get a clear look at him.

"I don't know who you are, buddy, but you'd best take your cart of food and beat it." I wasn't in the mood for some hotel gigolo. My concern turned to annoyance. I'd have the hotel manager's head on a pike for this. A secure room was the least they could provide.

I pointed to the hallway. "Get out now, before I kick your ass six ways from Sunday."

His response was a warm, sexy chuckle. The sound touched nerves at the base of my reptilian brain. I knew that laugh! I knew that aftershave!

"Graf!" I hurled myself at him. After a kiss that took my breath away, I smacked his arm. "You are vile. Why didn't you tell me you were coming to Chicago?"

"And spoil the joy of your warm reception? You were about to put me out on my ear."

"Damn straight." My heart was thundering with joy, but I played it tough.

"Aren't you even a little glad to see me?" He slipped the rose from the vase and lightly touched my neck with the soft petals. "Just a tiny bit? I had to track Cece down to find out where you were staying."

I conceded the game with a small moan as I kissed him. I wanted nothing more than to hold him tightly against me, to feel the lean muscles of his body pressed against me, his lips on mine.

He kissed me back with heat. "My god, I've missed you."

I hadn't acknowledged, even to myself, how much I'd missed him. Or how much I needed him to hold me in just this way. For the luxury of a long moment, I allowed myself to lean on him, to surrender to the support of his arms and his strong body.

He drew the kiss to a sweet close, then held me back and scrutinized me. "I ordered dinner for us," he said softly. "You look thin and tired. Cece—"

"She's been tattling on me."

"She's worried about you. And for good cause. Sarah Booth, you look . . . delicate."

While I might look delicate, something savage and wild was building inside me. I had no appetite for food or the bottle of champagne. I wanted Graf. I wanted to feel his skin and his touch.

I began to unbutton his shirt.

His hands covered mine. "No man could want you more, Sarah Booth. My strongest desire is to throw you down on that bed and make love to your for the next two hours. But I came to take care of you."

"Then do it, Graf. Take care of me." I freed my hands and snatched his shirt. Buttons flew around the room. "Stop talking and kiss me."

12

"Open wide."

I obliged, and Graf put the piece of steak in my mouth. "I feel like a baby," I told him as I chewed. He held the glass for me to sip the champagne.

"I hope I don't have to stay in Zinnia just to make you eat." He cut another piece of the cold steak. It was three in the morning. We'd made love with hot abandon, sating ourselves, only to start over for another session, this one tender and caring. With one appetite satisfied, another had risen to the forefront. I was starving.

"How about I call room service for some hot breakfast?" he asked.

"No, the steak is perfect." I didn't want to order breakfast. I didn't want the night to be over. Morning would bring a parting that I dreaded. My heart's desire was for Graf to come home to Zinnia with me, but I couldn't ask, because he'd put my wishes ahead of his dream. I'd never ask that.

He fed me another bite and took one for himself. As he turned to cut the steak, I took joy in his lean, beautiful torso. "You could model for an artist," I said.

"Flattery will get you everything you want—but in an hour or two. You've drained me."

"You are beautiful." I traced a finger over his thigh. "Handsome doesn't cover it."

"You're not so shabby yourself." He ran a hand gently down my hip. "But you've lost weight."

"I eat all the time."

"Sarah Booth, there's a bad virus or something in Sunflower County. I'm worried. You're in and out of the hospital and you aren't taking care of yourself."

He was right. "I'll get Doc to prescribe some super vitamins." I chewed and swallowed the steak he offered. "This isn't contagious, Graf. It's contained to four people, all of whom were on a particular piece of land. At first it looked like it could be a widespread matter, but now it appears to be limited. You don't have to worry about me on that count."

He cut another portion and fed me. "As soon as Oscar recovers, you'll come back to Los Angeles, won't you?"

I didn't know the answer until that moment. "Yes. I'll never leave Zinnia, but I'll be with you while you finish the film."

"We can make this work, Sarah Booth."

"We can do anything, Graf." I turned away to hide my sudden tears, but I wasn't fast enough. His hand captured my chin and slowly brought my gaze back to his.

"What's wrong?"

"My life is perfect. Everything I've ever wanted is mine for the taking. And Tinkie is losing everything."

He kissed me softly. "She hasn't lost everything. She still has you as a friend, and that's a big thing."

I inhaled, trying to pull my erratic emotions back into line. "I have to fix this."

"If anyone can, it's you." He got up and pushed the food away. "I brought you something."

"What?" I was naturally leery of surprises. Once burned, twice shy was my motto. I thought of Aunt Loulane and her fondness for adages and proverbs. My high school years had been lived by her cross-stitched samplers of sage sayings.

Graf removed a red-bound script from his bag. "Federico Marquez, your favorite director, asked me to give this to you."

Excitement made my skin tingle. "Have you read it?"

"I have." He handed it to me. *Crimson Swan.*

"What's it about?"

"A vampire enforcer who tracks down a serial killer in a small Mississippi town. They can film in Zinnia."

The script's weight was real and tangible. Graf offered another shot at my dream after the fiasco of my last film.

"Thank you."

"I'm merely the messenger. Federico sent it. It's based on a book by a Mississippi gal, Jeannie Holmes."

"Is there a part for you?"

"Varik, a dangerous man who nearly drains you of all your blood."

"Charming."

"Oh, I can charm you into offering that beautiful white neck to me."

I had no doubt of that. In fact, Graf had glamoured me so thoroughly that I wanted to do nothing but remain in bed for the rest of the week. If only we could stop time outside the hotel room, freeze everything tragic and bad happening to my friends, and give ourselves a week or a month or a year to truly explore the riptide of feelings swirling around us.

But that was not to be. The bedside clock showed another precious hour had slipped away.

"When is your flight back to L.A.?" I held the script as if it could somehow, magically, stretch the minutes.

"I have to be at the airport at six."

I did the calculations in my head. Our time was short.

"Sarah Booth?"

I gave him my full attention.

"I want to marry you."

My heart fluttered in excitement and fear. "Graf—"

"Don't answer me now. Don't. The timing is all wrong. I want to propose properly. But I didn't want to leave with those words unsaid."

"I can't imagine my life without you."

"That's a big step for you." He leaned over and kissed me. "One day you'll trust me completely. That's when we'll marry. When I prove I'm the man you can lean on."

I kissed him. We only had a couple of hours left before his departure. I intended to make full use of them.

When I exited the hotel, suitcase in hand, my cab driver was waiting. Graf had left in the predawn darkness, and I'd managed not to cry, though I was slightly teary as I climbed into the backseat of the cab.

My destination was the office of the superintendent of public schools. To my everlasting gratitude, the school system's records were computerized, and within half an hour I'd found Jimmy Janks's high school home address, 1024 Pompeii Street, and his father's name, Austin James Janks. I'd also looked up Sonja Kessler's school address.

I wasn't familiar with the street, but my resourceful cabby supplied me with a city map.

A stop at the nearest library gave me a peek at a reverse directory. John and Elsie McBane now owned 1024 Pompeii. The home where Sonja had grown up had also been sold. My time was limited and I had to choose.

"Pompeii is closer," my driver said.

"Go there." Sometimes a cabby with a good sense of direction makes all the difference in the world.

Janks's old neighborhood was quiet and middle-class. The homes were older, neatly maintained, the lawns clipped and trimmed. When the cab stopped in front of 1024, I hurried up the sidewalk and rang the bell.

"Can I help you?" Elsie McBane was a pretty young woman with a baby on one hip and a toddler banging his toys in a loud ruckus on the floor behind her. Instead of frustration, she wore an open smile and jounced the baby on her hip to keep it quiet.

I introduced myself and implied that I was attempting to find a member of the Janks family in regard to an inheritance.

"Oh, that would be wonderful," Elsie McBane said, obviously delighted to have an adult to speak with, even if it was a stranger. "The younger Mr. Janks, Jimmy, was such a nice man. He kept this house in perfect condition. Not a crack uncaulked. You don't find such care and detail in most homes."

"Yes," I agreed. "Do you know where I might find the elder Mr. Janks?"

She frowned. "Why, he's dead, I'm afraid. There was an accident involving chemicals." She shook her head. "I'm sorry, I don't remember the details. It was a long time ago, way before we bought this house. I only heard the talk. Jimmy hated to sell the family home, sentimental value and all, but he had to. An inheritance would be a wonderful thing for him."

"What did the father do?"

She grabbed a pacifier that the baby spit out and put it back in the infant's mouth. "Seems like he was some kind of chemist or biologist or something like that. I believe he worked for DeFoe, the chemical plant."

My pulse had begun to race, but I hid my excitement behind a bland smile. "Do you remember when he died?"

"I'm sorry, I don't." She leaned down to the toddler on the floor and removed a pot he was beating. "Charles, please stop banging for half a minute." She rolled her eyes. "He's fascinated by the sounds he can make. I'm hoping Emma here is a quieter baby."

The infant watched me from beneath a mop of dark curls. Never one to get sappy over a baby, I found this one striking. "She's a beauty."

"Takes after her dad."

"Thanks for your help, Mrs. McBane."

I jumped in the cab and we headed to the airport. As the city slipped farther and farther behind me, I examined the map my driver had so kindly provided.

The Janks house was less than a mile from the street where Sonja Kessler had grown up. As Cece had so succinctly pointed out, coincidences like this were hard to swallow.

After clearing security, I had forty minutes to kill, and I dialed Chicago information. The link to pesticides and Austin James Janks might be a dead end, but it was worth checking out. Time was critical. If there was an antidote to Oscar's illness, we needed it as quickly as possible.

DeFoe Chemical was unwilling to give out any information on employees, past or present. I had no alternative but to call in the law.

"Sunflower County Sheriff's Office." Bonnie Louise answered the phone.

"It's Sarah Booth. I need to speak with Coleman."

"Is this business or personal?"

I couldn't believe her, but now wasn't the time for a set-to over phone etiquette. "Business."

"He's in a meeting, but he should be out in just a minute."

"And you're his new receptionist?" Coleman had a long history of hiring difficult receptionists.

"I'm happy to help Coleman any way I can, even if it means answering the telephone for a half hour." She drawled the words.

"Any luck on the tests you've been running? I'm particularly interested in pesticides or chemical agents."

There was a pause. At last she answered. "The soil tests show nothing, so far. The cotton itself, while genetically altered, hasn't been treated with any detectible chemical or poison. The well water is fine to drink. My best determination is that pesticides aren't an issue."

"What about those strange boll weevils?"

"The good news is that they're confined to the genetically altered cotton. There's no danger they'll spread. It's not clear how this relates to the sick people."

An airline employee announced my flight.

"There has to be some link," I told her. "The last four people to step foot on the property are sick. If it isn't pesticides, it has to be the cotton or the weevils."

"The weevils appear to have mutated in some ways. They're still being examined, but it's going to take some time. I have to study their DNA, breeding, and reproductive cycles. Preliminary testing shows sudden changes in those areas."

It didn't take a brainiac to figure this boded ill. "How long before you get some answers?"

"I've consulted an independent expert, a brilliant man. Even Peyton is impressed with his skills and accomplishments and nobody impresses Peyton. He's dying to meet the doctor. I'm hoping to have some solid information soon."

The airline attendant began to shut the door to the flight ramp. "My flight is boarding. Tell Coleman I'll stop by to see him when I get home."

"He's got a full schedule, but I'll tell him."

Before I could say anything, she hung up. I hustled onto the plane that would ferry me to Memphis. Before take-off, I was able to leave Coleman a voice mail on his cell phone regarding Austin James Janks.

It was late afternoon by the time I got home and fed Reveler. Sweetie Pie and Chablis were asleep on the front porch, and I let them inside and defrosted some ground turkey to cook for them.

"Your mama will be home soon," I told Chablis. She was looking a little forlorn. I scooped her into my arms and gave her some kisses. Since Tinkie was practically living at the hospital, it was up to me to keep Chablis fed and loved.

As I'd driven south from Memphis I'd heard a country ballad on the radio about a prison hound. I held Chablis in my arms and sang it to her while Sweetie Pie accompanied me with a soft alto yodel.

A sharp knock on the kitchen door interrupted our duet.

"Who's there?" Most of my friends used the front door and didn't bother with formalities.

"Sarah Booth?"

The voice was deep, male, and one I recognized. Coleman Peters. At the back door.

"Coleman?"

"I didn't want to leave the patrol car in front of the house."

"Why ever not?" And then it struck me. He didn't want Beaucoup to know he was visiting Dahlia House. "Are you hiding the fact that you're here?"

"Not for the reasons you've jumped to."

I inhaled. Perhaps I had been speedy in my assessment. "Then why?"

"Everyone in town knows we have a history. And that you're in love with Graf Milieu. Why should we complicate things by stirring up gossip?"

Even though I could see his point, I was still a little hot. "I don't give a rat's ass what other people think, Coleman. You're the sheriff. I'm an investigator. Our friends are in trouble. We can talk about it at midnight in the cemetery if that's what we need to do."

His expression touched me. "You never change," he said. "That's a compliment."

"Want some coffee?"

"How about a Jack? I'm off duty."

Coleman seldom drank, and with Gordon sick, he was never off duty, but I fixed us both a short one without comment. God knows I could use a drink. I hadn't slept a wink the night before and I was running on pure adrenaline.

"What're you cooking?" he asked.

"Turkey and whole wheat noodles. For the dogs."

He stirred the pot with a big spoon. "Sounds like your

nesting skills are kicking in and the dogs are the beneficiaries."

"Chablis is virtually an orphan." I added the frozen peas and carrots. Though I had nothing fresh to cook, my freezer was well stocked.

The ground meat cooked quickly and while it was cooling, Coleman and I sat on the front porch to sip our drinks. While the days were warm, with night falling the wooden steps were cool. Soon the paint would be baking in the summer heat.

The fields around Dahlia House sprouted row upon row of tender green cotton, young plants that symbolized the South's tragic past and uncertain future. Even so, looking over the growing fields yielded a moment of serenity.

Coleman sipped the Jack. "I talked to the folks at DeFoe."

It was a good lead. I could tell by the way Coleman gripped his glass. "And?"

"Janks moved to Argentina, where he was a contract worker for a branch of DeFoe that creates crop pesticides. There was some trouble at the plant. They were reluctant to go into details, but it involved a breach of plant security and the theft of chemical formulas."

"What kind of chemical formulas?"

"There's a particular type of beetle in South America that destroys the roots of grass. It could devastate the beef industry there. Janks and several other scientists had reached a breakthrough on the pesticide, when someone broke into the plant. Janks was killed and the formula stolen. About a year later, a European company came up with a formula to resolve the beetles. DeFoe lost a lot of money."

"The boll weevil is a type of beetle," I pointed out.

"Exactly. The DeFoe spokesman glossed over the actual event. He'd only say that Janks was killed, burned to death in a chemical fire. He wouldn't come out and say it, but he hinted that Janks might have been involved with the break-in and the fire. I'd say the Janks clan is something to keep our eyes on." He lifted his glass in a toast. "Good work, Sarah Booth."

"Cece had a date with Jimmy last night? Did she find anything?"

Coleman, about to sip his drink, slowly lowered the glass. "I haven't spoken with Cece."

"She was supposed to call you last night. She went to Memphis with Jimmy for dinner."

"And no doubt to pump him for information." His forehead furrowed. "You haven't heard from her?"

I stood quickly. "No. I need to check right now."

Inside, Coleman dished up the turkey for the dogs while I called Cece's cell phone. The phone rang straight to voice mail. I left a message, asking her to call, and then tried her home phone. No answer.

The newspaper was closed, but I called, anyway, hoping she might be working late. When her voice mail picked up, I ended the call.

"I want to run by her house," I said.

"Let's do it." Coleman had his keys in his hand.

13

"Open up!" I pounded Cece's solid front door while Coleman went to the back.

"Cece!" I rattled the knob. The door was locked. Judging from the look of the house, no one was home. I amended the thought to no one *alive* was home. The sense of emptiness was palpable.

I retrieved my cell phone from my pocket and called information to get the home number of Amis Truesdale, the publisher and executive editor of the *Dispatch*. If Cece worked today, my fears were unfounded. But if—

"Amis Truesdale." His voice was crisp, no-nonsense.

I explained who I was and asked if Cece had been in the office that day.

"She didn't come in and she didn't call, which isn't like her." Concern was clear in his tone. "I sent a copy boy over to her house, but no one answered the door. He said her car wasn't in the garage."

The thud, thud, thud of my heart felt as if it would break my ribs. Cece had possibly been missing for twenty-four hours and no one had noticed. Until now. Even though I knew she was seeing Jimmy Janks last night, I hadn't worried about her. Swept into my own drama and Graf's arms, I hadn't even tried to call her.

Coleman returned as I finished my conversation with Cece's boss.

"If you hear from her, Mr. Truesdale, please call me or Sheriff Peters."

"What was Cece into?" Truesdale asked. "I could tell she was chewing on something, but she never discusses her stories. She's got attitude, but she also delivers."

"Sheriff Peters will explain when he has something to reveal." I hung up. "She didn't show up for work today. I don't know if she made it home from Memphis. She could be inside the house, hurt or . . ."

"Don't do that to yourself, Sarah Booth. Her car is gone, and in all likelihood, Cece is fine. When she's on a story, she doesn't think of anything else, but she's resourceful."

"And courageous," I added. "And sometimes lacks good judgment. But she *never* misses work." I leaned against one of the front porch pillars because my legs were unsteady. "She could be bleeding to death in there right this minute."

Coleman read my deep fear. "I get the point. Stand back."

I stepped aside so he could ram the door with his full weight. In high school, Coleman had been a standout football player. He'd gone to college on a scholarship. He knew a thing or two about bodily assault. It took him three tries, but the wood splintered, and we stepped inside.

At first, nothing appeared to be amiss. Except for the dishes in the kitchen sink. And the clothes tossed carelessly on the still-made bed. Cece was a neatnik, and wherever she'd gone, she'd left in a hurry. I could almost see her, getting ready for her date with Jimmy, rushing around, leaving the tidying up for later.

But if Jimmy had driven her to Memphis, where was her car?

"Where did Janks take her to dinner?" Coleman asked. He put a restraining hand on my shoulder as I started to the bathroom.

"She didn't say."

"What did Janks drive?"

"Black SUV. Tahoe, I think." I'd seen the plates when he drove around the building, but I didn't have a photographic memory to recall such details. "It had a Mississippi tag," I said. "I remember that because he said he was from Mobile."

"Let me get Dewayne to run a registration."

Dewayne Dattilo was Coleman's only other deputy, and the two of them had worked nonstop for days. For Coleman to call him in indicated great concern. "Do you think Cece's in trouble?"

"I think Cece is missing. The more we know, the quicker we can find her."

He borrowed my cell phone and placed the call to Dewayne. He returned my phone and shut the front door. "I'll get someone to repair the door. Let's get out of here."

"I can't just leave and—"

"We're going to Janks's hotel room. If he's there, and if he had anything to do with Cece's disappearance, I'll get it out of him."

135

The set of Coleman's jaw and his tone of voice convinced me it would be best to do as he said without a lot of questions.

Downtown Zinnia was a ghost town. Even Millie's was closed, and the two stoplights had been turned off. Each deserted shop front seemed an omen of tragedy as we sped through the town.

"How do you know where Jimmy Janks is staying?" I asked Coleman.

He drove for at least a mile before he answered. "Beaucoup had suspicions about him. The development deal on the Carlisle land depended on Erin being willing to sell the land for nonagricultural use. Janks seemed pretty sure the deal would go through."

"Good work on her part." I tried to sound sincere. It wasn't that I didn't respect Bonnie's intelligence. My problem had to do with the fact that she was a bitch. Much like Coleman's soon-to-be-ex wife. I had no stake in Coleman's romantic life but, as a friend, I hated to see him hook up with another harpy. "Coleman, Bonnie is—"

"She's devoted to her job, Sarah Booth." He cut me off. "And she's good at it."

"I never said differently."

"No, you didn't. And please don't. We're both feeling our way through this. You have your solutions and I have mine. But to answer your question, I made it a point to run down where Janks is staying. Just to keep an eye on him."

Strictly business. I could handle that. "And where is Janks staying?"

"At the Gardens Bed and Breakfast."

"Uh-oh." The Gardens was one of the most beautiful old homes in the Southeast. Live oaks lined the drive, and the house was surrounded with formal gardens designed and maintained in the style of European royalty.

Another small point—the owner of the B&B hated me.

Coleman chuckled. "I'll protect you from Gertrude."

"I don't need protection." I thought about it. "Well, I might. She really does hate me." She'd whacked me on the head—deliberately, in my opinion, though she'd said otherwise—when I was on a previous case. For an old bat, she had a pretty good swing.

"We're on official business. She'll understand."

"If it gets too rough, I'll call Tinkie. She knows how to keep Gertrude in line." Mentioning Tinkie's name made me realize that I hadn't checked in on her lately. I remedied that while Coleman drove.

She answered before the first ring could fully sound. "Where are you, Sarah Booth?"

"What's wrong?" I knew something had happened.

"It's Oscar. He had some kind of seizure and they took the ventilator out. Now he's trying to talk. He said your name. Can you come? He may talk again if he sees you. It's the first sign that . . . he isn't brain-dead."

The muscles in my neck and shoulders knotted so tightly, I could hardly turn my head. How could I tell Tinkie that Cece was missing and I couldn't come to the hospital because our friend might be in danger?

"Look, I'm on a serious lead right now. I can't leave. I'm . . . surveilling someone. It could be valuable and maybe lead to a clue about Oscar."

"Where are you?"

"I'll be at the hospital as soon as I can. I promise."

"I just thought if Oscar saw you, he might come back to us."

She sounded so forlorn and desperate. "As soon as I can," I promised as we pulled into the beautiful oak-canopied lane that led to the B&B. "I'll be there, Tink."

Gertrude, with her copper-wire hair sculpted into perfect obedience, stood behind the registration desk. Her smile was wide and welcoming. "Sheriff Peters," she said, "what can I do for you?" When she caught sight of me, the smile faded.

"I need to speak with Jimmy Janks."

She pinned me with her gaze. "Mr. Janks is a guest here. I'm not in the habit of letting anyone disturb my guests. Now if you get rid of the riffraff at your side, I might be amenable to helping you."

Coleman's temper was shorter than I thought. "Gertrude, I'll put you in jail for obstruction of justice if that's the way you want to play it."

Normally, he wouldn't stoop to a bluff, and I could have told him that Gertrude was smarter than the average bear. Too late.

"Do you have a warrant?" Gertrude pushed her glasses up her nose.

Coleman's sigh was an admission of defeat. "Gertrude, I can get a warrant, but time is critical. I need to check a room. It's a serious matter. You could play a big role in saving an innocent person's life. Will you help me?" He could turn on the charm when he wished.

"Sounds like a pile of rubbish, like what Adam Chandler would say when he's cooking up a plot on that soap opera." She sniffed and pointed out me. "Sheriff, I'm disappointed that you'd be swayed by Hollywood celebrity." She leaned on the counter, her breasts covering the blotter where guests still registered with an ink pen. "Why are you keeping company with Sarah Booth Delaney?"

"I'm under arrest," I told Gertrude.

"Grow up, Sarah Booth. You aren't even wearing handcuffs."

"Gertrude, please." Coleman struggled for patience. "Is Janks in his room?"

"Possibly."

"May I check his room to see if he's injured?"

"Okay, but only because you asked nicely." She pushed the register toward him.

Coleman scanned the open page. "Room two."

She checked the pigeonholes where she kept the room keys and produced one. "The rooms, as you know, open on the hallway and the back gallery. I don't keep up with the comings-and-goings of my guests. I'm not nosey."

Right, I thought, like Norman Bates wasn't crazy.

Coleman took the key to Room two. "Thank you, Gertrude."

His boots rang on the tongue-and-groove oak floor as he walked. I hurried after him, afraid Gertrude would try to stab me with her registration pen.

"Sorry," I whispered. "She hates me. I told you she did."

The hallway was illuminated with dim lights that emulated gas lamps. It was a nice touch, but not practical for good visibility.

When we got to Room two, Coleman inserted the key and pushed the door open. The room was a mess, complete with what looked like a bloodstain spattered across a beautiful hand-loomed carpet.

"Cece." I started toward the stain and stopped myself. The worst thing I could do would be to tromp in and destroy evidence. Taking in the disarray of the room, I thought Janks had left under duress—and while a few articles of clothing were scattered about, I didn't see a suitcase.

Janks had left in a hurry. Whether on his own or at the hands of someone else, I couldn't begin to guess.

"My carpet!" Gertrude had followed us and was about to charge into the room, but Coleman stopped her.

"You didn't hear anything?" he asked.

She glared at me as if this were all my fault. "I went to play bridge for a few hours. It could have happened then. There's no one in the rooms on either side. Mr. Janks asked for as much privacy as possible."

Coleman herded Gertrude into the hall and I followed. He called Dewayne to come and collect evidence. I was trying hard not to jump to conclusions.

"We aren't sure Cece was even in this room." Coleman tried to comfort me. "While the stain, if it is blood, indicates an injury, we can't judge the severity."

"But someone was hurt here," I pointed out.

"Don't jump the gun. It could've been an accident."

He didn't believe that. He wouldn't call Dewayne to process an accident scene. Coleman knelt beside the stain and surveyed the disarray of the room. "We'll have more information once we process the scene."

There was nothing else I could accomplish here. If there was a lead to Cece's whereabouts, Coleman would find it. I could perhaps accomplish something at the hospital. But how in the hell could I conceal this from Tinkie? She could read me like a book.

Coleman stood up. "Dewayne will be here in less than

five minutes. We'll get you to the hospital then. When I know something conclusive, I'll call you."

I ran down the freshly mopped hallway, the scent of pine forever reminding me of the long, heartbreaking days of Aunt Loulane's decline.

My world was under attack. Oscar, Cece, Gordon, the population of my homeland. And my own body was in revolt. Another wave of nausea swept over me, causing me to lean against the wall. The sickness passed, and I rushed on until I rounded the corner and saw Tinkie.

"Sarah Booth!" She rose to meet me, hope so evident that I slowed to a near standstill. "Oscar said your name." She grasped my arm, and I was shocked at how thin and cold her fingers were.

I covered her hand with mine, rubbing and squeezing as if I could press warmth into it. "What can I do?"

"I'll get Doc. Keep an eye on Oscar."

Oscar remained, almost unchanged, except the ventilator was gone. His color was still gray, his face and arms covered in sores. Tinkie said he'd had a seizure. Not even the kindest interpretation could paint that as a good thing.

Footsteps rushed toward me, and Tinkie returned with Doc. "Can he see me from here?" I asked Doc.

"He can see you, but he can't talk to you. You'll have to go in the room."

I was allowed what Tinkie was not. And I was scared. I didn't want to contract this sickness. No one thought it was contagious, at least not from person to person, but what if it was? I closed my eyes and prayed for courage.

In many instances of grave danger, Tinkie had come

141

to my rescue without thought or regard for her own safety. She had rushed into ambushes and attacked men and women with guns. She was fearless. I could be no less for her.

"Come with me. We'll get you suited up," Doc said. He led the way. "We don't believe this is contagious, Sarah Booth, but we aren't taking any risks. Until we figure out what this is and how to treat it, we're insisting on full isolation."

I had no problem with that. As Aunt Loulane would say, an ounce of prevention is worth a pound of cure.

"Tell him I love him," Tinkie said. She clung to my elbow. "Tell him he has to get well." Her voice broke. "Tell him that he's the most important thing in the world to me and Chablis. Tell him I can't live without him."

I wrapped my arms around her and held her tightly as she sobbed in deep gasps. Doc turned away, hiding the tears that brightened his own eyes. Doc had ministered to both me and Tinkie since we were born. Probably Oscar, too. He wasn't just a medical man, he was a friend, and it hurt him to see us suffer.

"Tinkie," I said as I rubbed her back. "Oscar is tough. He's made it this far. If he can make it a little longer, he'll pull through this."

"Why didn't he ask for me?" She wasn't jealous, just hurt.

"Because he knows you're guarding him. I'm the one who has to solve this. If he has information about the cause of the illness, he'll tell me. Oscar would do anything to keep you safe, which means keeping you out of that room."

She pushed her hair out of her face. "I don't want you to come down sick, Sarah Booth."

"I'm healthy as a horse and you know it. You haven't

slept in days. You're on the verge of a complete physical, emotional, and mental breakdown."

"I am not." She straightened her posture. "I just like hanging out at the hospital so I can flirt with the doctors."

That one act of bravery was almost my undoing. Worn to the bone, Tinkie had more courage than anyone I knew.

"Sarah Booth, we need to suit up." Doc gently took Tinkie by the shoulders. He kissed her cheek. "We'll figure this out, Tinkie. Don't give up yet."

14

The suit that Doc gave me was like something from a *Star Trek* episode. I wondered if Oscar, if he returned to consciousness from the coma, would recognize me.

"What, exactly, did Oscar say?" I asked Doc as I fastened the Velcro tabs.

"The seizure forced us to remove the ventilator. While he was struggling, he said your name."

"Anything else?"

"No."

"What should I do?" I felt helpless.

"Talk to him," Doc said. "Touch him lightly. Let him know you're drawing him back to this world."

I'd never talked theology with Doc, but his sentiments were clear. Oscar was hovering somewhere between life and the other side. I was to bring him back to the world of mortals. Too bad no one had given me a cape or magic powers. "Inadequate" didn't begin to describe my feelings.

"I'll try." The suit made me sound like some kind of wheezy insect-man.

The door to the isolation ward swished open, and I stepped into what looked like an airlock. Another door opened automatically onto the room where four very sick people appeared to sleep.

As I passed Gordon I lightly touched his shoulder. "You have to get well," I told him. Gordon was the only victim who remained on a ventilator. Regina and Luann breathed on their own. Though I had no medical training, they appeared to have more color and their sores seemed to be healing. Or it could just be they were less under the glare of unforgiving fluorescent lights.

As I approached his bed, Oscar moaned and one leg twitched. That had to be a good sign. He could move. He wasn't paralyzed.

My gloved fingertips grazed his cheek. "Oscar, it's me, Sarah Booth."

I dared a look at Tinkie, who watched each second with breathless hope from behind the glass. My stomach knotted, and I stroked Oscar's hand, avoiding the needles and tubes attached to every possible artery.

"Oscar, Tinkie said you wanted to talk to me."

His chest moved up and down so shallowly, I wondered if the ventilator shouldn't be reinserted. "Oscar?"

I needed a response. One that would let Tinkie know he was sound of mind and that the fever hadn't destroyed his brain function.

Moving to the side of the bed, I lifted his hand and held it on top of mine. "Oscar, I'm here. I'm here because you asked for me. You have something to tell me?"

It seemed an hour passed with only the rasp of his

labored breathing, but it was only seconds. I watched his face for any change of expression—for some indication that he was aware of me.

"Oscar, Tinkie is not twenty feet away. She's watching you. The only time she leaves your side is when we force her to rest or eat. If you're here, and if you can respond, signal with your hand."

The bandages had been removed from his eyes, and though they didn't open, I thought I saw the eyeballs shift left, then right. His index finger scratched my palm.

"Oh, Oscar." I wept then. I couldn't stop it. He was there, trapped in that body ravaged by pain and disease. He hadn't gone away.

His finger moved again, a light tap against the base of my forefinger. He was trying to comfort *me*, and that prompted me to get a grip on my emotions.

"Oscar, if you don't get better, and soon, I'm going to have to kill you." It sounded peculiar, but he knew what I meant. "Tinkie is about to worry herself to death. Gordon is very sick, as are two realtors. Do you have any idea what happened to you?"

One tap of his finger on my palm.

"You went to the Carlisle plantation?"

Two taps. A yes. He was communicating! But I had to test it to be sure.

"Shall I tell Tinkie that you love her?"

The finger tapped twice, with emphasis. He tried to grasp my hand, but he was too weak.

"It's okay. I'll tell her," I promised. "But we have to talk about what happened. You went to the plantation. Everything in the house was in order." I went over the facts as I knew them, and he confirmed them.

"And when you went out to walk the fields, you discovered the cotton was infested with boll weevils."

Two solid taps.

"Did you talk to anyone there?"

One tap. His lips pursed, and he made a dry rasping sound in his throat. I frantically waved to Doc. "Can he have some water?"

"I'd love it if he'd drink," Doc said. He disappeared through the airlock doors and came back with a glass and a straw. He wore the same hazmat suit that I wore, which made both of us a little clumsy, but Doc was able to put the straw to Oscar's lips. Oscar drew in a small amount of water and swallowed.

"Who did you see?" I was pressing him, but this might be the break we needed to find the source of his illness.

"Bugs." The word rasped out of his throat. "Cotton."

Doc frowned at me. He indicated the monitors, which showed elevated blood pressure and a spike in heart rate. My time with Oscar was limited.

"Did you see anyone there?"

His finger tapped once. His hand went limp and slipped from mine. His eyes darted wildly behind the closed lids before they rolled upward.

"He's gone," Doc said.

I froze. "No." It couldn't be. Not like that. Not after he'd come back to us.

Doc took my arm and moved me away.

"Wait, Doc. He can't be—"

"He's asleep, Sarah Booth," Doc said in a gentle voice. "He's exhausted by communicating with you."

Sweet relief. Oscar wasn't dead, he was only resting. I punched Doc in the arm. "You need to learn better phrasing."

"Do you realize what you did, Sarah Booth?" he asked, his face beaming behind the clear mask of his suit.

"What?"

"You brought Oscar back. You drew him out of that coma back to reality."

"He'll get well now?"

Doc looked at Tinkie, her face and hands pressed to the glass, watching her husband. "I can't say. Sometimes, a patient makes a rally, to deliver a final . . ." My expression stopped him. "At least there's no apparent brain damage. Not yet. If we can find a way to fight this, I believe they all stand a chance of recovering. That's a lot better than I felt this morning."

Doc didn't feel better for long. As we were stripping off the hazmat suits, I told him about Cece's disappearance.

"Do you have any idea who's behind this?" His face was strained. "Oscar and three others have contracted some illness. Now Cece has possibly been abducted. This has to stop. Does Tinkie know about Cece?"

The thought of telling her was intolerable. "No. Maybe I'll wait. Until we know something positive."

"She can't bear a lot more," he said.

If I was reading Doc's signals correctly, he wanted me to withhold the news of Cece's disappearance. A lie of omission didn't sit well, but the thought of sending Tinkie deeper into anxiety was worse.

"Point taken," I said.

"If there's any flak, I'll bear the brunt of it."

Exhaustion mixed with relief made me lean against the wall. "Oscar is still there. That's the report I'll give Tinkie."

When Doc didn't respond, I felt the weight of his doubts. His faith in a medical cure had been shaken.

While he practiced the art of healing, he relied on science to direct his skills. So far, science was thwarting him.

Tinkie waited outside the door. "He knew you! What did he say?"

"He's trying to help us."

"Thank goodness." She almost hummed with tension. "I was so afraid the high fever had damaged his brain."

I circled her with one arm and held her against my side, and we stood that way for nearly a minute.

At last she spoke. "He drank some water. You held his hand. Thank you, Sarah Booth. What did he tell you?"

I hesitated. "Things at the Carlisle place seemed normal, except for the weevils. It's apparent he went out into the cotton."

"And there wasn't a trace of evidence in the field?"

This was a sticky point, since Gordon had investigated the plantation after Oscar became ill. Before Gordon's report had been filed, he'd fallen sick. Only Bonnie Louise and Peyton had actually been on the Carlisle property since then.

"I need to examine the area," I said.

"You can't. It's too dangerous."

Arguing was pointless, and I didn't intend to stress Tinkie more. In my heart, though, I knew there was no other way. Someone had to go. While Bonnie Louise and Peyton might have the equipment, they didn't have the personal motivation that I did.

"One way or the other, we'll find an answer." If I had to beat it out of Luther Carlisle or Jimmy Janks—once we found him.

The worst possibility crossed my mind. What if Janks had dumped Cece at the plantation? What if she was lying there now, sick or dying because of exposure to something we couldn't identify?

"I've got to get some rest," I said, edging down the hall.

"You aren't fooling me, Sarah Booth. I know that look. You're going to do something dangerous."

"No, I'm really exhausted. I was headed to bed when Coleman showed up and . . ."

"And what?"

"And asked me to help him." My answer was feeble and wouldn't satisfy Tinkie for longer than two minutes. "I really have to go."

"What did Coleman need your help on?"

I waved a hand. "A lead."

"You're hiding something."

If I didn't get away, she'd break me and I'd spill everything I knew. "Please, Tinkie. I'm beat."

I couldn't discern if it was pity or exhaustion that slipped across her features. "We'll talk tomorrow. If you do anything that endangers your life, Sarah Booth, we're finished. No more partners. No more friends. If something happens to you—"

She focused her attention on Oscar, her mouth set in a firm line.

I found myself stranded outside the hospital with no wheels. Coleman had dropped me off, and in my desperation to get away before I spilled my guts about Cece, I'd forgotten to borrow Tinkie's Caddy. Going back inside wasn't an option.

The night was cool and sweet, lightly scented with an early magnolia on the crisp air. Above me, the stars glittered sharply. In high school I'd learned what made them sparkle. I couldn't remember such a long-ago lesson, nor did I want to. I preferred to enjoy the magic of their beauty.

Finding a ride home was almost more than I could manage. I could call Millie, but then I'd have to tell her Cece was missing and she'd spend the night worried. She had a café to run that demanded her full attention.

Harold was a possibility. Always urbane and never fussy, he would dress and pick me up with nary a complaint.

Coleman was busy. If he was making headway—any headway—I didn't want to disturb him.

Behind me the hospital door opened and Peyton walked toward me. "Ms. Delaney, are you okay?"

"I need a ride home."

"I'm happy to oblige." He pointed to a dark red SUV with the CDC logo on the side. I was so caught up in my own issues I'd failed to notice it in the parking lot.

"Thanks, Peyton." Here was opportunity—unexpected but greatly appreciated. "Would you happen to have one of those CDC hazmat suits that I could borrow?"

He opened the vehicle door for me. "You want to go to the Carlisle place?"

"Yes."

"I don't have one in the truck. Come by the office tomorrow and I'll see what I can do." He closed the door and went around to the driver's side.

"Could we run by there and get the suit tonight? I want to be sure . . ." A wave of nausea caught me unprepared, leaving as abruptly as it came.

"Sure of what?"

Phrasing was all important. Revealing the depth of my

fears would not benefit my cause. "A friend of mine is out of pocket. It occurred to me that she may have gone there."

"One thing I can assure you is that no one is on that property. You have my word. But I'm happy to take you there. Tomorrow. That's my best offer."

In the dark I could accomplish little, and if I continued to press, he might outright refuse. "Tomorrow, then. Why are you at the hospital at this time of night?" Peyton was on the job 24/7. His dedication was remarkable.

"I was running some tests and I needed to consult with Doc Sawyer."

I stopped in the process of buckling my seat belt. "Any results?"

He put the car in gear before he answered. "Progress, but no firm resolution."

Since he was driving, I had the luxury of studying his face. His lips were tightly compressed, his jawline firm and clear. Something—or someone—was eating him alive. The case had become personal for him. "What do you *think* you discovered?"

"It would appear someone has tampered with the DNA of those weevils."

"Like the cotton." Coincidence city here.

"Not exactly, but similar." He shot a look at me and then refocused on the road.

"You're saying someone deliberately created this new breed of beetle designed to devastate the cotton crop." Even as I said it, we drove past fields of new cotton. In the moonlight, the tiny plants stretched to the horizon, the future of many landowners.

He inhaled. "I'm saying it's possible."

"Another explanation is what?"

"Perhaps an experiment went awry."

That took longer to digest. "So someone could have

152

designed these weevils for a *good* cause and it somehow went bad?"

"It's possible." He was extremely defensive.

"Do you have an idea who may be behind this?"

"Absolutely not."

His response was so swift, so emphatic, I knew he was lying. He suspected someone, but he wouldn't share that name with me. Not voluntarily, at any rate.

"Have you connected the weevils to the illness?"

"No, but the connection has to be there. What else could it be, Sarah Booth? There are no soil contaminants, nothing in the water at the Carlisle plantation. The house has been tested for everything from radiation to chemical pesticides. I haven't found a damn thing."

The weariness in his voice revealed how his lack of success gnawed at him. Peyton was, perhaps, as driven as I was. He pulled up in front of Dahlia House.

"How did you find out about the mutation in the weevils?" I asked.

"The credit goes to Bonnie Louise. She made the breakthrough, with the help of her mentor at Mississippi State. Bonnie is a remarkable researcher, and the boll weevils have always been a primary interest of hers."

"Does Coleman know about this?"

"She's given him a full report." He chuckled softly. "She nearly killed herself getting over to the sheriff's office to report to him. Bonnie has it bad for the lawman."

I could only ignore his comment about Coleman. "Thanks for telling me about the report."

Peyton turned off the engine. "You're a loyal friend. Mrs. Richmond and Doc Sawyer sing your praises, Sarah Booth. They told me how much you gave up to return home and help your friend's husband. I wish Dr. Unger's report had been more conclusive. Beaucoup thought for sure he'd be able to identify the mutations of the weevils and give us a course of action. Unfortunately, progress is going to be much slower than I'd hoped."

"Dr. Unger?"

"Jon Unger. He's an international authority on insect development and, as I mentioned, Bonnie's mentor. She's been consulting with him on this case." He rubbed his face. "Unger works with the government on high-profile matters. Beaucoup thinks he's the second coming."

Bonnie Louise had mentioned him, but she'd been under the impression Peyton admired his work. I didn't read it exactly that way. "Is he coming to Zinnia?" I asked.

"I don't know. Bonnie and I have taken different paths on this investigation. I've hardly seen her. Unger may have been here already. I just can't say." He looked like he was about to slump over the steering wheel from fatigue.

"Thanks, Peyton." I slipped out of the car. "Get some rest. I'll see you tomorrow."

He drove away, his taillights blinking red in the velvety Delta night.

15

Sweetie and Chablis snoozed on the horsehair sofa in the parlor. Aunt Loulane would stroke out at the sight of the hound and the dustmop sprawled across the antique, whose history was almost as long as Dahlia House's. I merely felt bad that I'd had so little time to spend with the pooches.

Tiptoeing so as not to wake them, I decided to call Coleman from upstairs. I was bone tired. My body felt thick and sluggish, but my mind was like a panicked bird, flying in all directions. The sensation made me dizzy.

My foot was on the staircase when I felt Jitty's presence. Often she caught me by surprise, but this time I knew she was behind me.

"Please tell me you have some advice," I said. Normally I tried to avoid her dictates and sometimes obscure pointers, but I was willing to take help from any source, even the Ghostly Divide. "Just no more Great Depression costumes. I can't take it."

Shifting to sit on the staircase, I faced her. Gone were the rags and dirt. Instead, Jitty was unadorned—she was *contemporary*. No ball gowns, no tie-dyed, no outlandish *Star Trek* suits. She wore jeans and . . . "Is that my favorite red top you're wearing?" I asked.

"Oh, this? I found it in the closet."

Times had to be tough in Casperville if she was raiding my closet. "What's wrong with you?"

She sank onto the step below me. "I'm scared for you, Sarah Booth."

"You're always the one quoting FDR. 'Nothing to fear but fear itself.'"

"My fear is that you're gonna take some rash action that'll haunt you the rest of your days."

"Actions won't haunt me. That's what you're for." She was genuinely worried. Whatever fun I might have had at her expense, I couldn't enjoy it.

"The person behind all this woe is smart—and wicked—Sarah Booth. Not your normal run-of-the-mill criminal."

"Tell me something I don't know." I wished Jitty could resort to ghostly means to help me, but she couldn't. Or wouldn't.

"You're at a turnin' point in your life, Sarah Booth. A future that most women would kill to have is right there at your feet."

"That's true." How well I knew all the things I'd dreamed of—except for my family—were within my grasp.

"You've earned it. Success, love, a good man."

"What's wrong with you?" Jitty was always my champion, in a punitive kind of way. But she was never serious, complimentary, *and* contemporary.

"Big dreams come with big risks. Lord, Sarah Booth, be careful."

If I walked to the kitchen window, I could see the family cemetery where the people I'd loved most in my life were buried. Since Aunt Loulane's death, I'd been alone. I'd chosen to be alone. But that was changing now. With Graf, I had a shot at a family. I had no intention of getting myself injured.

"Something bad is happening in Sunflower County," I conceded, "but I'm not directly involved. Sure, I'm trying to figure it out, but so is Coleman, Dewayne, the CDC, and Cece."

She didn't have to say anything else. Cece was, after all, the reason for her visit this night.

I rose slowly, aware again of a draining weariness. "I'm calling Coleman and going to bed. Morning will be here in a few hours."

"Sleep tight. Don't let the bedbugs bite." She faded on a jangle of her silver bracelets.

Coleman was still at the B&B when he answered his phone. "The good news is that the blood on the carpet in Janks's room doesn't belong to Cece."

I sank onto the bed, afraid to believe it. "You got a DNA sample that fast?"

"Simpler test. Wrong blood type. Cece is B negative. This is A positive."

"How did—"

"Doc did some blood work on Cece before she had her sex-change operation. He knew her type."

"Can you match the blood to Jimmy?"

"It's much easier to exclude someone by type than match them. Even if Janks is A positive, we can't say this is his blood. Doc doesn't have any records on Janks, but he's got someone checking databases. So far, nothing. There is some news, though."

"What?" I slipped out of my shoes and jeans.

"One of Gertrude's residents overheard a heated conversation coming from Janks's room around eleven o'clock this evening. Two male voices. There was the sound of something breaking, then a door slammed. The guest, a salesman from Slidell, Louisiana, didn't see anything, but we did find a broken glass in the bathroom trash. The blood on the glass is also A positive."

"Do you think Janks has been hurt?" Janks was our best lead to find Cece.

"I wish I knew where they went to dinner."

Why hadn't I asked? Normally I was all over Cece's business.

"You don't think she might have said something to Tinkie?" Coleman asked.

"Nope." Inspiration struck. "But maybe Millie. I'll call you right back."

I dialed knowing I'd wake her. I'd hoped to spare her worry about Cece, but this was an emergency.

"Hello." Millie's voice was softened by sleep.

"Sorry to call at this hour, but it's important. Did Cece mention her dinner plans in Memphis?" I asked.

"What's wrong?" Millie was fully alert and concern permeated her tone.

"Cece's missing. Has been since last evening when she went to Memphis with Jimmy Janks."

"I told her not to get in a vehicle with him." Millie

was throwing things around. I heard something heavy strike a wall or the floor.

"She was trying to help Oscar," I said.

"I know that, but carrying on with a liar and cheat isn't helpful. Now she's missing and—" She stopped her outburst. "Sorry, I just get aggravated. I had a long talk with Cece before her date. I tried to make her see sense. She wouldn't listen. She was all hot to trot to investigate what that land developer was up to."

I hadn't even tried to talk her out of her plan. "She felt she could handle Janks."

"I'm thinking back over what she told me." Something else in Millie's house slammed into a wall.

"What are you doing?" I asked.

"Moving books. There's a *National Enquirer* here I need to find."

Millie loved celebrity gossip and had a yen for strange stories of alien babies and mobsters revealed to be living in Florida years after they were believed dead. "I hope it pertains to Cece."

"Of course it does. Memphis has all kinds of places to celebrity-watch. I gave her some tips. Now if I can put my hands on that magazine, I'll tell you where she and that Janks fellow went to eat."

Millie's mind worked in a fashion I couldn't begin to fathom. She had an uncanny ability to link daily events to tabloid trivia.

"Here it is!" Millie's voice was relieved. "There was a special segment on the ghost of Elvis visiting places he once loved to dine at. Cece was intrigued, because she thought about doing a story for the society pages. You know, kill two birds with one stone kind of thing."

"Millie, you are a genius."

Pages rustled and paper crinkled. At last, Millie gave a small cry of success. "Johnny Dino's Supper Club, where the blues play hot and the drinks are cool. Supposed to be some bookie action there."

"That sounds exactly like Cece. You've helped more than you know. Thanks, Millie."

"Call me the minute you find her."

"I will."

"And Sarah Booth, find her unharmed, okay? I can't take much more of this."

Information gave me the number to Johnny Dino's Supper Club. In less than a minute I had Johnny himself on the phone. Lucky for me, the place was closing and Johnny listened as I gave him a brief description of Cece and Jimmy.

"They were here. Had a nice dinner, looked like to me. Then all hell broke out."

"They had a fight. Like a fist fight?"

"Naw, nothin' like that." He hesitated. "Look, I don't eavesdrop on the conversations of my guests—"

"But?" I knew there was a but.

"But the woman was some kind of newspaper reporter." He lowered his voice. "That kind of talk ain't so good in a place like mine. Anyway, whatever she was askin' pissed the guy off. He was angry, but not physical."

"Can you tell me exactly what she said?" My ribs ached from the pressure of my thudding heart.

"Somethin' about an investigation. Some land deal gone sour. That she'd find the sister. I remember that. 'The sister' were the exact words, 'cause I wondered if it might be a nun she was lookin' for."

"And then what happened?"

"The guy just laughed and told her to dig as much as she wanted. He paid the tab and they left. They seemed okay when they walked out. That's the last I saw of them. Now I gotta go. Bernie's waiting to lock the door."

He hung up before I could ask another question. In truth, if I was going to get more out of him, I would have to make a trip to Memphis. Or Coleman would.

I was so tired, I was nauseated, but I made one last call to Coleman and told him what I'd learned.

"I'll ask the Memphis PD to stop by Dino's club. Their presence might help him remember more details. But at least we know Cece was with Janks and seemed fine."

"Are you and Dewayne still at Gertrude's?" Coleman and his deputy were as tired as I was. My stomach roiled and I thought of toast or crackers, but it was too much effort to walk back downstairs.

"We're putting up some crime-scene tape."

"Gertrude's going to charge the county the going rate for that room," I warned him.

Coleman laughed. "Maybe not. She's cooperative if you talk to her the right way."

"Sure," I said, "I don't speak Beelzebub."

"You're slurring your words, and I know you haven't been drinking," he said. "Hop in bed. That's an order. I promise, if anything breaks, I'll call you."

16

The low moan of a hound dog brought me out of a long, complicated dream of Bette Davis and Joan Crawford duking it out over a baby carriage occupied by Mia Farrow's child. I awoke to a world blanketed in heavy fog. From my bedroom window, Reveler and Miss Scrapiron were ghost horses as they cantered across the pasture.

Bleary eyed, I trotted downstairs to brew a pot of coffee, letting the aroma draw me to wakefulness. The dogs rocketed through the doggy door, barking in the fine spring morning. With a cup of java in hand, I finally went into the office I'd created for Delaney Detective Agency. I'd managed to avoid the place since I came home from L.A. Without Tinkie, the room was like a funeral parlor.

Turning on a computer, I did a quick Google search of Dr. Jon Unger. His list of research credits was impressive and his connections with the U.S. government, veiled in vagaries, told me he was a highly sought after fellow. A German-born scientist who'd permanently immigrated to America in the nineties, he'd been a guest lecturer and researcher at Mississippi State for nearly two decades. Bonnie Louise had brought one of the best minds in the world to the problem here in Sunflower County. Peyton was right about that.

I was on my third cup of coffee when the phone rang.

"Get over here quick." Millie spoke in an urgent whisper.

Before I could respond, the line went dead.

When I got to Millie's Café, Jimmy Janks and Luther Carlisle were sitting at a table near one of the front windows, sipping coffee and chatting as if the world were in perfect order. I nosed my car into a narrow parking space between two pecan trees. I could still see the men, but I was partially hidden.

I called Coleman's cell phone. "Janks is at Millie's. He's eating breakfast with Luther. Like nothing is wrong." I could clearly see Janks shoveling eggs and biscuits into his mouth. Cece was right. He ate like the fork was a new invention.

"Don't confront him." Coleman sounded a lot like Dirty Harry. "If he leaves, tail him."

"Where are you?" I didn't object to tailing Janks, but I had no arrest powers.

"I can't get there, Sarah Booth. Can you follow him?"

"Sure. But shouldn't you arrest him?"

"Just don't let him out of your sight. And don't attempt to detain him. For any reason."

Pondering Coleman's strange behavior, I put my phone away and slunk down in the seat. Janks was so interested in his food, he didn't spare a glance out the window. The thick ground fog also worked in my favor. The café was

163

lighted and gave me a good visual, but the fog shrouded my car.

Millie refreshed their coffee. Something she said made Janks stop eating. He looked up at her, a frown passing over his face. As Millie withdrew, a tall, lean man entered the café, zoning in on the table with Janks and Luther.

Whoever the stranger was, he was angry. Though I couldn't hear what he was saying, it was clear by the way he pointed his finger and his expression that he was hot under the collar.

When he left the restaurant, I got a good look at him—I'd never seen him before. As he left in a dark blue pickup, I was tempted to follow, but Janks was my primary focus. So far, he was the last one seen with Cece, which meant he was the man I wanted to grill.

Where in the hell was Coleman? If he were here, he could corner Janks while I tailed the stranger.

When I dialed his cell phone again, there was a busy signal. Still seated at a table, Janks and Luther were now in a heated debate.

Janks whipped out his wallet, threw money on the table, and stood.

Luther reached out and tried to mollify him, but Janks shook him off and started toward the front door.

Damn it to hell, where was Coleman? Our only link to Cece was about to leave.

The restaurant door opened and I pressed myself across the console, thanking my stars for the shelter of the pecan limbs. I heard his SUV door slam and the engine rev. Gravel crunched beneath his tires, and I sat up. My only option was to follow him, as discreetly as possible. The antique roadster wasn't the best surveillance vehicle because it was fairly conspicuous, but beggars can't be choosers, as my Aunt Loulane would say. It was my only ride.

Tailing Janks at a safe distance, I called Millie. "Who was that man and what happened?"

Plates clattered in the background. "His name was Joe Downs and he works for Mississippi Agri-Team. Sarah Booth, he accused Luther or Janks or both of them of doing something to Lester Ballard, the man who worked the Carlisle land. Mr. Ballard has been missing for two days. He returned from a trip and heard about the troubles here, so he came to see what the ruckus on the plantation was about."

Luther had mentioned Lester Ballard, Peyton had made a note about him, and Coleman had been trying to reach him for several days, but he was out of the country. Now another MAT employee was in town, hunting for Ballard.

"Did you overhear anything else?"

"I thought Downs was going to hit Luther, and Lord, he almost smacked Janks. He said Lester Ballard had been upset about some new cotton seeds and felt he'd been duped by Luther or Janks or both of them."

"Did Janks say anything about Cece?"

"Not a word. I didn't ask. I was afraid to meddle."

"Good thinking. I'm tailing Janks."

"Sarah Booth, be careful. I should have poured a pan of hot grease in Janks's lap and made him say where Cece is."

In the grand scheme of things, it wasn't such a bad plan. Once I caught up with Janks, I didn't intend to be much nicer. He would tell me where he'd left my friend, or I'd take necessary action despite Coleman's warnings.

"Where are you, Sarah Booth?"

"It looks like we might be headed to the Carlisle place." Talk about a racing pulse. The plantation was the location I most wanted to go to but was also afraid of.

"Don't you dare go on that property." Millie sounded an awful lot like Tinkie and everyone else.

"I'll take every precaution."

"Don't be a fool, Sarah Booth."

Janks turned north on a farm-to-market road that cut across Sunflower County. "He changed directions. I don't have a clue where he's going, but I'm on his trail. I'll call back when I know something."

Janks sped through the eerie fog, and I could only wonder where the highway patrolmen were when my speedometer never fell below eighty.

My stomach grumbled a big complaint. I hadn't taken time for breakfast, unlike Janks, who'd managed to shovel at least two pounds of grits, eggs, and bacon into his maw. He'd fueled up for the week.

Luckily I'd topped off my gas tank, but I wondered if Janks intended to drive straight out of Mississippi and into Alabama. We left the Delta behind and entered the hilly region that led to the Black Prairie and West Point.

Home of Lana Entrekin Carlisle.

Was this just another coincidence?

I opened my cell phone, a little annoyed that Coleman hadn't even checked on me. Over an hour had passed since Janks had high-tailed it out of the café and Coleman hadn't bothered to call.

"Sheriff Peters," he answered the phone. The foghorn of a tugboat sounded in the background.

"Where in the hell are you?" I asked.

"On the river."

That would be the Mississippi, not exactly a boundary of Sunflower County. "What's happening?"

"I don't know how to say this, Sarah Booth."

"What?" I kept Janks in my sights, but my driving was automatic.

"A tugboat captain saw a body floating in the river. I got a call from the sheriff over at Friar's Point. He let me know. We've got the rescue unit out searching. We're hoping the body caught in some of the trees or roots along the bank. The fog has slowed the search, and it'll take some time, I'm afraid."

"Who is it?" My heart ached.

"In the fog, the captain didn't get a good look."

"Is it Cece?"

"I don't know."

Janks was ahead of me and I had the most irrational desire to floorboard the gas and ram the back of his SUV. "I'll kill him," I said.

"The body in the river could be anyone, Sarah Booth. A fisherman, a vagrant, someone who fell off one of the tugs. Don't jump to conclusions."

"If Janks has harmed Cece, I'll kill him."

"Calm down and do your job. Stay on Janks's tail. I could have him picked up, but if he has Cece stashed somewhere, the best thing you can do is follow him. Maybe he'll lead you to her."

In his own way, Coleman had thrown me an emotional lifeline. "Did you talk to Millie?" Up in the distance, Janks hit a patch of sunlight. The fog, which had made the road so isolated, was lifting.

"I did. And I ran a check on Joe Downs. He's Lester Ballard's supervisor. Downs told me that Ballard came to Sunflower County two days ago and hasn't been heard from since."

167

"Criminy. He's missing, too? Since the blood in Janks's room wasn't Cece's, do you think . . . ?" Negotiating several stoplights on the outskirts of West Point required my attention.

"I wouldn't be searching for this body unless I thought it related to what's happening around Zinnia."

"Coleman—" But he couldn't assure me that my friend wasn't dead and floating in the river.

"As soon as I know something, I will call you."

"So what else did you learn from Downs?" I forced the question out.

As the fog lifted, I dropped back, keeping Janks in my sights but not so close as to draw suspicion that I was following him.

"Downs is angry and upset. He accused Luther and Janks of working together to destroy the agricultural value of the Carlisle land."

"Any word from Erin?" Perhaps she'd seen Cece and could tell us if she was safe.

"I called her studio in Jackson and left word for her to call me. She wasn't at work, but the receptionist said she'd return my call as soon as she arrived."

In the background I could hear Bonnie Louise saying something. While river rescue wasn't likely a part of the CDC mission statement, I knew a body search would accept any and all volunteers. The Mississippi River didn't like to give up her conquests.

Coleman came back on the telephone. "I have to go, Sarah Booth."

"I'm in West Point. I'll stay on—" Janks took that moment to execute a sharp left turn across traffic. There was no way I could follow him.

"Coleman?" I turned left at the next block, hoping to catch up with Janks. "Coleman?"

There was no answer from the sheriff, and Janks had vanished.

Disappearing acts were getting to be old hat—and I didn't care for them. Perhaps Janks had realized he had a tail and deliberately dumped me, or maybe Hell had opened and swallowed him whole. Whatever, he'd vanished.

Cursing did no good. Conjuring Janks wasn't in my power. A fifteen-minute cross-search of the town told me Janks had slipped by me. My only lead to Cece, tenuous though it was, had been severed.

I parked in front of the busiest shop in town, a place called Bits and Pieces. As I watched customers come and go, I tried Cece's phone. No answer. At home, on her cell, or at the newspaper.

Since I was in West Point, I decided to make my drive count.

I hurried inside the shop to see if anyone there knew the Entrekin family. Luck was on my side. The store owner, Bill East, not only knew the Entrekins but had gone to school with Lana. His fondness for her was easy to see.

"Gregory Carlisle was a handsome and wealthy man," Bill said as he organized a rack of wind chimes made from melted glass bottles. "Almost everyone in town thought Lana had made the catch of the century."

"Except you?"

He shrugged. "Folks say money can't buy happiness. I happen to believe that. Before Lana married, we talked a good bit. She wasn't totally convinced but felt she could make a go of the marriage and of living in the Delta."

"Did you see Lana after she married and moved away?"

He straightened a box of pens on the counter. "About two weeks before she died, she came home. Her parents were already dead, but she stayed at her old family home. I think she was homesick."

"Did she say that?"

He shook his head. "Not in those words."

"But you talked with her?"

"In town, on the street. Nothing personal. Just friendly conversation. I saw her one evening, at a party. My wife and I talked to her for half an hour. She waited outside until I went out to smoke a cigarette."

"And?"

"She was unhappy." He paced the narrow aisle filled with unusual relics, antiques, and original artwork. "She talked about our high school days for a few minutes and then she left."

"Do you remember what she said?"

"Nothing that made sense. She said the Carlisle name was more than just land and money but that it had never been her name. Not really."

"That was it?" No earth-shattering revelations that would clearly identify Lana's killer—if she was killed.

"She seemed sad. I offered to call one of her children, but she said no, she'd head back to Sunflower County in a day or two. And she did."

"Why did she come back to West Point?" I asked.

"I found out later, it was to buy a burial plot. A single plot, beneath an old magnolia tree at the foot of a hill in the West Point cemetery."

"She's not buried beside her parents?"

"No, she's alone."

He drew me a map of the town and showed me how to get to the cemetery, and then he shook my hand and bade me farewell.

17

Before I left West Point, I drove by the cemetery where Lana Entrekin Carlisle had been laid to rest. The last of the fog was lifting in wisps, revealing a well-shaped magnolia tree, the leaves a green so dense, they looked black against the bright grass. Beneath the tree was a single headstone.

As I approached, I saw that someone had left fresh flowers on the grave. Violets. Their deep purple contrasted with the silvery granite of the stone, and I gently picked them up.

Violets are delicate and wilt shortly after they're cut. I had a vague memory of gathering the shy blooms with my Grandmother Booth as we walked along one of the wooded trails behind her home. We'd always wait until we turned toward home to pick the wild blossoms that grew in clumps protected by leaves and shadows. Holding them for the short walk home took a toll on them.

The flowers in my hand were unwilted. Someone had gone to a lot of trouble to find fresh violets—not exactly the easiest plant to locate.

Movement in my peripheral vision made me swing around. Jimmy Janks sprinted from behind an oak tree and hauled ass across the cemetery. He jumped gravestones like hurdles.

"Hey!" I took off after him, dropping the flowers and my purse. "Janks! Stop!"

He ignored me. I put on a burst of speed, hopping the graves behind him, amazed that my old track instincts kicked in. Aunt Loulane would never approve of such disrespect for the dead, but I had to catch the fleeing developer.

"Janks! Where's Cece?" He was drawing away from me, and I was tiring.

He looked back over his shoulder once, then vaulted the wrought-iron fence that encircled the cemetery. By the time I climbed the fence, he was driving away.

I'd lost him.

Again.

I caught my breath before I went back to retrieve my purse, forcing the images of a dead body floating in dark river water out of my head.

As a matter of respect, I gathered up the violets and returned them to Lana's grave. Her stone marker was simple and plain. "Lana Entrekin Carlisle," the dates of her birth and death, and one small quote: "Home Forever." A pain touched my chest at those words.

No matter how many questions I had, Lana couldn't answer them. As I started up the slope toward my car, I saw a woman kneeling in the Saint Augustine grass, tending a grave.

Once the introductions were exchanged and I explained my pell-mell rush across hallowed ground, I realized that Lucille Armstrong was a sharp-eyed observer of human nature. She'd not only seen Jimmy Janks, she'd watched him.

"He put the violets on the grave," she said, "then stood there. I think he might have been talking."

She was too far away to hear the conversation, but she was astute at reading body language.

"He cared for Lana." She removed the gloves she wore to pull weeds. The grave she cleaned belonged to Bobby McKnight. Born 1926, died 1981.

"Why would you think he cared about Lana Carlisle?" I was curious to hear her take. It was just as possible he'd been cursing Lana, though the flowers did support an emotional connection.

Lucille thought for a moment before she answered. "I knew Lana when she was a young girl. I taught her, actually. That child loved purple, and she often wore silk violets woven into her hair. Whoever that man was, he knew what Lana preferred. He knew and cared enough to bring her favorite."

Janks was a good twenty years younger than Lana. Likely not a lover. If Janks grew up in Chicago, where had he met Lana?

"Could you tell by the way he behaved what he was feeling?"

Lucille pointed to the grave. "Bobby McKnight was my father's best friend. He taught me to drive. He let me ride the horses on his farm and encouraged me to go to college." She brushed a spot of dirt from her forehead with the back of her hand. "He introduced me to my husband, Norman. I care for Bobby's grave because I loved him. The way that man stood at Lana's grave, I think he cared about her."

Lucille was attributing her feelings to Jimmy Janks. I wasn't certain the transfer applied, but it was certainly worth considering.

"Why wasn't Lana buried in the Carlisle family cemetery?"

She motioned to a bench not far away. We walked over and sat in the shade of a live oak. "There were rumors floating around West Point that Lana didn't want to marry Gregory Carlisle and move to the Delta." She took a breath. "I always thought the gossip might have been motivated by jealousy. People saw Lana had snatched the gold ring on the merry-go-round of marriage and so sullied the tale as much as they could. There were rumors of Gregory's infidelities, but never any evidence."

"You changed your mind?"

"I don't know. Lana's wedding was big society news in the South. Then she was gone. She had two children. Whenever she visited West Point, I'd see her on the street; she seemed happy enough. I think, though, that she was homesick for this area. Sometimes, Miss Delaney, the land calls a person home."

How well I knew that sentiment. The sun was nearing its zenith, and while the background on Lana Carlisle was interesting, it didn't explain Jimmy Janks or help me find Cece. "Thank you, Mrs. Armstrong."

"My pleasure." She rose and returned to the grave of her father's friend.

When I pulled away from the cemetery, she was weeding again, a short woman determined to honor someone who'd been good to her.

When the outskirts of Zinnia filled my windshield, I settled on a plan of action. Coleman, wherever he was, had no cell phone signal. Dewayne, who sounded as heartsick as I, hadn't heard from him.

I stopped by Cece's house, then the newspaper. No one had seen her. The publisher, Mr. Truesdale, literally wrung his hands. "Please call me when you find her," he said.

I left the paper and pulled up at a four-way stop. Half the day was already gone—with nothing to show. Janks was the ticket to Cece, and I'd lost him.

A car behind me honked, reminding me that I was sitting at a stop sign. I eased forward as my cell phone rang.

"Sarah Booth," Coleman began, "we've found Cece." I could tell from his tone that the news wasn't good.

It took all of my control not to burst into tears. "How did she die?"

The pause lasted only milliseconds, but it was enough for Coleman to grasp my thoughts.

"Cece is alive. She's been beaten, but she's alive. The body in the river is Lester Ballard."

"Cece's alive?"

"Yes. I left you a message on your phone about Lester Ballard. He was shot in the back and dumped in the river. I thought you knew."

His call must have come in while I was chasing Janks through the cemetery. It didn't matter. What mattered was that Cece was alive. "Where is she?"

"She's in the hospital in Jackson."

My heart lurched. "How bad is it?"

"Serious. I'm tied up at the river, so Harold has gone to check on her. If possible, he'll have her transported back here to Zinnia. He's halfway to Jackson by now."

"Is she going to be okay?" I dreaded his answer, but I had to know.

"The beating was severe, but the doctor didn't feel the damage was permanent. She managed to get to the emergency room before she collapsed. She just regained consciousness and gave them her name."

A wedge of emotion almost choked me.

"She's going to be okay, Sarah Booth."

I pulled the roadster to the side of the highway. I didn't trust myself to drive. Or to talk.

"Do you think Jimmy Janks is responsible for what's happened to Cece?" I asked. I would carve out his gizzard with an iced-tea spoon.

"The Jackson PD is investigating, but Cece hasn't been able to tell them much. She's heavily sedated. What the officer was able to piece together was that she was attacked in the parking lot in front of Erin Carlisle's studio."

"I lost Janks in West Point. At Lana Carlisle's grave."

"That's an intriguing twist. Don't worry. He won't get far. We'll get him." He hesitated. "Look, Beaucoup is calling. She helped in recovering the body, but she had to rush back to conclude some tests. Maybe she's found something. I'll call you when I hear anything."

I leaned my head against the headrest of the car. My world had turned upside down again. I was at sixes and sevens, and while I knew I needed to go check on Tinkie and Oscar, I had no faith that I could conceal the truth of Cece's condition.

My life in Hollywood hadn't been easy or problem-free; it had been surreal, almost as though it were happening to someone wearing my skin. *This* was too real and too awful.

Easing the car back onto the road, I drove to the CDC offices. Peyton might be in, and it was possible he'd have more information. No matter that Cece had been found,

I still wanted to investigate the Carlisle plantation for myself.

The CDC used the back entrance rather than traipse through waiting rooms with wall-to-wall moms and children who needed vaccinations or medical attention. Once inside, I saw Peyton's door was cracked and I heard him on the phone.

"That is Bonnie Louise's area of specialty. I'll pass that information along." He made a few more affirmative sounds, then replaced the phone.

"Is someone there?" he asked.

The man had bat-hearing. I'd barely shuffled on the linoleum. "It's me, Sarah Booth. I came for the hazmat suit."

Peyton came to the door and waved me in. There was a glint of excitement in his dark eyes.

"Do you have anything on the illness yet?"

He paced the room. "We took samples from the blood, mucous lining, skin scrapings, tissue samples from all of the sick people."

I didn't dare interrupt him but said a silent prayer that, at last, something useful had been discovered.

"The reason Oscar and the others haven't responded to antibiotics is because this isn't a bacterial infection."

"But it doesn't appear to be viral, either," I said.

"True. None of the tests for viral agents have been conclusive."

I couldn't help jumping ahead. "If it isn't bacterial or viral, what is it?"

"Fungal."

After Katrina, thousands of homes in New Orleans and along the Mississippi Gulf Coast flooded and became infested with mold. Some owners became very ill. But we hadn't even had a good rainy spring in Zinnia.

"We're talking mold, right?" I wanted to be sure I hadn't gone off on a tangent.

"Some form of mold or spore. The patients must have inhaled the spores." He lifted both palms. "That's an educated guess. I don't have all the facts yet, but at least I have a direction."

"Where did this mold come from?"

He closed the office door before he sat on the edge of his desk. "This can go no further, Sarah Booth. I'm trusting you with information that I may not share—just yet—with the sheriff."

"You have to tell Coleman. He's working to resolve this just like you are." I didn't see why he would withhold any information.

"In good time, Sarah Booth." His tone warned me to back off. "I should probably keep this to myself until I have something solid."

"Someone deliberately infected the Carlisle plantation, didn't they?" I asked. Even speculation would be helpful to me.

He hesitated, then finally spoke. "That would be my guess. The problem is that I've not been able to identify a spore that would cause these exact symptoms."

"A mutation."

"Exactly. But until I have more information . . . I don't want to send this investigation down a rabbit trail, understand?"

I saw his point. Peyton was talking serious crimes. "The mold, by itself, is it harmful?"

He shuffled some papers on his desk until he found one sheet. Pulling it to the top of a stack, he looked it over. "Bonnie and Dr. Unger have worked nonstop on the weevils. They'd found a very different breeding cycle. It may be attributable to the mold."

"So how do we find out about this mold? What will counter the effects in Oscar and the others?"

"I'm running tests on the cotton. Bonnie Louise is working on the weevils. Now Doc can address the mold. Between the three of us, we should find an answer."

"How long?"

"Mold is insidious. Now that we know to look in this direction, we have a focus, but it isn't as simple as A follows B to conclude with C."

"Oscar and the others don't have a lot of time, Peyton."

"I know that. We'll get the answer you want, Sarah Booth."

I was about to ask for the hazmat suit when the door flew open and banged against a wall.

"I want to talk to the CDC." The tall, lanky man from Millie's Café entered armed with a bad attitude. Joe Downs was making the rounds of Zinnia and, judging from the redness of his face, he was still pissed off.

18

"Who the hell are you?" Peyton was as cool as a crap shooter on a winning streak.

"I'm Joe Downs. Mississippi Agri-Team leases the Carlisle plantation. I have a murdered employee and some land that I'm told looks like a biblical plague struck." He jabbed his pointer in Peyton's direction. "If those weevils spread to other plantations, this could be the ruination of the economy here."

Peyton pulled up another chair. "Have a seat, Mr. Downs. This is Sarah Booth Delaney."

Downs gave me a nod of acknowledgment and eased his angular frame into the chair. "I know 'er. Knew her dad. He did some legal work for my father. Knew his business and treated folks fair."

I didn't get a chance to thank him before Peyton cut in.

"First of all, Mr. Downs, I regret the situation you're in, but I have nothing to do with it. The CDC is studying an illness, and I have to point out, the boll weevils are a secondary matter."

"Look, Lester Ballard was a friend as well as an employee. He's dead. Murdered. Shot in the back! People who went out to that plantation are seriously sick. A strange crop is infested with weevils, and all I can get from the sheriff is a bunch of guff. I want to know what you've found and what you're planning to do." Downs gripped the arms of his chair.

"We're doing everything in our power." Peyton went to a carafe, poured a glass of water, and handed it to Downs.

If what Peyton suspected was true, someone had created the problems with the cotton and weevils. And that someone had something to gain. "Did MAT have a written agreement with the Carlisle family for the use of the plantation?" I asked.

"Of course we did. Used to be a handshake was good enough, but not any more. We had a signed lease. Good for another six years."

"Were you aware that Luther Carlisle intended to sell the land?" I pressed.

"The first MAT heard about this was a week ago. Lester was fit to be tied. He tried to talk to Luther, but the coward wouldn't take Lester's calls. Lester had some business in Central America, but he returned and was on this Sunflower County matter quick as he could be."

"What are the terms of the land lease?" I asked. "Can it be terminated?"

"For cause. From our end. I find it mighty interestin' that contamination is about the only reason MAT would halt the lease."

I found that equally fascinating. "You've never had trouble with the Carlisles before?"

"Not a bit of it. Luther was glad enough to take our money and have us manage the land. That Jimmy Janks came in here and got Luther all goo-goo eyed with greed over his development scheme. Janks is the scoundrel who's trying to turn good farmland into a subdivision, and I'd lay money he's behind these weevils."

"Do you know if Mr. Ballard spoke with Janks?"

Downs sipped the water. Talking calmed him. "Lester said he was meeting Janks. Lester had found some other land that wasn't so fertile. He meant to propose a swap with Janks so he could develop the poorer land. He said he had a meeting set up, but Janks didn't show, so he was taking the meeting to Janks. That's the last I heard from Lester. This morning Lester didn't answer his phone. He wasn't in his hotel room. I knew something awful had happened."

I got up and refilled Downs's glass. He'd lost a coworker and friend, and he wanted answers. My sympathies were with him.

Downs sipped the water and continued. "Luther, that greedy gut, is tryin' to roll over his own sister." Contempt dripped from his words. "Still, I never figured him for a killer. Too squeamish. Goes against that genteel pose he strikes. But there's no tellin' what greed will do to a man. If he's behind this, he'll burn in Hell, because I'll send him there."

"Threats aren't necessary," Peyton said softly. "Sheriff Peters will find the guilty party."

"I'm sorry, Mr. Downs," I said. "I know this is a terrible loss for you."

"Lester was a good man. A decent man. He didn't deserve to be killed and thrown into a river. And you can call it a threat, but I consider it a promise. Someone is going to pay." He stood up. "While this is personal, it also involves an entire industry. If those weevils get loose on the rest of the cotton, it could destroy us."

"Mr. Ballard, I know you're worried. My associate, Ms. McRae, has a unique knowledge of the boll weevil. She isn't here now, but when she returns, she'll call you and update you on her studies regarding the insects."

"I'm not nearly as concerned in studyin' them as I am in killin' them. I heard most of the cotton on the Carlisle land is destroyed. I can't even get out there to check it."

It intrigued me that Peyton failed to mention the weevils had only attacked the genetically altered cotton. That might give Downs a little solace, but I trusted Peyton had his reasons for staying mum.

"We're hoping to have some answers soon. Then you'll be able to check the property." Peyton was kind but firm.

"Can you give me a time when this might happen?" Downs asked.

"I wish I could. This is our highest priority."

Once Downs got to the land, based on the descriptions I'd heard of the cotton, he'd have a hissy fit for sure.

Downs rubbed his chin. "I talked with some of the experts at MAT. There's a new chemical, a pesticide. I'd like to give it a try. See if I can't salvage something."

Peyton's jaw flexed. "I wish I could say yes. I honestly do. But finding the cause of an illness comes first."

Downs rattled the ice in his glass. "They didn't catch what they've got from cotton or weevils. That's crazy talk that'll get folks stirred up and make trouble like you've never thought about." He leaned forward. "It sounds like something Luther and Janks cooked up to scare people. Fact is, I wouldn't put it past Janks to be the one who sent Lester that new cotton seed."

This was a lead to pursue. "We've been curious about the cotton on the Carlisle place. It's . . . unusual." If Peyton wanted to yield the details, he could. Again, he kept silent.

Leaning a boney elbow on a knee, Downs thought a moment. "Lester told me something about the seed, but I don't clearly remember the whole story. Take it up with Luther Carlisle. He's involved. You can count on it."

"Thanks." It was a solid tip.

"Listen here, you two. MAT has worked that land for a long time. If there's something sick about it, someone brought it and put it there and it wasn't Lester."

He unfolded from the chair. "Call me when I can see that land."

Downs hadn't been gone a minute when Bonnie Louise pushed through the door. She wore scrubs and a lab coat and looked as if she hadn't slept in a week. "Peyton, I need your help." She acknowledged me with a look. "Dr. Unger believes the mold comes from the weevils. He's not sure of the source, but this is a big step. He wants us to gather more specimens from the field."

Peyton stood quickly. "Let's go."

"Oh, yeah, Sarah Booth, Coleman asked me to call you an hour ago and tell you Cece left the Jackson hospital. She should be here in Zinnia any minute. Sorry, I got busy and forgot to call."

A little advance notice would have been nice. To prepare Tinkie for Cece's condition. "I'll get that suit later," I told Peyton.

"Sure thing." He locked the door behind the three of us as we hurried out of the building.

I walked across the potholed parking lot and driveway to the hospital's back doors. They were supposed to lock automatically, but that wasn't the case. Some enterprising family member of a sick person or a hospital employee sneaking out for a smoke break often disabled the lock with a bobby pin. When I tugged lightly, the door opened wide. Folks had been working that stunt since Aunt Loulane was in the hospital fifteen years ago.

I approached the hallway where Tinkie sat on the edge of the cot, slumped with fatigue.

In my year back in Sunflower County, I'd rarely seen Tinkie less than perfectly turned out. She wasn't a woman who wore her feelings on her sleeve. Somewhere in the Daddy's Girl rulebook, there's something about how neither rain nor sleet nor snow nor emotional and physical exhaustion shall ever interfere with looking good.

Tinkie's clothes were flawless; it was her body that needed ironing. In the week of Oscar's illness, her muscle, bone, and skin had shifted. That realization scared me into action.

"Tinkie, you have to get out of here for a while." I came from behind and startled her so badly, she jumped up.

Using her own momentum, I spun her and marched her down the hall. "You're going home. We'll pick up Chablis and Sweetie. Maybe I'll cook something."

"French toast? Sans the Mickey, right?"

"Cut me some slack. You need to sleep, but I won't drug you again. And you can have breakfast or dinner, whatever you want." Where had the day gone—it was mighty close to supper time. "Eat something and if you can't sleep, I'll bring you back here. I'll call your mom to come sit while we're gone."

"You promise?"

"Scout's honor." I wanted to get her outside in the sunlight to tell her about Cece. I made the arrangements with Mrs. Bellcase as we walked down the corridor.

"What's wrong?" Tinkie asked, when I held the back door open.

"I have some bad news." We crossed the parking lot, and then I told her about Cece. All expression fell from her face, and she scuffed her toe in the gravel like a first grader.

"Tinkie, are you okay?"

"Is she seriously hurt?"

She didn't resist when I opened the passenger door and put her in the car. I slid behind the wheel before I answered. When I was buckled in, I took a deep breath. "It must be pretty bad. Harold went to facilitate transferring her here. They'll be here soon."

"And Coleman doesn't have any more details than that?"

"Coleman has his hands full, Tink. There's been a murder." I filled her in on what I knew of Lester Ballard's death.

"I don't want to go home. Let's stop by the sheriff's office," Tinkie said.

"You look like a puff of wind could blow you away. You need something to eat and some time with your dog."

"I need to find out what's happening to the people I love." The quiet tone of her voice made me hesitate. Tinkie was in bad shape, but she wasn't a lightweight when it came to friendship. Cece was as big a part of her life as mine.

We sat in the roadster at the edge of the health clinic parking lot while I decided which way to go.

Tinkie grasped my wrist and squeezed. "I've been helpless, sitting there with Oscar. I need to do something. Maybe I can help figure out who hurt Cece."

And that was all it took. I pressed the gas and headed to the courthouse. While Tinkie needed rest and food, she also needed to get involved in something outside Oscar's illness.

19

Dahlia House was out of the way, but I ran by to pick up the dogs. Tinkie needed the comfort of her hound, even if her canine was a dustmop that looked more like a stuffed toy than a real dog. Chablis was tiny, cute, and had the heart of a lioness. She could give Tinkie what I could not— the sense that her family was still complete.

"I'll be back with the dogs in a flash," I told Tinkie as I hopped out of the roadster. Tinkie didn't look as if she had the strength to climb the stairs to Dahlia House.

I entered the front door and stopped. Cigar smoke curled in the light from the front windows.

Someone had been smoking in my home. And cigars! I didn't know anyone who smoked those things.

"Put your hands in the air." The voice was cold and menacing. I complied, my mind jumping backward to

Cece and her beating and ahead to Tinkie and what a weakened target she would be if I failed to handle this.

"What do you want?" I asked.

"Turn around."

I was reluctant to face my attacker. Most criminals preferred not to leave eyewitnesses alive.

"Do it. Now."

I moved slowly. The man standing in the shadows of the parlor wore a pin-striped suit, a hat, and held a machine gun. Though his fedora concealed his features, I could see a thin mustache that emphasized the narrowness of his lips. He was slender, and the cock of his hat told me he was bold.

I'd never seen him before.

"Where are the dogs?" Concern for Sweetie Pie and Chablis made me step forward.

"Desperate times call for desperate measures," he said. Beneath the harshness of his words was something else, an echo of another statement . . . another voice.

I studied him, noting the slender frame and the tiny little curl of a smile.

"Damn it to hell and back, Jitty. You scared me." I dropped my hands. "Now I need to change my pants. I hope you're happy."

Instead of the chuckle I expected, Jitty only tipped up the brim of her hat, revealing her luminous eyes. There was sadness there, not humor.

"Did you know John Dillinger was a hero to a lot of people in America? They cheered him on in his robberies."

Now it was a history quiz? "Give me a break." I filtered through the little bit I knew of 1930s gangsters. "He was viewed as a Robin Hood of hard times. He robbed banks and shot cops. Except to my knowledge he never gave a dime to the poor."

Jitty shrugged. "J. Edgar Hoover wore a dress."

I rolled my eyes. "What is this about? Tinkie is in the car. Cece has been severely beaten. Coleman is fishing a dead man out of the Mississippi. Oscar is still sick—what's your obsession with outlaws gunned down by the FBI?"

"Times were different when John Dillinger was on the loose."

"Your point is?" I had good cause to act brusque. The chance to make things right was slipping away from me hour by hour.

"Wanted posters of Dillinger were everywhere, but hardly anybody recognized him on the street. Folks didn't expect to see a bank robber passin' by on the sidewalk. No television to show his mug. No Internet. No cell phones. None of the things that make life so dang complicated today."

Doggie toenails scrabbled on the hardwood floor as Sweetie and Chablis launched themselves through the swinging kitchen door and rushed me. I patted and stroked, but Jitty was trying to tell me something. Jitty never actually helped me with a case, but sometimes she helped me with a much bigger problem—me.

"Okay, Dillinger remained on the loose for a long time. I'll give you that. And some folks did protect him. Willingly." That summed up my knowledge of the outlaw.

Jitty stubbed out her cigar in a leaded-glass ashtray. Had I committed such a violation of Delaney antiques, she would have badgered me for weeks. "The FBI shot and killed Dillinger in front of the Biograph Theater in Chicago. It was a Sunday, July 22, 1934."

Jitty had lived—or haunted—through most of this; far be it from me to argue with her. "Fascinating. But why should I care right now?"

"The FBI knew Dillinger would be in that theater."

Something niggled at the back of my brain. A betrayal. A huge one. "A woman called the FBI, right?"

"Bingo!" Jitty laid the old-fashioned tommy gun on the table beside the sofa. The prop department in the Great Beyond could obviously furnish anything.

She continued talking. "Ana Cumpanas, her married name was Ana Sage, was the madam of a brothel. She's the one fingered Dillinger to the FBI. She told them the theater, the time, the film, and she even went to the movie with Dillinger and his latest girlfriend."

A factoid floated to the surface of my brain. "She wore a red dress. That's how the feds identified him."

"Actually, it was orange, but in the lights of the theater's marquee, it looked red. He was shot in a nearby alley. Some folks dispute as to whether he ever even pulled his gun."

"Okay, so how does all of this apply to me?"

"Ana believed she'd be deported to Romania if she failed to deliver Dillinger to the FBI. She came over from Romania and had some run-ins with the Indiana law. The FBI supposedly promised her the deportation action against her would be dropped."

This was going to have a bad ending.

Jitty brought out a cigar from the inside pocket of her elegant suit jacket and twirled it between her fingers. "She was deported in late April 1936. The only thing she got out of her betrayal was a portion of the reward money for Dillinger. Five grand."

"So the moral of the story is never trust a madam in a red dress." I had hoped to make her laugh, but not so.

She started to fade, but I could still hear her. "Think about it, Sarah Booth. Trust is the issue."

"Jitty, what are you telling me? Should I trust or not? Will I be betrayed by someone in a red dress?"

Even though I listened for nearly a full minute, there was no answer. Like Elvis, Jitty had left the building.

I was left with one more puzzle to study on top of the pile I already had.

Tinkie cuddled Chablis to her chest as we rode through the cool April evening. Sweetie Pie sat in the backseat and occasionally leaned over to slurp Tinkie's neck or cheek. The top was down on the roadster, and the wind whipped a bit of color into Tinkie's face, but the fine lines and wrinkles that hadn't been there a week before testified to the stress she was under.

Though the plan had been to go to the courthouse, by the time I got into town, Tinkie had fallen asleep.

I shook her shoulder lightly. "Tink, I'm taking you home." Besides, I wanted to check out Cece before she saw the damage done to our friend.

When she didn't argue, I knew how exhausted she was. "If I find something, I'll fetch you," I promised her. "The best thing you can do is sleep."

She was so far gone, she didn't acknowledge me. With Chablis and Sweetie keeping me company, I drove to the big house on the hill that Tinkie called home.

By the time Tinkie was settled on the sofa with Sweetie Pie beside her and Chablis curled in the nook of her arm, she was sound asleep. A quick call to the sheriff's office garnered the information that Cece had arrived at the hospital. From Dewayne's voice, I could tell things were dire.

Fighting images of what I was likely to discover, I parked in the hospital lot beside the Sunflower County sheriff's car. As I marched toward the door, I struggled to weave some plausible story from all that had happened.

But there was no connective tissue—that I could see. Turning the pieces every which way, I couldn't make them lock together.

While the Carlisle land was presumed to be the source of the disease or infection or mold that had leveled Oscar, Gordon, and the two realtors, no one had proven it.

The boll weevils—and the strange genetically altered cotton—were an added twist. Was this some form of agri-terrorism? But why Mississippi and why a crop like cotton with no application for use in weapons or the drug trade?

Jimmy Janks was a viable contender for prime suspect, but he wasn't alone. Luther and Erin Carlisle, despite Erin saying she wouldn't sell the land for development, both stood to profit if the plantation was sold for premium development dollars.

And thrown in the middle of the Carlisle family intrigues was Sonya Kessler. Was she truly a half sister willing to sit outside the warmth of the fire while Luther and Erin divided the spoils?

Also connected to the Carlisle land was Lester Ballard, shot to death and his body dumped in the Mississippi. He'd been supposed to meet with Janks.

Add to that the attack on Cece—while allegedly on a date with Janks—and none of it made sense.

Speaking of Janks, what was his connection to Lana Carlisle? Why would he visit her grave across the state in West Point?

Like a web spreading wider and wider, the facts had one central source—the Carlisle plantation. In some way, everyone connected back there.

"Trust is the issue."

Jitty's latest impersonation nagged at me as I pushed

open the door and stepped into the familiar hospital smell.

A nurse told me Cece's room number. Hand on the knob, I gathered my courage and opened the door. At first, I thought I might faint. The Delaney fortitude gained control, and I closed the door softly behind me.

An oxygen tube fed into her nose and other machines beeped and blinked. Her face was a mass of bruises, and she'd need reconstructive surgery on her nose, which was smashed beyond recognition.

As I approached the bed, she lifted a hand. I grasped it gently, and her fingers curled around mine.

"You're home now, Cece. We'll take care of you." If I'd ever doubted the power of those words, I didn't any longer. Cece was home, and so was I. To be anywhere else in the world would have been wrong.

Cece kept the pressure on my fingers until I patted her hand and withdrew mine. I brushed her blood-crusted hair from her forehead and tried not to flinch at the battered contours of her face.

"Has Coleman questioned you?" I asked.

"I don't remember much."

"Do you see your attacker?"

"No." The word was whispered.

"Did Janks do this?"

"I don't know. He took me home and left." A tear leaked down the side of her face. I wiped it away, feeling a surge of rage so hot and pure that I was afraid I'd burn her skin.

"Why did you go to Jackson?"

"To see Erin."

"Erin Carlisle?"

"Yes." Her voice was like wind shifting dead leaves.

Images started to flutter through my head. Cece had

been found in the parking lot of the strip mall where Erin's studio was located.

"Erin was with you in the parking lot?"

"Yes."

"Was she there when you were attacked?"

She hesitated. "We were walking across the lot to her studio. I don't know what happened to her."

"I'll be right back," I said before I raced out of the room.

I skidded around the corner on the slick linoleum tile and almost slammed into Doc Sawyer.

"Whoa, there, Sarah Booth. Coleman's looking for you," he said.

"Where is he?"

"Down in the cafeteria with Mrs. Bellcase. They went for a cup of coffee."

"Thanks." I wheeled and ran to the cafeteria. Sure, running wasn't allowed in hospitals. A foolish rule when it was Death they should have been trying to govern.

When I pushed through the swinging doors of the cafeteria, Mrs. Bellcase stood alone, a cup of coffee in her hand. Dazed, she failed to hear my approach.

"Where's Coleman?" I asked.

"He got a call . . ." She staggered a step, and I caught her and helped her to a table. Tinkie's entire family balanced on the thin edge of exhaustion. Instead of sitting down, she started toward the door. "Oscar needs me."

"Did Coleman say where he was going?"

Judging by the look on her face, she'd forgotten all about Coleman. "No, he didn't. Wait. He found a relative of Gordon's in South Dakota. He said she's coming here to be with Gordon. He doesn't have anyone else."

"You need some rest," I told her gently. Bossing Tinkie's mama didn't strike me as smart. I opted for suggesting. "Can I call someone to relieve you?"

"No." She squared her shoulders. "Sorry, Sarah Booth, my energy level plummeted for a minute. I'm fine, and Tammy Odom has offered to sit a while. She'll be here soon." She gathered herself. "Coleman never said where he was going, but he got a call that seemed urgent. I know he's terribly worried about Gordon. His temperature spiked to 105. The two women appear to be improving a tiny bit, but the men . . ."

"I'm glad Coleman found Gordon's cousin." Gordon's father had been the sheriff of Sunflower County at one time—a very corrupt man. Gordon had endured and overcome that family reputation to become Coleman's trusted right hand. I'd once suspected him of murder, but he'd earned my respect and my thanks, and it tore at me to see him so ill and helpless and alone.

While I was tempted to stop by the isolation ward and mojo up some kick-ass energy for the patients, I had other fish to fry. Erin Carlisle might be in danger, and both Tinkie and Cece needed my attention. But first Jimmy Janks. Coleman and Dewayne had searched Janks's office and come up with nothing criminal, but there were things about Janks that didn't add up.

Toke Lambert reclined on a wicker chaise lounge on the front porch of his home in a gated community. Each house on the cul-de-sac was a McMansion, an architectural statement that had become the equivalent of the brick ranch houses of the 1970s. Like the general American population, the style of houses had gone from functional to opulent and obese. Toke's house had to be at least eight thousand square feet.

"Hello, Toke," I said as I plowed through the lush centipede grass of his manicured lawn. "Looks like life is treating you well."

He waved a hand as if to dismiss his surroundings. "You know, Sarah Booth, it's all about management skills. Some of us have it, some don't."

I'd never cared for Toke, and he knew it. The pleasantries were over. "What do you know about Jimmy Janks?"

"He's wanting to develop the Carlisle land. Or at least he was before all this ruckus started." He picked up a frosted glass and sipped.

"How did you meet Janks?"

"Tell me why I should answer another question, Sarah Booth. What's in this for me?"

I wanted to say that if he gave me something worthwhile I wouldn't bother smashing his face, but such threats were ridiculous. "Oscar Richmond is very ill, and I'm on the case. I'm sure Mr. Bellcase at the Zinnia bank would want you to cooperate."

Five houses in Toke's neighborhood were up for foreclosure. Despite his claims of managerial genius, he required credit. One word from Mr. Bellcase and Toke's credit line might disconnect.

Toke wiped his mouth with a linen napkin. "Luther introduced me to Jimmy. He'd arranged a dove hunting party last winter and Janks was there. Talk about a fool with a gun. He almost pulled a Cheney on one of the men. We took Janks's shells away from him."

"Didn't you go to school with him?"

Toke laughed. "I don't think so."

"Not even for a semester?"

"What's with you, Sarah Booth? I said no."

Toke, even though he was a lazy lout, had the inside scoop on Delta entrepreneurs. "Where does Janks get his money?"

He sat up. "At last, you ask something interesting? I've wondered exactly the same thing. He blew in here with a line of credit that none of us can understand, especially when credit's tighter than Dick's hat band."

"So what did you find out?" Toke would have pursued it. One thing about a birthright Buddy Clubber—he knew how to track the money source.

Toke tossed down the rest of his drink and swung his legs off the chaise. "Jimmy Janks has big wealth in his grasp. His line of credit is unbelievable. And it comes from a source outside this country. That's all I could find. Offshore banks in the Caymans."

So Janks's development project was bankrolled by foreigners. A foreign money source, genetically altered cotton, mutated weevils, a strange illness that would be fatal without intensive medical care but one that was also contained to a specific location. When I added those things together, I got something frightening.

"Thanks, Toke." I trudged back across his lawn.

"Don't mention it, Sarah Booth."

As I got in my car, I heard him yell out to his wife to bring him another gin rickey.

The small strip mall where Janks had an office was totally deserted when I passed by. A more perfect opportunity might never be found.

I U-turned and parked so that my vehicle was blocked from sight by a Dumpster. The front door was plate glass, but a regular steel door closed the back. Picking locks wasn't my expertise, but I'd made up my mind to take a shot at it.

Before I tried my hand at B&E, I called Erin Carlisle. Her home number was listed, but she didn't answer. She wasn't at the studio—no surprise there. I left messages in both places, then walked over to the back door of Janks's office.

I rattled the knob for good measure. To my surprise, it turned easily and the door opened as if a magic spell had been cast. Which disturbed me.

Nonetheless, I stepped into the inky void of a storage room, giving my eyes time to adjust. The room was empty except for a half-dozen cardboard boxes.

A muffled crash came from the front office, followed by a curse.

No wonder the back door was open—someone had entered before I did. Moving quietly toward the sound, I wished for a gun. Tinkie had given me a canister of pepper spray that I had clipped to my key ring. I gripped it at the ready.

If Janks was in the office, I had to detain him.

Something else tumbled over. Whoever was up front was ransacking the office pretty thoroughly, or so it sounded.

Step by step, I made my way out of the storage room and into the hallway. The sounds were clearer now. Someone else had come to search through Janks's records.

With the pepper spray held in front of me at arm's length, I left the safety of the hallway and entered the main office.

Joe Downs, on his knees, yanked files from a drawer. Chaos reigned in the office. Papers floated everywhere. Drawers had been dumped, the contents strewn all over the floor. Downs might call this searching, but to me it looked like rampant vandalism.

He clutched a fistful of files and threw them behind him onto the floor. His hand closed on another batch.

"Stop," I ordered him.

His reaction surprised me. Instead of yelling or being startled, he calmly lowered his hand. "Miss Delaney," he said, "what are you doing here?"

"Looking for evidence. What about you?"

"The same."

"It would seem you're more intent on destroying evidence than finding it." Was it possible Downs was in cahoots with Janks? Even to the point of killing his friend and employee Lester Ballard?

"Janks sent those cotton seeds to Lester. I know he did. I intend to prove it. I'll sue that developer for everything he owns. I'll get the CDC, the EPA, the FFA, the FBI, the CIA, and the KGB after him if that's what it takes."

"An impressive list of alphabet agencies." I held the canister at the ready. "Move away from the papers and call the sheriff's office."

"Surely you don't intend to bring the law into this." He wasn't scared, just annoyed. "You entered illegally, as I did."

"Good point. Doesn't make a damn." I motioned to the phone. "Call the sheriff's office now." I gave him the number.

When Dewayne was on the line, I took the phone. Joe Downs made no effort to stop me. He eased to his feet, perched on the edge of the desk, and waited quietly.

"Is Coleman back?" I asked Dewayne.

"Miss Bonnie Louise called and he took off. Something I can do for you?"

Downs reached into his pocket and brought out a

sheet of paper. He held it toward me. "You're wasting valuable time," he said. "I'm trying to help."

"Sarah Booth, are you okay?" Dewayne asked.

"I'm fine." Right or wrong, I came to a decision about Downs. "Dewayne, could you ask the Jackson police to make sure Erin Carlisle is okay? It's possible she was with Cece when Cece was attacked in Jackson. She might be a witness. Or she might be a participant in the beating."

"I'm on it right now, Sarah Booth."

"Thanks, Dewayne." I replaced the phone and pointed to the paper that Downs still held toward me. "What is that?"

"Read it for yourself." He passed it to me. "I found it here."

I scanned the description of the life cycle of the boll weevil. Written in hand at the bottom was a notation for a particular strand of cotton.

Downs pointed at the paper. "I've grown cotton in this area all my life. That's not a type of cotton MAT has ever planted. I'm telling you, Janks is responsible for all of this. Now do you believe me?"

"This doesn't prove anything." It didn't. But it painted Janks a darker shade of guilty.

Downs let his hands fall to his lap. "I spoke with the sheriff about an hour ago. He was able to match the blood on the carpet in Janks's hotel room with Lester Ballard's blood. Lester's hand had a cut on it. Any fool can see they got into an argument and Janks murdered my friend. If I have to go to jail to prove it, I'm ready to do so."

Downs was only trying to do the same thing I was. I clipped the pepper spray back onto my key chain. "Let's take this place apart," I said.

20

Though Joe Downs and I turned Janks's office inside out, we found nothing else. I wasn't certain I trusted that Downs had found the paper on the weevils and cotton at the scene. It was possible, in his need to avenge his friend's death, he'd brought it to the office himself. On the bright side, Tinkie was diving into Janks's investment background and Tammy Odom, a high school friend known as Madame Tomeeka, was sitting watch with the patients. Tammy had some serious psychic ability, and she never turned down a friend.

I returned to the hospital to finish my conversation with Cece. When I found her dozing, I considered waking her, but a phone call from Dewayne side-tracked me.

"Jackson PD got in touch with Erin Carlisle's reception-ist. Erin hasn't been at work for two days. The receptionist didn't know what to do, so she never filed a missing persons report."

"Thanks, Dewayne." This was not good news.

When I peeked into Cece's room again, she was still asleep, so I took the opportunity to speak to Tammy. Perhaps she'd had a dream or vision or message. I'd take help from any source available.

Tammy had not only come to sit, she brought a plate of food big enough to feed three starving timbermen. Pork roast, greens, cornbread, and sweet potatoes. Before anything else, Tammy insisted that I eat something. I took the plate to Cece's room and watched as the delicious aromas worked their magic.

Her eyes blinked open and one side of her mouth moved into a smile. "What smells so good?"

I listed the menu items. "Want a bite?" The oxygen tube had been removed, and though she'd suffered broken ribs, some internal bruising, and a broken nose, she was on the mend.

She opened her mouth, and I gave her a taste of the sweet potatoes, which she didn't have to chew. Corn bread with fresh butter was next. We shared the plate in companionable silence.

"I haven't even tasted it, but I've heard hospital food sucks, dahling," she said.

I laughed, mostly with relief. There was just a hint of "society Cece" in that statement. What I had to tell her, though, might be upsetting. I waited until she'd eaten her fill before I broached the subject. With Cece, it was best to jump right in. She wasn't much for pussy-footing around. "Erin Carlisle is missing. She hasn't been at work since the night you were beaten."

Cece's breathing was loud in the room. "She said someone had been following her." The damage to her face made her words short and irregular.

A million questions flooded my brain, but I took it slow. Cece was fragile. Though she liked to present the image of being tough as nails, she had her breaking point too, and being battered into a bloody pulp had to be close to the edge. "You went to Memphis with Jimmy. He took you home?"

"He did. We had a tiff about the Carlisle land. I told him I was going to interview Erin." She took a moment to breathe again.

"Was he angry when he took you home?"

"Not angry. Unsettled."

"You obviously got in touch with Erin, and she agreed to meet you at Image Photography."

"That's right. You're a virtual telepath, dahling."

I rolled my eyes. "Did you talk to her?"

She shook her head. "We arrived at the parking lot at the same time, and we were walking to her studio when a car flew across the asphalt. We both dove out of the way. Before I could get up, someone hit me with a club or something. I think Erin screamed. Then I blacked out."

"Can you say whether Erin was attacked or abducted?"

"No."

Damn it. Cece was normally sharp and remembered details, but she'd been clocked from behind.

"Do you have any idea where Erin might be?"

"She said she was catching a flight to Chicago. She said she was going to meet her sister."

"Erin knows about Sonja Kessler?" This was unexpected.

"Didn't say her name. Just her sister."

"Think, Cece. Can you remember anything about the car that almost ran you down?"

"It was big. Dark. Maybe navy or black." She closed her eyes. "It happened so fast."

Jimmy Janks drove a big, dark SUV.

A nurse came into the room with a syringe. She injected the contents into the drip that fed into Cece's arms. Within seconds, Cece's eyelids fluttered.

"Thank you, Cece. You've been a big help." The search for Erin now had to be extended into the Windy City.

"Tomorrow." Cece's voice was a mere wisp of sound.

I kissed her forehead. "Is only a day away," I whispered in her ear. "Tomorrow you'll feel like hell, but all of your friends will be here to torment you."

"Cheerful bitch," she replied before she gave herself to sleep.

I stopped by to talk with Tammy and found her staring at Oscar, her face filled with that same determination Tinkie always showed.

"Don't give up hope, Sarah Booth," she said when she heard my footsteps and faced me.

"I'm too tired to hope *or* give up." The idea of walking to my car exhausted me. In fact, the cot in the hallway looked pretty damn good.

"I'll stay the night," Tammy offered.

"I promised Tinkie I would do it." It was a matter of honor that I support Tinkie in her battle against death.

"She'll be fine if I stand guard. You need to sleep. Both of you. I won't let any of them slip away in the dark hours."

Tammy had a better grip on things of the spirit than I ever would. My only connection with the other side was Jitty, and somehow I didn't think she was a reliable source of information or inspiration. I felt hollow and drained, with just a vague twinge of nausea. Sleep was much needed.

"Will you call me if anything changes?" I asked.

"I will." She patted my shoulder. "Sarah Booth, I've had a few dreams about you."

Adrenaline shot a rush of energy to my limbs. Tammy's dreams were never trifling. They always had meaning. "Should I ask, or should I leave it alone?"

"I'm not sure. Most of the time I understand a dream, at least on some level. These images are confused. And troubling."

Tammy was a tall woman, nearly six feet. The turban she wore made her look even taller. The orange, green, and yellow caftan hid her curvaceous figure. She was an imposing figure, especially when she was talking about troubling dreams and visions.

"Tell me," I said with trepidation.

"Do you have any relatives left, Sarah Booth?"

The immediate answer was none, but Tammy didn't ask questions without a reason. "None that I know of." I was thinking of Erin and Sonja. Was there a sister or brother somewhere out there I didn't know about? The idea excited me—and gave me a sense of hope. I would love to have a sibling, especially a sister.

"There's fresh dirt turned in your family cemetery. That I saw clearly." Before I could ask, she held up a hand. "No, it isn't you."

"I can't think of anyone. Except . . . Sweetie Pie." The thought of my dog being injured made my throat close with emotion.

"Not the dog." She patted my arm. "Sweetie Pie has future adventures. As does her little friend, Chablis."

"That's good to know." Now that Sweetie and I were out of potential psychic danger, a load lifted from my shoulders. If there was a family member alive, I wasn't close to him or her. Well, that was a major understatement. I was so un-close I didn't know he or she existed. But for the life of me, I couldn't even come up with a third or fifth cousin. I was truly the last of the Delaney line. My mother was an only child of only children—so there were no descendants on that side of the family either.

Jitty had a point when she fussed at me to "breed up." If I didn't, what would become of Dahlia House?

"Do you see a future for Oscar?" I asked.

Tammy hesitated. "I haven't looked at his cards. Or Tinkie's. Sometimes when a deep friendship is involved, I'm blocked as to what I can and can't see."

She wasn't playing games. Tammy always told the truth, even when it hurt.

"Did you have any other visions about me?"

She rubbed her forehead, pulling at one of her dark curls. "You're on my mind a lot, Sarah Booth. There's someone else in Dahlia House, isn't there?"

My heart almost stopped. Tammy had been in the house a few times, and each time I thought she'd sensed Jitty, but she'd never said a word. "No one else lives there." Talk about splitting hairs, but I didn't want to outright lie to Tammy.

Her smile was conspiratorial. "There are many people who've crossed the River Jordan who watch over you. Many. While they can't keep hardship and pain from your door, they're always right beside you whether you know it or not." She arched one eyebrow. "And I think you know that better than you let on."

"If Oscar was going to die, would you know it?"

She looked through the glass and studied the sick bay.

"There's a darkness in the room, Sarah Booth. Not necessarily death, but a presence. Something that's absorbing the light."

"Where is it coming from?"

She kept her gaze riveted on the patients. "I can't find the source. All I know is someone, or something, dark and twisted is involved in this."

Her words generated a keen sense of dread. "Can we get rid of the darkness?" I asked.

"We can stand vigil against it."

Tinkie had been right all along. She'd sensed something none of us except Tammy understood. And she'd fought for the man she loved and her friends.

"Thank you for being here tonight." Tammy was a far better watcher than I was.

"Get some rest. Tinkie will be back tomorrow, and I keep hoping Doc and some of those experts will come up with some way to cure our friends."

"My hope exactly." I thought again of what Peyton had told me about the possibility that mold was at the source of this illness. Someone had to get to the bottom of this, and while I wasn't an expert on mold, I was an investigator.

First thing in the morning, I was heading to the Carlisle plantation.

21

My dragging feet thudded across the front porch of Dahlia House, and tired as I was, I missed my hound. Sweetie Pie was guarding Tinkie, and she was exactly where she needed to be.

Madame Tomeeka's dreams and visions filled my head as I climbed the beautiful curved staircase to my room. I was too tired even for the comfort of a few moments with Jack, my old Tennessee friend. Sleep was my only requirement. Perhaps, if my brain rested, I could see the facts of the case more clearly.

Such as—how had Erin found out about Sonja?

When I was in Chicago, Sonja had presented herself as a woman happy with her lot in life. She'd said she had no desire to make Erin aware of Gregory Carlisle's indiscretions. Yet Erin had said she was flying to Chicago to meet her sister even as Sonja was informing me of her desire to stay in the background.

So who told Erin about Sonya? Erin had trusted the source of her information enough to plan a trip to Chicago. Luther was the logical choice, but there was no love lost between the Carlisle siblings. And certainly no trust.

Jimmy Janks was the next suspect. He stood to gain plenty if he could unsettle Erin enough to shake her blockage of the development of the Carlisle land. Maybe he'd hoped to make Erin so disgusted with her father's conduct that she'd yield the fate of the property to Luther.

According to Cece, Janks had dropped her at her home. He'd been aware of her intentions to drive to Jackson and speak with Erin. He could have followed Cece. But why? And why beat her so brutally?

Which begged a third question—had Erin vanished willingly? I didn't know her. She might have a habit of lost weekends—or lost weeks for that matter. She could be living it up in San Francisco or halfway around the world in Tahiti for all I could say.

As I struggled through the elements of the case, I removed my jeans and shoes and considered a hot bath or quick shower. Instead, I fell backward onto my bed. Cleanliness came second to sleepiness, at least for this night. My eyelids felt like cement blocks were tugging them downward.

From a far corner of the room came the lively sound of a big band. I could not believe this. I kept my eyes closed and willed the sound to disappear. I recognized the catchy tune as a dance number from the 1930s—"Tutti Frutti." Somewhere I'd seen film clips of energetic teenagers bobbing and swinging in complicated steps that required agility and a talented partner.

"Jitty!" I yelled. I was dying for the sandman's visit, and she was tormenting me with a full orchestra.

"Any hepcat would know the difference between an orchestra and a disc." Jitty materialized right in front of me. The white shirt closed at the throat with a black tie. The black skirt and saddle oxfords made me sit up in bed. Sleep fled the room.

"Get out!" I pointed at the door. "You are not allowed to read my thoughts like that." I hadn't said anything aloud. She'd stepped over the line.

"Be a rootie-tootie and find yourself a cutie," she sang back at me, wagging her finger and dancing around the bed.

"Jitty, I've been awake for days." I wanted to throttle her. "I could die. My death will be on your head."

"Sarah Booth, I think you got some anger issues."

Dear God, if she were not dead, I would gleefully kill her. "I have some sleep deprivation issues."

The music faded and she sat on the edge of the mattress. "I'm sorry, you do need your rest."

I flopped back against my pillow. "Then go away. If I don't get some shut-eye I may burst into flames."

"Sarah Booth, did you ever think about how the whole world relies on the young for true hope? Like those young boppers and swingers, they kept the spirit alive. The Great Depression, all of that. If it hadn't a'been for the young-uns, folks woulda given up and crawled off to die."

I opened one eye to see her expression. Surely she was messing with me. "Did you ever stop to think that I could sell this place and you with it?"

She gave a little shake of her head. "No call to get all uppity. If you had a politically correct bone in your tired ole body, you wouldn't talk about sellin' me. Not to no-body, nowhere, no time."

I sighed. "You know what I meant."

"Yes, I do. No offense taken." She smiled, and in the moonlight filtering through the blinds I saw that her dancing and sashaying hid a deeper sadness.

It was hopeless. I couldn't fly to the arms of Hypnos if she was genuinely troubled. "What is it?" I asked.

"When do you think we cross the line between youth and gettin' old?"

This age thing was heavy on Jitty's mind. "You'll always be young. And sexy. And thin." I flounced in the bed seeking a more comfortable position. "I'll hit middle age and my middle will age and spread, but you'll always be just the way you are today. Somehow that's not fair."

"Middle age isn't old!" She hesitated. "Sometimes I forget you don't have a model for such things. Your mama died so young, and all your relatives are gone. There's no one left to show you the way."

"That applies to most of the situations of my life," I admitted. "I'd give almost anything for ten minutes with my folks. They could help me."

"Somehow, Sarah Booth, you'll figure it out. You're comin' to the last of your youth. Transitions are always the toughest part. Life's still got some fine surprises in store for you. I believe that for sure." Her eyes danced with mischief, and I wondered what she knew that I didn't. It wouldn't do any good to ask, because Jitty was a master at keeping secrets.

"Maybe middle age will be easier," I said. "Wisdom, serenity, those are what I perceive as the gifts of maturity."

"Best to hide those lights under a bushel if you want to get you a man."

Jitty wasn't kidding. And she was wrong. "Graf loves me *because* I'm smart."

"I'd say it's more like *despite* the fact."

"Men have changed since your time. They admire women of accomplishment."

Jitty executed a quick dance step. "Men, down in the bottom of their hearts, want a woman who makes them feel needed. When a man feels that he's the king of his domain, then he's the happiest he's ever gonna be."

"Because a woman is smart doesn't preclude the man from feeling needed." Why was I arguing the merits of the metrosexual man with Jitty at midnight when I felt like someone had thrown glass dust in my eyes?

"Not if it's done the right way. Take a tip from your partner. Tinkie has always been smarter than Oscar, but when you first met her, you saw only what she wanted you to see—another ditzy sorority girl who'd achieved the Nobel Prize of the DGs: a secure marriage."

That was true. I'd not only underestimated the depth of Tinkie's character, I'd never noticed the greatness of her heart. Time had taught me who she really was, despite the trappings of the Leader of the Pack of Sunflower County DGs. "Okay, I concede that point. But do you think Oscar realizes how smart Tinkie is?"

"He knows what she wants him to know. And he'll never doubt that he's the top priority in her life." She sat back down on the bed. "Dancin' and datin' aren't the priority of your life anymore, Sarah Booth."

"They never were, Jitty."

Her eyes were brown pools in the moonlight. "I know that. When your parents died, they took your youth with them. Can't be helped, but you missed out on the carefree time of bein' a young adult. Now you're all serious bidness. A man wants to see your softer side."

"Graf knows I have a soft side. He's seen it." I was feeling way too defensive for so late—or so early, as it were—in the morning.

"Allow yourself to be tender, Sarah Booth. Tender and nurturing. Will you do that?"

"Can't say 'til I get there," I told her.

"I think the best thing about bein' young is that you believe anything is possible."

I thought about her statement, despite the fact that she was keeping me from much needed rest. "I'd agree with that. But then I'd say the best thing about being an adult is *knowing* that anything is possible."

"Touché, Miss Wish-Upon-A-Star. And I was gettin' worried that you were growin' cynical."

Jitty's drawl was slow and thick, and for a moment I closed my eyes and allowed myself to relax into the safe comfort of it. All of my life I'd been surrounded by women with a slow, easy drawl. Women who were strong yet tender, smart yet compassionate—the very qualities Jitty advocated that I practice.

"I'm not cynical, Jitty. I'm tired. Was there anything else?" Sleep once again hauled at my eyelids.

"Tomorrow, listen to some of those old records your mama loved."

"Okay." The word rolled out of my mouth.

"There's a song there for you."

"Okay."

"Good night, Sarah Booth."

"Okay," I mumbled.

The last thing I heard was the warbly echo of her whistling. "My Blue Heaven" drifted over me like a soft blanket.

It was bright and sunny when I finally rejoined the living. I'd slept so hard, my back was stiff and my muscles sore. Fleeting dream images disturbed the glow of the sunshine, but I pushed them back and sat up. There was work to be done, and I was rested and ready to do it.

First was a check with Tammy at the hospital. "It's all fine," she said when she answered my phone call. "Tinkie has called about eight times. She needs a lift up here."

"Can do." I'd forgotten I'd left Tinkie stranded at home. It was a sign of her genuine concern for me that she hadn't called and awakened me. She was undoubtedly champing at the bit to get back to the hospital and Oscar.

"I'm baking some biscuits," she announced when I called. "I'll feed you breakfast for a change."

Now that was a turnabout. Normally I played chef to Tinkie's breakfast desires, but after I'd spiked her French toast, I gathered she didn't trust me with a spatula. "I'll be there soon."

I raced through a shower and my toilette and picked up my car keys on the table in the foyer.

I headed out the front door and nearly tripped over a special delivery package. When I picked it up, I noted the California return address. Graf! My heart tumbled at the thought of him.

Before I went another inch, I tore into it. The black velvet box that slipped from the packing made me close my eyes. I knew what it was. Although I hadn't anticipated it, I wasn't surprised. Graf had become the kind of man who honored his word.

I briefly considered waiting until I got to Tinkie's, but somehow that was a violation. This was a private moment between Graf and me. I opened the box, awestruck by the way the light caught the facets of the yellow diamond. The simple solitaire was set on a band of twined gold. A pattern of ivy had been carved into the band.

A small note was crammed into the ring box.

I love you, Sarah Booth.
Please wear this symbol of our love.
Graf.

How clever of him to send the ring in a way that allowed me to accept or reject it without the pressure of him standing—or kneeling on one knee as I felt he would—in front of me. There was a deep traditionalist streak in Graf, yet he'd pushed it aside to consider my nature, my fears.

He knew me well enough to realize that I would have to think about this moment, about what I was promising, and about how this would change who I was—in my eyes as well as in the community I loved.

I slipped the ring on my finger. It was a perfect fit. In every way.

Jitty's words from last night came back to haunt me. If I wore this ring, I had to commit to allowing myself to soften, to trust Graf enough to let him be strong. While I might chafe at the idea of playing a role, I had to accept the wisdom of Jitty's advice. A good relationship required consideration of the needs of "the other."

My cell phone broke the moment.

"Sarah Booth, the biscuits come out of the oven in five minutes. Don't you make me eat cold biscuits." Tinkie's voice sounded better than I could remember.

"I wouldn't dream of that." I ran down the steps and jumped into my car.

Good for her word, Tinkie had breakfast on the table when I walked in. Crisp bacon, hot biscuits with butter and mayhaw jelly, fresh coffee, and grits.

"This is delicious," I told her. We were both eating fast. "If I slowed down, I could taste it better."

"No time for slackers," Tinkie said. "Tammy has a client to read for at eight, so we're on a tight schedule."

I shoved half a biscuit in my mouth and grinned at her.

"The ring is beautiful," she said, her total attention on her grits. When she finally looked at me, there was only happiness in her expression. "Of all the guys in your life, Sarah Booth, Graf wouldn't have been my pick until I saw the two of you together in Costa Rica. The man adores you."

"I can't believe I've accepted an engagement ring." Just like that. The ring slipped onto my finger and now I felt as if it had always been there.

"Have you set a date?"

The idea floored me. Engaged was one thing. Married, with all the trappings of an official ceremony, was something else. "No. We haven't even talked about one."

She laughed. "Don't worry, once Cece recovers, she and I will take over all the wedding plans. It will be spectacular."

That was a troubling word. "Maybe we could just go for intimate and lovely."

"That, too."

Now wasn't the time to argue with Tinkie about the size, shape, or tone of a wedding far in the future, so I let it slide. "Have you met Beaucoup or Peyton?" Both of the CDC workers had been in and out of the hospital, but Doc had handled passing information to Tinkie.

She ground pepper on her grits. "Mr. Fidellas stopped by yesterday while he was at the hospital. He's a handsome guy and said some nice things about you." She checked to see if I was taking the bait. When I gave her only a bland look, she continued. "He asked some questions about off-shore banking accounts. I told him to talk to Harold."

"Did he say why he asked?"

She passed the salt and pepper to me. "Some angle his partner was working, I think."

"Yes, Beaucoup." Obviously Coleman was sharing everything with her. "So what do you think of her?"

"Bonnie Louise—I refuse to call her that vulgar nickname—stopped by the first day she got here. You know, I remember her family well. It was so hard on Oscar to put them off their land. They'd been on that acreage for generations."

The biscuit I held in my mouth turned as dense as concrete. "Oscar put them off their land?"

"Didn't you know?"

I slowly shook my head. "I didn't. Beau—Bonnie—said she was from Sunflower County, but I don't recall where. From the way she talked about leaving the land, I assumed boll weevils or drought or too much rain had ruined their crop and bad times got tougher."

"The weather was a part of it, but it was a combination of bad decisions and miserable luck, just like what's going on around the country now. Bad loans, poor judgment, and not reading the tiny-tiny print have gotten a lot of people in trouble. But Oscar has never done business that way. The McRaes had a straight-up loan. Her family got in over their heads and they lost everything, but she doesn't appear to hold a grudge or any hard feelings. She's asked about Oscar several times."

I buttered my second biscuit. I had no evidence against Beaucoup for any wrongdoing. But my gut told me there was more to her than met the eye. Now that I knew her history, I had an inkling of her agenda. How biblical would it be for an heir of a foreclosure victim to somehow poison the banker responsible for the loss of the family farm?

"What's wrong, Sarah Booth?"

"I feel sick." It was true. The revelation of Beaucoup's background had given me such a violent mental twist that it made me nauseated. I rose unsteadily from her kitchen table.

"I'll be right back." I ran to the bathroom and knelt beside the toilet. Sleep or no sleep, I had to make an appointment with Doc. This was getting to be ridiculous.

"Sarah Booth, are you okay?" Tinkie called.

I rinsed out my mouth and studied my reflection. As I lifted my hand to straighten my hair, the light caught in the diamond and flashed sparkles around the room. I felt like a kid with the best present in the world. "I'm one hundred percent fine. Let's roll," I said as I walked to the front door.

22

I dropped Tinkie at the hospital and headed to the chancery clerk's office. Land records were sometimes snarled, but Attila proved his warrior spirit when he attacked the paper trail that led to a time when Bonnie Louise and her family farmed a tract of land in the northeastern corner of Sunflower County.

The deeds were cut-and-dried. Mr. McRae defaulted on his mortgage, and the property was sold at auction from the courthouse steps on December 23. Talk about rotten timing. Oscar, acting for the bank, oversaw the foreclosure and sale. No doubt a horrible Christmas for the McRae family and for Oscar.

Bonnie Louise McRae had one helluva motive to hold a grudge against Oscar.

In a plot designed by a mastermind—if my suspicions were correct—Beaucoup was also *the* primary element in identifying Oscar's peculiar, and potentially fatal, illness. A conflict of interest, I would say.

It was possible I'd terribly underestimated the gray matter between Beaucoup's ears. Her bodacious bubble butt, the way she cooed in Coleman's ear, and her bitchy attitude had perfectly distracted me from what lay beneath the exterior.

"Ms. Delaney, are you ill?" Attila asked.

"No. I'm okay." The record room was stuffy, and I was light-headed from the blast of reality that had rocked my world, but I was fine.

"High interest rates forced a lot of folks off the land, just like now," Attila said. "I wasn't chancery clerk then, but I remember this event. Mr. McRae brought his family to the courthouse for the auction. They stood and watched, the children crying and clinging to their father's leg, begging him not to let someone take their home." His finger ruffled the pages of the deed book. "Oscar was almost as upset as the McRae family, but he had a job to do."

"Not a job I'd want." My imagination supplied me with plenty of visuals.

"Back then, banks were particular about who they lent to. Folks had to meet criteria to qualify for a loan. What happened wasn't anyone's fault. Farming is a gamble, you know that."

"Do you recall what went wrong with the McRaes?" Where did a family go once they'd been evicted from their home?

Attila took a seat at the table where we'd been working. "Mrs. McRae was diagnosed with breast cancer. Farmers back in those days often didn't carry health insurance. They were self-employed and that's always been a hard row in this country. McRae insisted that his wife go to

Houston for the best treatment they could get. He fell into debt. Then we had a drought. He gambled on cotton and lost that year. It was like a hurricane swelling over a rowboat. There was nothing he could do."

"Did Mrs. McRae recover?"

He looked at the shelves of land deeds. "No, she didn't. She died about three years later."

"And McRae?"

"Drank himself to death from the grief. He lost his wife, his land, his family. Had a big insurance policy that paid off the debt, though. In the end, he did everything he could to take care of his family. Gabe McRae seemed to be a good man. He got caught between a rock and a hard place."

What was there to say? The newspapers were once again full of average, normal people being ground to dust by huge financial organizations, a failing medical system, and greedy corporations. Beaucoup's father was one of the silent victims of the last economic turmoil.

Bonnie Louise McRae had a right to hard feelings and a lot of pain associated with Sunflower County.

Hard feelings could turn into hard actions. I thought of Bonnie Louise, with her blond, country girl charm and soft drawl. Looks could be deceiving. In fact, they often were.

"Thank you, Attila. You've been a tremendous help."

I left the bowels of the courthouse and stopped for a moment in the sunshine. Standing on the courthouse steps, I saw that in the days of Oscar's illness, the last vestiges of winter had retreated. Oaks around the courthouse sported new green. The scent of magnolia frascatti, like ripe bananas mingled with honey, danced on a gentle breeze.

The shrub was in Addie Ruth Bennett's yard. I'd often

ridden my bike there and crawled under the branches to inhale the wondrous scent, so exotic, that excited all sorts of fantasies and adventures. I'd had a magical childhood, and Bonnie Louise had seen her family disintegrate. Loss of that nature could drive a person over the edge.

It seemed like years had passed since I'd been by to have a cup of coffee with Millie, and now was a good time—between the breakfast rush and lunch crowd. I could also pick up something tempting for Cece and take it to her in the hospital.

I left the courthouse and walked the few blocks to the café. The day was hot but not too humid, and I passed the shops where I'd purchased outfits for Hollywood with help from Tinkie and Cece. My cell phone rang.

"Sarah Booth," Coleman said. "I've received a copy of the report from the Jackson PD. Erin Carlisle is officially a missing person. The only evidence they could find at the scene was Cece's blood. The Chicago police attempted to contact Sonja Kessler, but she wasn't at home. If she works, they haven't been able to find an employer."

"Is there any sign of Erin in Chicago?"

"No record of a plane ticket in her name. Law officers are checking both airports, but I don't think Erin went to Chicago."

Which meant she'd most likely been abducted.

"The Jackson police are checking Erin's phone records," Coleman continued. "If she spoke with Sonja Kessler, we'll know it. We'll also know who called Erin. Someone had to tell her that she had a half sister, and it's a fifty-fifty chance that information came via the phone."

"What are you thinking?" I asked.

"Based on the brutality of the attack on Cece, I'm concerned for Erin. She's the key to unlocking the Carlisle land for development. If she's not around . . ."

"Then Luther can develop it any way he chooses." I'd come to the same conclusion. "Do you think Luther is smart enough to plan all of this by himself?" If Coleman could come to view Beaucoup as a suspect on his own, it would be much better than me pointing the finger at her.

"Information on Lester Ballard has also come through. The blood in Janks's room gave us a DNA match to Ballard. There was a cut on Ballard's right hand, which we believe was sustained during the argument overheard by the man across the hall."

"Do you think Janks killed Ballard?"

"Initial evidence points in that direction, but I don't have absolute proof. Ballard wasn't killed in the B&B. We don't have a crime scene yet. Wherever he was shot, he was taken to Friar's Point landing and dumped in the river."

"Thanks, Coleman. I'll let you know if I find anything."

I'd made it to Millie's, and I opened the door on the smell of home cooking. Millie was wrapping silverware in the back, but she came over with cups and a pot of coffee. Other than two customers deep in conversation at the counter, we had the place to ourselves.

I ordered Millie's world-famous chicken and dumplings for Cece and some dewberry cobbler for Tinkie and waited while Millie passed on the order to the cook.

When she was back at the table, she picked up my left hand and examined the ring.

"I'm so happy for you, Sarah Booth." There were tears in her eyes. "Graf won me over, I have to say."

"I'm still adjusting to this." I twisted the ring on my finger. The fit was perfect, but the image of myself was a little disconcerting. Sadie, Sadie, married lady wasn't a role I'd ever aspired to play, despite Jitty's haranguing.

"Allow yourself to be happy, Sarah Booth." Millie

refilled my coffee. "Finding a man to share your life, if you're really partners, will be better than anything you ever imagined. Remember how happy your mother and father were?"

Of all the role models she could hold up, none was more potent. "My parents loved each other very much."

"There's great happiness in real love. Strife and conflict, too, but much joy. I'm glad for you."

"Thank you, Millie."

The doorbell jangled and a group of women entered and sat at a large table. The bell on the counter rang—my order was up. Millie stood. "Gotta get busy."

With the piping hot containers of food wafting delicious aromas under my nose, I left the café and retrieved my car. As I drove to the hospital, I tried to call Graf, but I'd missed him at home. Because I couldn't stand it, I left a message on his cell.

"The ring is incredible, Graf. It's beautiful. And it's on my finger. For better or worse, I will marry you."

It wasn't a traditional proposal or acceptance, but our life together would never fit into a neat box. We'd figure out how to live it our way. And we'd do it together.

Tinkie still retained the chipper look that a night's rest had given her, and when I scanned over the patients, it was clear to me that the two realtors were improving. Luann sipped juice through a straw, and Regina was able to speak a little. Neither had a clue what had happened to them.

Standing beside Tinkie, I pointed at the women. "This is great news, Tinkie. They're better."

"I'm afraid to hope," she admitted.

"Hope is what you do best, Tink. Don't stop now." I offered the cobbler.

Tinkie had chosen to wear Oscar's favorite red slack set, and the toll of the last week was evident. She'd lost at least ten pounds. But her hair was coiffed and her makeup was flawless. Perhaps the worst was behind us.

She took the container. "Take Cece her food. Knowing her, she's famished. I went down earlier, but she had a consult with a plastic surgeon. Doc says they're going to work on her nose soon. Put it back right."

The longer I spent with Tinkie, the more obvious it was that her perky attitude hid a deep depression. Grabbing her shoulders, I asked, "What's wrong?"

"Cece wouldn't be hurt if she hadn't been trying to help Oscar."

"Cece was on a story—you know that. Wild horses couldn't have kept her away from following a lead."

She looked down at her feet.

"You know that's true." I felt her bones as I tightened my grip. "And Oscar will get better."

"I don't know." The words leaked out of her.

There are all kinds of pain in the world, but the jolt of hurt that slammed into me almost made me stagger. Tinkie was the heart of Delaney Detective Agency. She believed in miracles, in real love, in the doctrine of the Daddy's Girl manual, and in the goodness of at least 10 percent of the human population. To see her stripped of those values was unbearable.

"Tinkie Bellcase Richmond, snap out of it." The only thing I could do was shame her out of her blue funk. It's exactly what Jitty would do for me—or to me, depending on your point of reference.

"It's the truth." She grew defensive, which in my book was a step forward.

"Oscar's hung on this long, I can't believe you'd let him slide away now."

"I'm not letting him."

"When you give up hope, you are. You're the anchor that holds him here. Madame Tomeeka said as much. You're the guard against Death. You, Tinkie, are his salvation."

She bit her lip and it popped out in an old gesture that made grown men beg for mercy. "You sure know how to make a girl feel bad."

I kissed her forehead. "That's what friends do. When necessary. And this time it was necessary. Now get back to watch so you can kick the Angel of Death in the ass if he dares to show up here."

She nodded, and there was firm commitment to the set of her chin. "Let me know if you hear anything about anything."

"Roger that, Captain Tink."

Cece's room was on another wing, but the food was still hot when I got there. She appeared to be dozing, so I hesitated.

"If you leave with that food, you're a dead woman, dahling," she said without opening her eyes. "They say people with a broken nose can't taste because they can't smell. Now that's a crock of she-it if I've ever heard one. I can taste those dumplings from here."

Whatever else was wrong with Cece's nose, she could still smell. I put the food on her rolling table and sat on the edge of the bed to feed her. While her face looked worse, with all the bruising and swelling, her overall color was better.

"They're going to do a rhinoplasty ASAP. What do you think of Nicole Kidman's nose?" She pushed up in bed and opened her mouth like a little bird so I could put a fat, juicy dumpling into her mouth. Cece was enjoying the role of invalid.

"I think Nicole would be really mad if you took it."

"Ha, ha," she drawled. "I asked for a caterer and they sent a comedian. And not a very good one, but one with an impressive rock on her left hand. Let me see that."

Cece had bounced back like a red rubber ball. I perched on the bed and took a deep breath and held out my hand for her to examine the ring.

"Very nice, Sarah Booth. The man is not cheap, I'll give him that."

"The ring suits me to perfection."

"And you slipped it on without being prodded by your friends. Which tells me a lot."

"He's a good man."

"And he has a very elegant nose, dahling," she said. "If I were a man, I'd want his nose."

It was nice to visit a sick person with a good prognosis and a healthy ego. "Speaking of noses, what about Erin Carlisle's? I thought it was classic yet pert. That would suit you. If you go too prissy, it won't match your personality." I stopped. "What?" She was giving me this look like I'd sprouted a halo—or horns.

"What are you talking about? Erin Carlisle's nose is aristocratic, that's true, but I don't think the upswept tip works with my bone structure."

Now I was the one trading strange looks. "What are you drinking? Erin has a straight nose. More Sandra Bullock."

"Not the Erin Carlisle I met in Jackson."

And there it was. Just like a sledgehammer to the temple.

"Shit," we said in unison.

I called Dewayne. "Can you find a picture of Erin

Carlisle from the driver's license bureau or maybe an online Jackson newspaper and bring a copy by Cece's room?"

"Sarah Booth, I—"

"I wouldn't ask if it wasn't important. Hurry, Dewayne. Where's Coleman?"

"He said something funny about some boll weevil studies at Mississippi State University. He had to make some calls about them."

My fingers clutched the phone. "Please tell him to come by to see Cece as soon as he can."

"What, you're calling a departmental meeting?"

Ah, another comedian. But Dewayne was trying. "Maybe a break in the case, but it sounds like Coleman is pursuing the same theory."

"Should I place a bet?"

"You're frisky today for a man who's had six hours' sleep in the past week."

"I'll tell him. And I found a photo of Erin Carlisle on her studio Web site. It's printing now."

When I closed the phone, Cece looked at me. "Where is the real Erin Carlisle?"

"A damn good question." Likely one with a tragic answer, but I didn't say that. "You were supposed to meet Erin at her studio. What happened?"

Cece was now feeding herself, tired of waiting for my distracted attention to return to her gastrointestinal needs. "I called her when I got back from Memphis and asked for a meeting."

"And she agreed, even as late as it was? What time was it?"

"One in the morning." Spoon in midair, Cece paused. "She didn't even blink at the time. And I didn't consider it strange. I had a ten a.m. deadline, dahling, and I had bait to entice her. Jimmy Janks told me more about his development plans, which was what precipitated the argument in Memphis. I told her enough to whet her appetite and she instantly agreed to talk with me."

"Why at her studio?"

"She said something about being on her way there anyhow—some phone call or something." She frowned in concentration. "I got there a little early. The studio was locked tight, and then she arrived in the parking lot. She was slow getting out of her vehicle and waved me over, so I went to meet her."

An empty parking lot in the middle of the night in a city with a problem with violence. Right. Cece had been set up. But why? "I'm thinking whoever this woman is, she had Erin inside the studio. She'd already grabbed her."

Cece nodded. "My thoughts exactly. There was something strange going on. The front of the studio is plate glass, and I kept trying to see inside. I thought I saw movement in the back, but it wasn't clear."

"But it would be enough to warrant an attack on you. This imposter had to have an accomplice. If we're right, and Erin was being held in the back, then they had to neutralize you. They couldn't chance that you'd seen something and would call the police."

"I wish I'd seen something important," Cece said.

"Maybe you did. First we make sure the woman you spoke with wasn't Erin."

"Do you have any idea who's behind this?" she asked before she spooned another dumpling down.

"If I had to pick, I'd say Luther Carlisle. He stands to benefit from Erin's disappearance. He'd hoped to inherit full control of the Carlisle lands upon the death of his parents, but Erin was named equally in the trust. If Erin dies, he'll likely inherit and he can sell the plantation and pave it all."

"Somehow, I don't think you'll let him do that."

There was a knock at the door and Dewayne entered with a wry expression and a shake of his head for Cece. "You look like hell, Cece."

"Thank you, dahling. I'm undeniably hot, and I'm glad you see it."

He held out the photo to me, taking note of my engagement ring. He didn't say a word, and I handed the photo to Cece.

"That is *not* the woman I met in Jackson. The hair color is right, but the face is all wrong."

As I reached for the picture, Cece snatched it back. "Nonetheless, she does have the perfect nose for me. Sandra Bullock, but better. My doctor will want to see this."

"Just so long as you don't get your priorities confused," I said. "Dewayne, let me walk you to the patrol car. I have some ideas."

23

Taureans are slow learners when it comes to the hard lesson of restraint. By nature, we want to bullishly charge into a situation and kick butt as fast and furious as our little legs will pedal. While extremely satisfying initially, this modus operandi often opens the door to the twin sisters, Grief and Remorse.

Standing in the parking lot with Dewayne, I thought of my natural inclination to act and the consequences that could follow. A dust devil swirled across the asphalt, blowing a few of last winter's brown pecan leaves along a slow path. In the distance, a mockingbird squawked hysterically. No doubt a cat was eyeing its nest.

"Whatever it is you're thinking, don't do it." Dewayne opened the cruiser door and leaned against it.

"I want to go to the Carlisle place."

"Sarah Booth, you won't do anyone any good if you get sick like Oscar."

"True, but I intend to wear a hazmat suit."

"Yeah, they got a big sale on them down at the Casual Corner. Maybe get one in all colors for the summer season."

Dewayne's wit had sharpened considerably. "I'll borrow one from the CDC."

"They won't even let Coleman use one," Dewayne said. "He had to order one from the Feds."

"Could be because they don't have one to fit him," I pointed out. "I'm not but an inch taller than Bonnie Louise. I can use hers."

"Fat chance. The truth is the CDC has quarantined the plantation, and they aren't going to let anyone on it. The sheriff hasn't even been there and he has the inside track with Ms. McRae."

I ignored that comment. "The CDC can't supersede county authority."

"That's *legally* true," Dewayne said. "Coleman invited them into Sunflower County, and they technically answer to him. But the real truth is they've shared very little information with him." He frowned. "That woman is always poking around the sheriff's office trying to find out what we know, but she hasn't told us much of anything useful."

Dewayne had just tightened the knot around Bonnie Louise's neck another notch. Coleman should have put it all together by now. He must have.

"Dewayne, I'm going to the Carlisle plantation. There has to be something there. I'm telling you, because someone has to know. In case . . ."

"In case you keel over with an unidentifiable illness that may fry your brain and destroy your lungs and heart?"

"You ever thought about seeking a PR job promoting plagues, famines, and boils?"

"As soon as Coleman returns, I'll tell him where you are. Maybe he can figure out a way to talk some sense into you." He gave me a hard look. "But I doubt it. Be sure your cell phone is charged and on."

I checked it while we were standing there. Months ago, Tinkie had insisted I carry one, and while it was a major pain in the butt, it did have its uses. "I'm good. Do you know where Bonnie Louise is right now?"

"Haven't a clue."

"If she shows up at the sheriff's office, try to detain her. And I need for you to do a complete background check on her and Peyton Fidellas." When I'd quickly checked their CDC employment records I hadn't seen anything suspicious, but Dewayne had the authority of law. He could find out a lot more than I could.

"Check both of them?" He was obviously seeing Bonnie Louise in the same light I did.

"It can't hurt. And you can play it like a regular background check, without arousing suspicion. If you only ask about one . . ."

He nodded as he twisted his hat in his hands. "Be careful, Sarah Booth."

"I promise. Let Coleman know this about Erin."

He gave me a half salute and drove away. As I was walking back to the roadster, my phone rang. I snatched it out of my pocket, "Coleman!"

"Wrong man. If I were the sensitive type, my feelings would be hurt." Graf's voice was steady and sure and gently teasing.

"Graf! I didn't expect to hear from you at this time." I figured he'd be on the set shooting. "The ring—" To my utter surprise, my throat closed with emotion.

"Are you really wearing it?" Graf's voice was warm with humor.

"I am. Tinkie, Millie, and Cece think it's incredible."

"Then I've passed muster with the Zinnia Gang of Four. Whew! That's a tough group."

His grace and wit eased me over the hump of emotion. "I wish you were here."

"It does my heart good to hear you say that, Sarah Booth. You're so independent, I don't ever want to crowd you."

"I love you, Graf." Those words, spoken over a cell phone to a man a thousand miles away, came more naturally than I'd ever expected.

"I promise you, Sarah Booth, while in the past I may not have realized the incredible gift you're offering me, I do now. I've never loved or wanted anyone or anything as much as I do you. I promise whatever you want or need in life, I'll do my best to provide it."

How was it possible that while the world of Sunflower County was falling apart around me, I could feel such elation and joy? "We've traveled a long road, you and I. You've made me believe in 'happy ever after' endings."

"Now that's a miracle." Graf's humor was perfectly on target, but this conversation deserved a face-to-face. The telephone, while an impressive instrument, wasn't cutting it.

"How is it that you're calling me at this time in the morning?" The shooting schedule for his film was rigorous.

"We're on break. One of the horses got overheated, so they're checking him over. We're leaving for a location shoot in the desert in a couple of hours. We'll be back tomorrow, but we'll be out of touch for at least twenty-four."

"Is this the big chase scene?"

"It is. They've already shipped the horses. Speaking of horses, how are Reveler and Miss Scrapiron?"

"Good. I haven't had much chance to ride. Things have been . . . busy here." I was tempted to tell Graf of my plan, but it would only worry him needlessly.

"Did you get a chance to read that script?"

Damn it, I'd put it on the table beside the bar and hadn't picked it up since. "I haven't. Things are hectic, but I'll look at it tonight."

"Just a gentle reminder, Sarah Booth."

Graf wasn't applying pressure, but even as little as I knew about the movie business, I realized the producer would want to start the process of gathering the millions necessary to put a film together. The pieces of the business plan had to mesh all at once; the actors and actresses who signed on were an important element in raising the cash and garnering studio interest.

"Tonight. We'll talk about it later." Instead of moving my car, I started to the health department on foot. It was only a short distance, and it was nice to walk and talk with Graf, to pretend that he was beside me.

"We may take a break in filming next week. Are you up for a visit from your fiancé?"

My heart lifted. "I'd like nothing better."

"Then I'll make it so. Hey, they're waving me back to the set. I love you, Sarah Booth Delaney."

"Don't break your neck on a horse." Damn. Now that I'd finally given him my heart, I felt totally vulnerable and at risk.

"Horses are manageable. *You* don't get crossways with a villain. I'm a lot safer here than you are. We don't use real bullets, you know."

He made me smile, and I loved him even more for that.

I was tripping up the steps to the temporary CDC offices in the health department when my cell phone rang again. This time it was Coleman.

"No time to talk," he said, and I heard the tension in his voice. "Sarah Booth, There's something strange going on with Bonnie Louise's mentor, Dr. Jon Unger. I did some checking and he didn't exist until 1992."

"I told you he emigrated around that time. Did you check Germany?"

"No such person exists. It's like he was created out of whole cloth when he got his emigration papers."

"But he's been teaching at Mississippi State University. Surely they checked his credentials."

"He was never on faculty. He's been conducting research there. Boll weevil research. Private research."

"Bonnie didn't tell you this?" I asked as gently as I could.

"She told me a lot of things, but not once did she mention this private research." His tone conveyed the chill of an iceberg.

I wanted to tell him I was sorry, but I didn't. For all of the truth that I sometimes ran my mouth recklessly, this was one time I wisely refrained. The idea of being used by someone who pretends romantic interest is a painful wound that only the owner can lance.

There was an element I had to speak about. "Peyton thinks the illness may be related to mold. Has he spoken to you about it?

"He has. That strange green cast to the weevils at the Carlisle plantation may play into this somehow."

I hadn't seen it for myself, but I'd been told about it. "This could be the breakthrough we're hoping for, Coleman." I hesitated. "You might want to check Bonnie Louise's past."

"I've done that." The silence stretched.

"So what are you thinking?" *He* had to say it.

"Bonnie Louise is my prime suspect. Have you seen her today?"

"I haven't. Where are you, Coleman?"

"I'm on the trail of a criminal," he said. "I'll speak with you in person before long."

There was the click of a disconnect and he was gone. I had my answer. Bonnie Louise was in his sights now, and no matter what he felt for her, Coleman would arrest her. Perhaps the whole ordeal for Oscar and the others was coming to a close.

"I need to borrow a hazmat suit." I sat in Peyton's office with the door closed.

He got up and left the office, returning with what I presumed to be Bonnie Louise's suit. "Be careful," he said, handing it to me.

"You aren't going to try to stop me?" This was a surprising twist. I'd figured he'd attempt to argue me out of my stated intention of examining the Carlisle property.

"I've searched every inch of that place. Maybe you can see something I've missed. We have to conclude this business. I'll go with you, if you like, but first I want to take this information to Doc." A grin spread across his face.

"Hot damn! You found an answer!"

His right eyebrow arched. "At least a partial answer, and one that spawns more questions."

"Tell me."

"The mold is a variant of a common species. That's what stumped me for so long—it isn't extraordinary. Yet in this instance, it's incredibly toxic."

"Where does it come from?" I asked. If we could find the source, then we'd have a better chance of uncovering how all of this happened—and possibly how to reverse it.

He picked up some reports from his desk. "It's too early to say. Doc will have to answer that, not me. He's the medical expert. What I can tell you is that the mold I've studied, taken from the weevils, produces spores, and mycotoxins." When I started to interrupt, he held up his hand. "Sarah Booth, the government has been studying molds for use in biological warfare."

"Holy crap." In the research on Dr. Unger, I'd learned that he'd been involved in government work. The implications of this case extended far beyond Sunflower County and the revenge machinations of Bonnie Louise McRae. If she was actually behind this, then she'd opened Pandora's box. "Have you called Homeland Security?"

"Not yet. I want to discuss this with Doc and the sheriff." He straightened some folders on his desk. "Mold is extremely difficult to diagnose. In cases of mold-induced deaths, there's often no evidence found in an autopsy."

"Was this mold created in a lab or did it . . . sprout naturally?"

"Impossible to say at this time," Peyton said. "It could have mutated on its own, but that honestly doesn't matter. What is of importance is how quickly we can organize against it."

"How do you treat mold? In a person."

"That's a complicated issue. The delivery method needs to be determined, whether ingested or inhaled. That's why I need to talk to Doc."

"Time's a'wastin'," I said, already on my feet and at the door. "Let's tell him so he can begin to find a way to help the sick people. And we have to find a way to stop this right now. Before anyone else is exposed."

"I'm right behind you."

Doc sat behind his desk and listened to Peyton's explanation. He sipped a cup of the witch's brew he called coffee and made notes, but he didn't interrupt until Peyton had finished.

"The delivery system could have been ingested," he said, "but I'm willing to bet it's contact. Regina and Luann are well enough to speak, and they've admitted to cutting across the cotton field. Oscar walked through the fields, likely brushing against the weevils and sending the mold into the air."

"And Gordon walked through the fields looking for evidence of foul play," I said. "All of them could easily have stirred the spores into the air."

Doc ran a hand through his wild hair. I'd hoped for some exclamations of joy, some jubilation that the source was revealed and now a cure could be found. Doc's behavior was worrying.

"This helps, doesn't it?" I asked. "It's mold. Like mildew. It can be killed, right? And if the mold is dead, then Oscar and the others will improve."

"Mold is tricky, Sarah Booth. Great strides have been made in understanding it. The genetic code of aspergillus mold was cracked in 2005, which may be how this particularly lethal variation was created."

He'd said *created,* as in masterminded in a lab. But that could wait. Curing the four sick people was the primary issue. "There are drugs, right? Pills or injections . . . medical things?" I didn't like the look on his face.

"The antifungal drugs themselves have side effects." Doc looked like a strong gust of wind could knock him over. "We've had the patients on steroids . . . Sometimes the damage is irreversible."

"But—" But what? Doc would do everything he could.

"Sarah Booth, mold can have serious consequences," Peyton said. "Most people aren't aware of invasive aspergillus." He glanced at me with pity. "It can attack the vital organs, including the brain."

Doc rubbed his cheek, drawing my attention to the stubble on his face. Usually he was meticulous in his grooming, which showed the degree of stress he was under. When he spoke, his voice was soft. "These weevils, where did they come from?"

"Ms. Delaney and I intend to answer that question immediately," Peyton said. "We're going out to the Carlisle place to take some samples and see what we can discover."

"I'm not certain that's a good idea." Doc squinted at me. "You look a bit peaked, Sarah Booth. I don't think you need to expose yourself. A weakened immune system is an invitation to terrible complications."

I started to argue the hazmat suit, but Peyton signaled me to remain silent. He cleared his throat and drew Doc's attention back to him. "I've given this some thought. Perhaps the whole plantation should be sprayed with chemicals strong enough to kill the weevils and the mold. The crop is lost, anyway. An aerial spraying would remove the threat of the weevils spreading."

Doc sighed. "I'm not the one to make that decision, Mr. Fidellas, but I'll support you. As much as I hate the idea of spewing chemicals across a thousand acres, I think we have to stop this any way we can."

"I'll speak to the sheriff," Peyton said as he rose. "If I have any additional breakthroughs, I'll be in touch."

"Thank you, Mr. Fidellas. I'll start the evaluation now for the best route to fight this. Because I'm out of other options with Oscar and Gordon, I'll start treating them while I set up a CT and some cultures for mold. I'll consult with authorities at the Mayo Clinic to develop a protocol." He stood up slowly, obviously eager to be on his way and as obviously near exhausted collapse. "If you'll excuse me, time is running out. I need to apply this information now."

"How are the patients?" I asked.

Doc wouldn't look at me. "As I said, Luann and Regina are improving."

"And Oscar and Gordon?" My voice cracked, because I knew by his phrasing that things weren't good.

"No improvement. In fact, we've found some bleeding in Oscar's lungs."

"Why?" I asked. "Why haven't they improved? If the realtors are better, why not Oscar and Gordon?"

"I have no idea, Sarah Booth. That's the damnedest part of it. I have no idea."

Peyton put his hand on my back, a gesture of support. "This is a mutant strain, Sarah Booth," he said. "What we're dealing with here is a wild card."

As I stepped toward the door, the room spun. Doc said something and someone grabbed me as I toppled sideways. Whether I hit the floor or not, I couldn't say. I telescoped swiftly into a black void.

"Sarah Booth! Sarah Booth!" Doc called my name.

The most noxious odor, sharp and caustic, made me start and struggle to sit up. Blindly I reached out and captured the hand with the bottle easing under my nose. "Whatever the hell that is, get it away."

"Old-fashioned smelling salts," Doc said. His face came into focus and I saw relief in his eyes. He wafted the bottle under my nose for good measure. "Ladies who wore tight corsets often carried a bottle in their reticules."

"I'm not wearing a corset," I grumbled.

"Then we'd better run some tests and find out why you swooned," Doc said.

"I agree." Peyton hovered just behind Doc's shoulder, his face a mask of concern.

I'd forgotten where I was or that he was with me. Pushing myself up, I reconnoitered the room. Sure enough, it was Doc's office. The coffeepot was a dead giveaway.

"I didn't swoon." I was insulted by the term. "I just got a little dizzy." I sat up the rest of the way. From this angle, Doc's office was even more cluttered than I'd thought.

"You're going to have some tests done, Sarah Booth. I'm stepping in as surrogate parent." Doc looked about as frazzled as I'd ever seen him. He was worried about me, and he already had a plateful of worry.

"Okay," I agreed. "Tomorrow morning."

Doc considered. "You promise you'll show up?"

I studied the possible turns of phrase I might use. Lying to Doc wasn't an option. "I promise."

"Be here at eight. We'll get some labs, go from there. But before you leave, I'm checking your blood pressure and drawing some blood."

He disappeared into the hall and returned with a blood-pressure cuff, which he put around my arm. In a moment he removed the instrument. "A little low, but nothing to worry about."

"See, I'm fine. I haven't slept much or eaten properly. That's all it is. I'm not sick."

"We'll make that determination tomorrow." He tied off my arm and inserted the needle, filling a vial. Once he was finished, I got on my feet before he could change his mind and slam me onto a stretcher.

"Ms. Delaney," Peyton said as he opened the door of Doc's office, "let me assist you." His hand under my elbow was firm.

Great. The one image I didn't want to project to the man who controlled the hazmat suits was weak and ineffectual. I moved briskly away from his hand. So as not to put the wrong spin on it, I said, "Thanks, Peyton. Doc wanted to pop me into a bed on the spot."

"It isn't normal to faint, Sarah Booth. I'd hate to see you as collateral damage in this situation." His hand lightly brushed my forehead, and I stepped away from his touch.

"We're on for the Carlisle place, right?" I forced a smile.

"Are you certain? If you're ill, the consequences could be terrible."

"I'm not ill." Having to repeat myself made me grumpy.

"Sarah Booth, if anything happened to you, I'd have to blame myself."

He was certainly intense. I looked down the hallway. "I'm fine, Peyton, but thank you. I want to get this resolved. Can I pick you and the suits up in about fifteen minutes? I need to speak with Tinkie first."

"I'll be waiting."

Taking a deep breath, I went to see my partner and best friend. I had good news for her. I could only hope it hadn't come too late for the man she loved.

24

Tinkie stood, straight-backed and stoic, looking through the hospital window at Oscar. I told her about the mold, about the potential for treating it, and I promised I'd find the person responsible for bringing this plague to Sunflower County.

She said nothing.

"Tinkie, you can't give up now. Doc can fix this. He will fix it."

Eyes riveted on her husband, she finally spoke. "Regina is drinking fluids on her own. Luann is sitting up and even talking on a cell phone. Their families are celebrating, and I'm happy for them. But look at Oscar and Gordon."

In contrast to the women, Oscar appeared worse. His pallor matched the sheets, except for the oozing pustules on his skin, which were red and angry. Beside him, Gordon seemed equally bad. How had this mold thing taken down two strong, healthy men yet passed over two women with lesser devastation?

"I'm helping Peyton with something, but I'll be back." I resisted checking at my watch. "We're going . . . to look for the source of these weevils." Tinkie was so depressed, she didn't bother to question where I was conducting this great research.

"It's too late." She spoke so simply.

While I wanted to argue with her, I couldn't. If I had to guess a time schedule, I didn't think Oscar would last through the night. "He's fought hard," I said.

"He's tired."

She was killing me. I could actually feel the tissue that held my heart in place begin to rip. When was it right to offer false hope and when to help a friend accept what appeared to be the inevitable? "Tinkie, what can I do?"

"Will you help me with all the . . . necessary arrangements?"

"We can talk about this later."

"I have to let him go, Sarah Booth. I've held him here, selfishly, because I can't imagine my life without him. Now, though, I accept he has to leave me. He won't be far."

Tinkie, unknowingly, had just stomped all over my own private wounds. Despite the fact that my parents had been dead for two decades, I hadn't let them go. I couldn't.

"How do you know Oscar is ready to go?" My voice quavered. There were times that Tinkie seemed to brush against another reality. She had a strong faith and a true belief that the veil between this world and the next was penetrable. When I was in Tinkie's company, I could believe it, too.

"I sense it," she said. "He's fought so hard. Trapped inside his body that's shutting down around him, he still fought. I felt the struggle. Now, he's still. It's almost as if a part of him has already left."

Hell, why not scoop out my heart with a soup ladle? "He's still because he's tired. I'll tell Doc to hit him with some speed. Now isn't the time to throw in the towel. Let me have the rest of the day."

At last she looked at me. "I can't ask him to suffer longer, Sarah Booth."

I would not have this. "You damn sure can. Think of the things he put you through. Think of the ba—" Oscar's passion for a planned life had cost Tinkie greatly in the past.

She put her hand over my lips. "You fight dirty." She looked a little shell-shocked at my tactics.

"You're damn right. I'll fight dirty *and* underhanded. Make him hang on. Just until midnight. Give me that, okay? Doc is going to start the antifungals now, even before the cultures and tests come back. And I'm going to find out who did this. Oscar would want to live to see justice, I can guarantee that. Sure he's tired of suffering. He's been through it. But he isn't the kind of man who folds his tent and slips away into the night. And you're not the kind of woman who would let him. Buck up and put the pressure on him to stay."

I took her chin in my hand and pointed her at the window. "Do that thing with your lip. Let it pop out of your mouth."

She frowned as if I'd spoken Celtic.

"Don't play innocent with me. I'll bet Doc will move Oscar to a private room. He isn't contagious. He doesn't have to be isolated. When he moves, you get in there and do whatever you have to do to remind Oscar of the pleasures of the flesh. He's a man—wherever he is, he'll return for that."

"That's unethical, Sarah Booth. He's helpless."

"Ethics be damned. You tell Oscar from me that he can't leave until I figure this out."

Tinkie pressed her fingers into the glass. "He hears you. See, his hands are twitching."

She sounded less defeated, but I didn't have time to push her any harder. And I didn't want to. There is a limit to how much bossing a friendship can take. "Move him to a room and do your worst," I whispered.

I rushed down the hall before she could respond—either negatively or positively—to my unusual tactics.

The CDC office was locked up, but Peyton had left a note on the door for me.

"Exciting development in the mold. May be able to offer more help to Doc. Have gone to Jackson to a bigger lab. Bonnie Louise still unaccounted for. Will call. Peyton. P.S. The hazmat suit is in your car."

While everyone else thought I was nuts to go to the Carlisle place, Peyton had faith in me. The suit was in the passenger seat of the roadster. I climbed behind the wheel and pointed the car for the one place where evidence against the instigator of this plot might be found.

I parked at the front gate and donned the suit. From the road, nothing looked too bad, but once I made it past the house and into the fields, the devastation was like a biblical plague. The cotton, which I'd been told was two feet high and lush, was a scraggly vista of dead stems and curled, brown leaves. Weevils were everywhere. They crawled along the brown stalks. I'd never seen anything like it, but I could easily grasp the direness of the situation if this moved on to the next plantation. I didn't need Jitty at my side to tell me that this looked like a scene from the

War Between the States. Or a glimpse of the future on a globally warmed planet. This was devastation of a man-made order.

With the cumbersome suit impeding my movements and vision, I entered the field. Behind me, the gracious structure of the old plantation rose like a specter of the past, a lone sentinel of a way of life that no longer existed.

A curtain fluttered briefly in a window, and I was reminded of the ghost I'd encountered in Costa Rica. Spirits lingered in old houses, but it wasn't a supernatural presence that I sought now.

Working from what I knew of Oscar's and Gordon's actions, I began my careful examination at the edge of the fields nearest the house. Before I left the property, I intended to search the old plantation, but I had to find out if Oscar and Gordon had seen something in those fields that drew them both into danger.

Moving through the rows, I ignored the insects. With the leaves mostly gone from the cotton plants, the activity of the weevils was like a maddened army on the march for food. They moved relentlessly. When I peered closer, I realized that some of them were dead.

Others were dying.

I watched in fascination as fire ants pursued the weevils. Huge mounds of the poisonous ants had sprung up in the cotton rows. Stories of elderly people falling into ant beds were Southern lore. Injured and unable to get away, the infirm died from the venomous bites.

The ants were on the attack, pursuing the weevils. Right in front of my eyes, the balance of nature was reasserting itself.

The suit protected me from the ants, so I knelt down to study the action more closely. Some chemical or spore or pheromone or something in the weevils compelled the fire ants to attack. Hordes of the burnished red insects raced in pursuit of the weevils.

The battle was fascinating, even for someone who didn't have a scientific bone in her body. Inching forward on my knees, I examined the dying weevils. The ants appeared to be stinging them to death—and then carrying them away. As I leaned over to watch a dozen yeomen ants hauling a weevil twenty times their size, I saw a key ring. Half-covered in dirt, it caught the glint of the sun. As I brushed the dirt away from it, I recognized the fake, pink diamonds that formed the initials BLM.

Bonnie Louise McRae.

A single key dangled from the chain.

Bonnie had been in the fields—it was part of her job. The key ring wasn't proof positive of any wrongdoing. Her job required her to examine the weevils. But what the key might open could be the coup de grâce for the CDC scientist. If this linked her to the weevils in any criminal way, the proof of her complicity would be irrefutable.

The suit was hot and uncomfortable, and I started to rise. The house needed to be searched, just in case. While I certainly hadn't done a thorough job of the fields, it would take longer than a day to walk a thousand acres. I had to get the key back to town and into Coleman's hands.

As I lumbered toward the house, the first blow landed on my left side at my waist. It came out of nowhere and knocked me sideways. The next one caught me in the stomach, and I blindly grasped what felt like a baseball bat.

Through the tiny window of the suit, I couldn't see anything except dead plants and dirt.

My body doubled over, and though I hung on to the weapon, I couldn't retain my grip. The last thing I felt was a whack to the head that sent pain sparkling behind my eyelids. Starbursts gave way to blackness.

"Don't move, Sarah Booth." Coleman's face peered down at me through the face mask of a hazmat suit. His voice sounded almost strangled.

When I tried to sit up, his hand pressed me back into the dirt. "Be still, you're bleeding."

I reached up to touch my face, but could feel no blood. "Where am I?"

"Be still, Sarah Booth. Please. The ambulance is coming." His hand on my chest held me motionless.

Sirens whined in the distance, and I squinted against the bright sun. I was outside. I turned my head and saw the dying cotton. Beside it was the helmet for a hazmat suit lying in the dirt.

My hands moved down my body and I felt the silken material, ripped in places, and realized where I was and what had happened just as a sharp pain tore through my abdomen.

"I've got to pick you up," Coleman said. His arms slid beneath me. "I have to get you out of here so the paramedics can work on you. I'm sorry." When he lifted me, the pain was unbearable and I couldn't stop the cry that escaped.

When I glanced down, I saw the blood. Dark and red it saturated the ground. A pool of it. My blood.

"What's wrong with me?" I gasped the words as he carried me away from the fields toward the house, toward the approach of the sirens.

"Someone hit you and left you to die in the fields."

"They took my helmet off."

I felt the muscles in his chest contract. "I know."

We both knew the implications of that.

"Doc will take care of you, Sarah Booth. You'll be okay. And when I find the person who did this . . ."

The fingers of my right hand clutched some object. I tried to lift my hand, to show him, but neither my hand nor arm responded. No amount of concentration could force my fist to rise to my chest.

"I'm paralyzed," I told him. Additional observations and complaints were cut short by the kind of pain that felt as if my torso were being squeezed by a giant. I had no doubt my pelvic bones would snap in two. "What's wrong with me?" I demanded.

"Save your strength." He kept walking, his steps steady, determined. "Don't worry about a thing, Sarah Booth. I've got you. Just don't worry."

He spoke to me as if I were a small child and he soothed my fears. When he'd carried me all the way to the main gate, he stopped but continued to hold me in his arms. "Just hang on a few more minutes. Help is on the way."

The ambulance drew close, and when it stopped, he gently deposited me on the stretcher. The eyes of the EMTs, visible through the helmets they wore, were grave as they set up a drip. So Coleman had gotten suits for emergency personnel as well as the sheriff's office. That was smart.

"She's bleeding out," one of them said.

"Stop it." Coleman's voice wasn't raised, but it was clearly a command. "Whatever you have to do, stop the bleeding."

"We've got to get her to the hospital," one of the paramedics said.

"I'll ride with her." Coleman wasn't asking, he was telling.

There was no argument. Coleman climbed into the ambulance beside me, his strong hand gripping mine.

The ambulance took off, and though I tried hard to stay awake, I couldn't. I heard voices, soft and glowing with warmth, calling me into the safety of sleep. The pain was unbearable, and I yielded to the peace offered by unconsciousness.

When I came back to myself, I was some place quiet and cool. There was a tiny beeping noise, the shush of some pneumatic machine. In the distance I could hear people talking. Tinkie—I recognized her voice. And Cece. She was there, too. A masculine voice. Doc.

"Don't tell her until she's stronger," Tinkie said.

"Sarah Booth is tough," Doc said. "She'll handle this." There was a pause. "She was due to come in for tests tomorrow morning. I never suspected."

"I called Graf," Cece said. "He's in the desert without phone reception. They promised to get word to him and get him on a flight."

"Did you tell him she lost the baby?" Doc asked.

"I did. I wanted him to know, but it won't matter," Cece said. "His concern will be Sarah Booth. She was out in that field, with all that stuff. Someone hit her, took off her protective gear, and left her out there to inhale that mold and die."

Tinkie lowered her voice. "I wouldn't want to be the person responsible for this when Coleman catches him."

The conversation made no sense to me. I felt like I was disembodied, floating around a room where people spoke of me as if I were dead. But it couldn't be me they were talking about. Someone had lost a baby, and I'd never been pregnant.

"Wait, she's moaning," Tinkie said.

Her cool hand, so small, stroked my forehead. "Sarah Booth," she whispered, "you're going to be okay."

"Tinkie . . ." That one word cost me a lot. I tried to open my eyes, but they wouldn't cooperate. "Paralyzed?" I had the sense that no part of my body would respond to any command.

"No, darling, you're not paralyzed." She kissed my forehead. "You're hurt, but you'll heal just fine."

"Happened?" If I could formulate a sentence it would be nice. I sounded like a poorly trained parrot spitting out one nonsensical word after another.

"You were attacked in the Carlisle cotton fields. Luckily Dewayne knew where you were. Coleman found you and got an ambulance. Someone hit you very hard with something. You're mighty bunged up, but you're too tough to kill."

She sounded so spritely and upbeat that I knew I was badly injured. I felt another pair of hands lift my wrist, and Doc leaned down.

"Gave us a scare there, Sarah Booth. You lost a lot of blood, but you're going to be fine."

There were more questions to ask, but I couldn't hold on to one long enough to speak it. "Graf?" I asked.

Cece fielded that question. "He's on his way."

Doc fiddled with the drip hanging by my bed. "I'm going to give you something more for pain. Just sleep, Sarah Booth. That's the best thing you can do for your body right now."

There was no time to sleep. My mother was calling me. I was suddenly among the oak trees at Dahlia House, a place behind the family cemetery. When I was a child,

I'd gone there to play with the fairies while my mother read books or entertained me with games only the two of us knew. It was our special place.

"Sarah Booth!" She sounded worried.

"I'm here." I walked among the trees, uninjured, whole and complete. At last I saw her, sitting on her favorite limb, one that swooped to the ground and formed a perfect seat. "I can't believe you're here."

And she was. As beautiful as I remembered. The sunlight caught in her dark brown hair, and her eyes danced with laughter. "You've grown into a fine woman," she said. "But I never had a doubt you'd be a looker. You stole your daddy's heart when you were born."

"You came back to me." I hardly dared to breathe for fear she'd evaporate. For twenty years I'd hoped for this moment, this time to be with her.

"Only for a short while," she said. "Jitty surely has told you there are rules here. I had to break a few even for this brief time."

"You know about Jitty?"

She laughed. "I know a lot of things." Her hand linked with mine and we walked among the shadows cast by the beautiful trees and the dapples of sunshine. "I know the woman you've become, and I want to tell you I'm proud of you."

"Why can't you come home if Jitty can?"

She squeezed my hand. "Sometimes love calls for sacrifice. I never want to encourage you to linger here, waiting and hoping for me. You have to live, Sarah Booth. Waiting for the dead isn't living."

"Tell me what to do."

My very serious request was met with laughter. For one split second I was sitting in the kitchen in Dahlia House, home from school, explaining how I'd gotten a spanking for tossing ink on Homer Kilgore. My mother's laugh was rich, warm, effortless. It was that same laugh, as if I'd told a funny story.

"Please, Mama, I need you."

"No you don't, Sarah Booth. You want me and your father. But you don't need us. And that makes me very happy. This is a hard blow for you. The loss of a child . . ." She searched my face, her hand brushing a few of my stray hairs out of my eyes as she'd often done when I was young.

"What about the baby?" I asked her.

"You'll grieve, but you'll recover. You're strong, Sarah Booth. And I'll never be far."

"Why did you have to die in that wreck?" I'd never understood how, out of the night, an accident had happened that changed everything I'd ever known. The Delta is flat. The roads run straight and mostly empty for miles. She and Daddy hadn't been drinking. "Why did Daddy lose control on a road with perfect visibility?"

"The past is dangerous, Sarah Booth. Don't linger there. No good will come of it. Live in the moment, and know that your father and I are close."

"Will you come back?"

Instead of answering, she kissed my cheek, the sweet, sad fragrance of jasmine the last part of her to disappear.

25

When I opened my eyes, it took a moment to realign myself with reality. I was in the hospital. I'd been gravely injured, and I'd lost the baby that I hadn't known I carried.

Listening to the sounds around me, I deduced I was in a private room with the door open. The oxygen mask had been removed. Someone sat beside the bed turning the pages of a magazine.

"Well, dahling, all I can say is that I'm so glad you avoided the draining pustule phase of the toxic mold business. In fact, you're something of a medical miracle." Cece's voice was very nasal, as if she had a terrible cold. She rose into my line of sight, a copy of *Cosmo* in one hand and a chilled pink cosmopolitan in the other. Her face was heavily bandaged.

"You had the nose job?"

"And you're lucid, too. How wonderful. Now you can explain your total stupidity in going to the Carlisle place alone." She took the sting out of her words with air kisses to both my cheeks. "Dahling, I was dis-traught."

"How long have I been out?"

She waved away my concern. "Long enough for Coleman to send battalions of crop dusters over the Carlisle plantation. That's all you've missed. I swear."

"I need to talk to Coleman." I remembered the key ring; he had to pursue that lead.

"Oh, there was something else. Bonnie Louise McRae has disappeared, and they finally found a witness in Jackson who saw Erin Carlisle arrive at her photography studio about fifteen minutes before I got there. She unlocked the front door and went inside. Coleman believes her abductors were already there, waiting to ambush her."

"And then the woman posed as Erin and they attacked you." My mind was a little fuzzy, but I'd put a few things together.

"Janks knew I meant to talk to Erin about the development deal." Cece tried to hide her feelings with a breezy attitude. "I've gone over every single thing he told me, and I still can't find anything that would provoke Erin's abduction . . ."

"Or the severe beating you got." I shifted so that I my head was raised. Obligingly, Cece stuffed a pillow behind me. "Cece, Lester Ballard is dead. They could have killed you."

"And Tinkie would have thrown herself on the pyre as a martyr to guilt. You ladies do guilt like no one else." Cece had recovered her droll tone and unflappable attitude. She was full of juicy tidbits—though she was doling them our like expensive caviar. The whole case would be solved and I would be lying in bed, whimpering whenever I had to get up to pee.

"Did Coleman find Erin?"

This time Cece wasn't so pert. "Coleman is afraid she's dead."

My body ached and my head throbbed. Moving set off jolts of pain, but I struggled to sit up completely. "I have to speak with Coleman right now."

Cece pressed the nurse call button. "Doc wants to talk to you first. He told me to notify him as soon as you regained your faculties. Of course, I told him that would be the Twelfth of Never because you'd always been half a bubble off. Still, he insisted he had to speak with you on a matter of great urgency." She worked hard to entertain and never let the conversation shift to the place where it eventually had to go.

"I'm not in a mood to be fussed at." I couldn't bear it if Doc confronted me about what had happened in that cotton field.

Cece's sophisticated façade cracked—as did her voice. "No one is going to fuss at you, Sarah Booth. I'll tear out their vocal chords. We're all so very sorry."

I held up a hand. "Do not go there." I knew what had occurred, but somehow, I had to keep the full impact of it at bay. If one person offered sympathy or tenderness or compassion, I would be overwhelmed by emotion.

"I understand." She tapped on a page of the magazine she held. "As soon as the swelling goes down in my new face, I'm going to buy this dress."

Even beaten, bandaged, and bruised, Cece could shop. I, on the other hand, was feeling out the edges of a black, consuming fury. While I couldn't begin to deal with the loss of my baby, I could relish the idea of revenge.

There was a rap on the door and Coleman entered.

Something passed between him and Cece, and she picked up her magazine and empty cosmopolitan glass. "I need to call the photographer at the newspaper to bring another drink—I need more anesthesia. Rhinoplasty may be considered elective surgery, but, dahling, it hurts like hell." She sashayed out the door.

Coleman seemed to fill the room, and I could find nothing to say that wouldn't open a floodgate of emotion. I couldn't even look at him.

His hand covered mine on the sheet. "When I saw you in the field, with all that blood, I thought you were dead. I've never felt such—I'm sorry about the baby." He stopped to clear his throat.

"Thank you for finding me, Coleman, but please, let's don't talk about it." I stared at the white sheet that covered my legs and stomach. Someone, I realized, had brought a beautiful green satin pajama set and dressed me. The 1940s Hollywood design was classic Cece. She did more than look at fashion magazines—she purchased from them.

Coleman pressed gently on my fingers. "If I could undo this, I would."

I nodded my thanks and understanding, but I had to move us beyond this moment. "I found a clue, but then I lost it. I'm sorry. I can describe it and maybe you can find it again."

He held up the key ring. "You had it clutched so tightly in your hand that I couldn't get it until they knocked you out."

"What does it go to?"

"A storage unit in Starkville, Mississippi."

"Is there anything in it, anything useful?"

Coleman's smile said it all. "Only enough to put Bonnie Louise McRae behind bars for the rest of her natural life."

While I should have felt elation, there was only emptiness. So Bonnie Louise had been driven mad enough by the need for revenge that she'd damaged innocent people, endangered a county, and stolen something irreplaceable from me. "What was in the unit?"

"The special equipment she used to raise the mutated weevils, a computer disk with notes on the process, how the mold was a by-product of damaged feed. Her step-by-step enactment of the plan to release the weevils and injure Oscar was all documented." His grin widened. "Also included was the name of the pesticide that's one hundred percent effective in killing the weevils. There's nothing left alive in those fields now."

The land had effectively been raped; people endangered and used as lab rats for her experiments. "The whole thing makes me sick. What did she hope to gain, other than revenge?"

"A lot of money. Her work might have been worthy of a scientific award had it been put to good rather than evil. It's a damn shame."

"I'm sorry, Coleman." On many levels.

"I can't begin to understand it," he admitted. "Bonnie had so much going for her. On the surface, she had everything." He returned to the bedside. "Sarah Booth, we found footprints in the dirt by where you were attacked. I've matched them to a pair of Bonnie's shoes she left in the Dumpster behind the health clinic. She's the one who attacked you."

"Where is she?" The numbness was fading. I wanted to see her behind bars—after I'd beaten her to a pulp.

"We haven't captured her yet, but we will. There's a national alert out. She won't get far."

That wasn't what I wanted to hear, but Coleman

wouldn't rest until he had her in custody. "She didn't achieve this alone."

"Luther Carlisle is in lockup right now. He was her partner, though I can't say how deeply involved he was. At the moment he's refusing to say anything except that he's totally innocent. If he knows where Erin or Janks are, he isn't talking."

"Janks is in this up to his ears, isn't he?"

"As yet, his role is undetermined."

"Have Bonnie and Janks skipped out together, leaving Luther to hold the bag?"

"If that's the case, once Luther realizes he'll do the hard time for them as well as himself, that'll grease his jaw hinges."

"You really have a way with words, Coleman."

The relief that touched his face told me how deeply he'd been worried about me.

"I'm going to be fine," I told him. There was no room for argument in my tone.

He didn't say anything, but a swallow worked down his throat. I remembered the stricken look on his face as he'd lifted me in the cotton field and carried me to the road for the ambulance.

I'd never doubted his love for me, but we'd been star-crossed from the get-go. Jitty was right. My life had gotten out of order with Coleman. Our attraction had grown before he was free to offer the anchor of his love that would have held us safe against the winds.

"Congratulations on your engagement, Sarah Booth." He didn't glance at the ring. "I wish you all happiness." He stepped back from the bed. "Doc is waiting for me to finish. There's something important he has to talk to you about."

"Call me if you find Bonnie or Janks or Erin." I felt the need to take action. "I'll be on my feet soon." The idea of lying in bed, tracking over and over events, was unbearable.

"Will do." He gave me a sharp nod and made his exit before either of us could say or do anything that would cause further pain.

The door had barely closed when Doc came in. He checked the drip and the monitors that charted my vitals. When he finished, he put his hand on my forehead and felt my temperature the old-fashioned way.

"Sarah Booth, there's something medical I need to discuss with you."

"I can't have another baby, can I?" There it was, the dark fear hidden in the corner of my mind. The one question I'd dreaded asking.

"Why would you say that?" he asked kindly. "I see no reason you shouldn't be able to have a child."

A mental image of Jitty wiping her brow flashed before my eyes. "Then what is it?"

"You haven't even considered why you aren't ill, like Oscar and Gordon, have you? No fever, sores, or coma."

The truth was that I hadn't. At all. I checked my arms and threw the covers back to reveal my feet. There weren't any sores, as Cece had pointed out. And I was talking and moving—and *not* comatose. "Why not?" I asked.

"That's what I need to find out. I'm onto something. Something that might make a world of difference for Oscar and Gordon."

"And Luann and Regina?"

"Interestingly enough, they're doing much better. In fact, they'll make a full recovery with nothing to remind them of this except a few scars from the skin lesions."

He sat on the edge of my bed. "So what do you and the two realtors have in common?"

It took me a moment. "We're all women?"

He nodded. "And you haven't suffered the autoimmune symptoms, even though you were left in the cotton field longer than Oscar or Gordon. You had more exposure, plus a devastating attack on your body. Yet you are unscathed by the illness."

I knew then what he was driving at. "Because I was pregnant."

He nodded again. "I think there's something here, something unique in the female system, that's able to fight this. I want to take some blood and run some tests. Will you consent?

"You didn't even have to ask, Doc. Just get busy."

"I knew that's what you'd say. That's why the tech is standing in the hallway." He kissed my cheek. "Come on in, John, she's ready for you to draw the blood. Just be careful, she doesn't have a lot to spare right now."

When John was finished and I was left alone in my room, I tried to avoid facing what had happened, but the damning reality was upon me like the Harpies.

In the year and a half I'd been home, Jitty had deviled me relentlessly to get pregnant. I hadn't considered such a thing, because my life wasn't settled enough to have and raise a child. Without conscious effort, I'd managed to get pregnant. Had I not been viciously attacked, Graf's and my baby would still be growing inside me.

Madame Tomeeka's strange prophecy came back to me. A new grave in the Delaney family cemetery was the vision she'd seen. Never in my wildest imagination had I considered it might be the grave of my unborn child, a child that had barely existed.

Tears spattered the crisp whiteness of the sheet, and I made no effort to stop them. I'd lost my grip on anger and a desire for revenge, and what I was left with was only loss. There was nothing that could be done to change what had occurred.

If I could turn back time, I would never have gone to the Carlisle place alone. But that wasn't being fair to me, either. My life was solving cases, and that brought danger into my world. I couldn't live in a bubble, completely protected from anything that might harm me. That wasn't living—that was only existing. My parents hadn't been like that, and neither could I.

The memory of my mother came back to me, and a sense of peace came with it. In my direst time of need, she'd appeared. All of these years of wanting just a moment with her, just a conversation. And she'd come because there was no one who could comfort me the way she could. While most people would call it a dream, I knew better.

The soft knock on the door drew me from my introspection, and I wiped at my tears. Tinkie entered the room, her face a reflection of my own tear-stained one.

"Is Oscar—" I couldn't finish the sentence.

"He's barely hanging on, but Doc is working on something." She came to the bed and put her hands on my face, gently wiping away my tears. "There's nothing I can say that will take away this pain. I grieve with you."

She was the truest of friends. "I know."

"If your blood somehow saves Oscar . . ."

The irony wasn't lost on me, but irony is a weak and pitiful counterthrust to tragedy. "Doc looked more hopeful than I've seen him in a long time. He's onto the solution this time."

Tinkie had suffered her own loss, and I could read the sadness in her face. "Sarah Booth, I'm so sorry. If only—"

"You didn't hit me, and neither did Oscar. The person who did this is responsible for a lot more than me. There're bad people in the world, and whether they're hiding at an old plantation or lurking in a mansion in Costa Rica, we can't spend our lives trying to avoid them. I was just thinking about this before you came in."

"I feel like my life has been stripped away." She sat on the edge of the bed. "The two people I love most in the world are both in this hospital. Both have been terribly injured." She smoothed the sheet. "If I ever doubted that I could do bodily harm to someone, I know now that I can."

Tilting toward her, I whispered, "Don't let the other Daddy's Girls hear that. You'll be banned from high society."

Her smile was worth the effort it cost me to lean forward.

"Doc says you can go home soon. He said you're young and healthy and that you'll be back in fighting form with no permanent damage."

Funny that the human body could adjust so quickly to such a horrific emotional loss. Not so the heart. "Bonnie Louise is still on the loose. And Janks, whatever his role was in this."

"Do you think she waylaid you, or do you think it was Luther?"

"Coleman found footprints that match Bonnie's shoes."

Tinkie nodded. "It's just that the attack was so vicious. Of course, no one knew about the baby. But still, why would she beat you that brutally?"

I thought for a moment, remembering her attraction to Coleman. It was possible that Bonnie Louise was one of those people who had to harm anyone she perceived as in the way of what she wanted. "I don't know. Look at what they did to Cece."

"Luther's in jail caterwauling about a lawyer, but Coleman is stonewalling him." Tinkie shrugged. "If he had a hand in this, I hope he rots in prison."

I told Tinkie about the key chain and what Coleman had discovered. Anger bloomed in red splotches on her cheeks. "Well, the good news is that the weevils are dead. And I promise you one thing, if Bonnie Louise McRae did this because Oscar had to do his job and foreclose on their farm, she's going to pay big-time."

"Let's focus on Doc helping Oscar and Gordon. Let Coleman handle Bonnie." Even as I said the words, I knew they were false. I had a personal score to settle with Bonnie. "I love having you here, Tinkie, but I know you need to be with Oscar."

She rose slowly. "You're going to be fine, Sarah Booth. You'll mend, and Graf will be here soon. Cece finally got word to him. He was on a shoot in the desert and we had a little trouble getting in touch. But he's doing everything he can to get here. The two of you have many good years ahead."

"I know."

She kissed my cheek. "I love you like a sister."

I caught her and held on. "Right back at you."

She was at the door when my phone rang. I picked it up. Coleman's voice came through the line.

"Sarah Booth, I've found Janks."

"Where is he?" I had every intention of going there and confronting him.

"His body was dumped in Goodman's Brake. He'd

been shot in the head. I'm waiting here for the forensic team before the body is transported."

"He's dead?" The scenario of guilt I'd developed collapsed. "How long?"

"The coroner will be able to give us a time when he gets here, but my best guess is at least a day. Maybe two. I'll keep you posted. Just recover."

"Thanks for letting me know," I said, caught in the sense that somehow, through all of this, Coleman and I had found our footing again as friends. I closed my cell phone.

Tinkie waited at the door and I relayed the information.

"Bonnie's cleaning up her accomplices. Luther should be glad he's in the jail," she said.

I swung my legs over the side of the bed. The pain was like a cannonball slamming into my torso, but I took a breath.

"What do you think you're doing?" Tinkie asked.

"Getting my strength back." I didn't have time to mope around a hospital bed.

26

Doc was furious when he discovered me walking up and down the hallway. Thank goodness he had other fish to fry. Instead of corralling me, he had to save Oscar and Gordon, but he made it plain he was upset.

"I won't be responsible for the consequences if you persist in this hardheaded conduct," he told me darkly as he tried to steer me back to my room.

"Erin Carlisle is missing. Lester Ballard and Jimmy Janks are dead. You're going to cure Oscar and Gordon." I took a breath and shook free. "And I'm going to nail the person who did this to me."

"You're a strong, healthy young woman, Sarah Booth, but your body *and* your heart require time to mend."

"Trust me, hammering the person responsible will help me recover a lot faster." I couldn't deny the wisdom of his words, but Doc hadn't suffered my loss.

"What do you hope to accomplish? Coleman is on the case, why not let him handle it?"

I had my reasons. "I'll be fine."

"I won't sign your release form."

Doc's stubbornness was an indication of his concern. "I would expect nothing less."

Wearing the beautiful green pajamas that Cece had ordered, I walked out the front door of the hospital only to realize my car was likely still at the Carlisle plantation. I called Harold.

"I'm standing on the front lawn of the hospital in green pajamas. Can you give me a lift home?"

"Did Doc release you?"

Harold knew me a little too well. "Don't start. I can't lie around in the hospital with nothing to do." Every step sent little flares of pain over my bruised body, but it was bearable. "And bring me a pack of cigarettes, please."

"Not a chance. I'll drive you to Dahlia House, but I will not be a party to your smoking."

I smiled. By asking for something I knew Harold wouldn't do, I'd maneuvered him into doing what I wanted. Maybe some of Tinkie's skills were rubbing off on me.

The bank was only a few minutes away, and Harold's fancy red sports car whipped up to the curb. He was out in a flash, opening my door and assisting me into the car. Good manners are comforting in the strangest way. I felt safe with Harold.

"I'm calling Coleman as soon as I settle you at home," he said.

"Call all you want. Coleman isn't the boss of me."

"Exactly the mature response I expected."

"Bite me."

"That bat whack to your head must've scrambled your

269

brain back to junior high." He took a curve about forty miles over the appropriate speed. He was a fine one to talk. Put a stick shift in a guy's hand and some power beneath a gas pedal and he'll revert to Hot Wheels every time.

"If I survive your driving, there's little anyone else can do to harm me."

Harold slowed to a more sedate pace. "I'll take the rest of the day off. Whatever you're up to, you aren't allowed to do it alone. Have you taken a look in a mirror?"

"No." I put my fingers to my face. Even without a looking glass, I deduced that one side of my head was swollen. I undoubtedly resembled a badly formed melon. "Wait until I get my hands on that bitch."

"Ah, vanity overrules common sense. I knew that despite the jean-clad exterior and the disdain for society, you are female to the core." Harold swung down the drive to Dahlia House. My heart lifted at the sight of the sycamore trees lining the drive, the trunks pale against the new cotton in the fields.

"Joke all you want, Harold."

When he braked in front of the house, he locked both doors. "This isn't a joking matter, Sarah Booth. I'll help you do whatever crazy thing you've concocted, but I will not leave you alone."

He wasn't kidding. Whatever action I felt necessary to take, Harold would help. Legal, illegal. Whatever. That kind of friendship could never be taken lightly. "Thank you, Harold." If I went all maudlin on him, he'd hustle me inside and make me soup. "I'm okay. Yes, I'm bruised, but nothing life threatening. And don't call Coleman, please."

My cell phone rang before the last word slipped off my tongue. Coleman was on the line.

"Doc says you're off the reservation," he said.

"Harold has brought me home." I tried to sound subdued.

"Let me talk to Harold."

"He's busy." I wasn't about to let the two of them gang up on me. "Where are you?"

"I'm still at Goodman's Brake."

The brake, an untamed area of wilderness and swamp, was a clever dumpsite for a body. The brakes in the Delta were often hunted, but since the season was out, the location was isolated. "What's the story on Janks? Have the forensic people gotten there?"

"The preliminary assessment is that Janks has been dead for at least a day," Coleman said. "You may have been the last person known to see him alive when he was in West Point."

"Did they determine anything else?"

"Janks was shot at close range with a small caliber weapon. Probably a .22. We'll know for sure after an autopsy."

"Can you connect it to Lester Ballard's murder?"

Loud voices babbled in the background, but when Coleman spoke, I heard him clearly. "They were both killed with a small caliber. Until ballistics are matched, though, no one can say more for certain."

"No word on Erin?"

"None. Luther is still in jail. I can't hold him forever unless I charge him, and I don't have the evidence to charge him. Yet."

"Coleman, I'm going back to the Carlisle plantation."

"Not a good idea."

"The weevils are dead. Peyton ought to have more information about them. Have you talked with him?"

"I've left messages, but he hasn't called me."

"He went to Jackson, but he should have returned

long ago." Worry sparked. "Do you think Bonnie Louise has done something to him?"

Coleman didn't answer, which told me he was leaning toward a bad conclusion.

"Look, he might be out at the Carlisle place. I'll check over the house and look for him."

Coleman wanted to argue, but he had his hands full with Janks's body, a missing woman, and a psychopathic killer on the loose.

"I'll call in every half hour." I wanted to reassure him.

"I wish Graf would arrive in town to ride herd over you," he said.

"Nice try. I gotta go." I closed the phone and met Harold's studious gaze.

"I'll be your chariot," he said.

I'd managed to elude Doc and Coleman, but Harold had the only set of wheels at Dahlia House. It was either ride with him, walk, or hitchhike. I conceded with minimal enthusiasm.

As lovely as my new pj's were, I couldn't wear them on a case, so I left Harold in the parlor with Sweetie and Chablis and I hurried upstairs to take a quick shower and change.

My image in the mirror stared back, swollen and bruised. The side of my face was a ghastly shade of yellow beginning to darken. Good thing I didn't have a movie role in the next four weeks. The only work I'd be able to snare would be as a plum on a Fruit of the Loom commercial.

When I removed my jammies, I saw the bruises at my waist, hips, thighs, and stomach. Someone had worked me over with great brutality. I got under the hot spray, hoping to begin the process of washing away the hurt and loss.

I dressed and combed out my wet hair. Makeup

couldn't begin to cover the damage, so I didn't try. I grabbed my purse and met Harold at the front door.

Sweetie and Chablis danced and barked, hoping for a sign they could go. Not a chance. While the weevils were dead, the potential of contaminants in the cotton was too dangerous. Chablis had a varied wardrobe of glitter bows, cashmere sweaters, and booties, but not a single canine hazmat suit.

"I'll be back," I told them. "Soon." When I looked outside, I realized there wasn't much daylight left. If I intended to investigate, I had to shake the lead out.

I lived with a ghost at Dahlia House, but the sense of being haunted didn't bother me at home. Not true of the Carlisle plantation. Foreboding hung over that place like a funeral shroud. Color me uneasy.

Harold idled down the driveway, and in the fading late spring light, the devastation in the fields was heartbreaking. Not a single sign of life was in evidence in the long vista of cotton fields—not plant or insect—as far as the eye could see.

In the distance, the grand old house looked shabby and abandoned—by living entities. If the theme from *The Exorcist* started playing and dead leaves began to blow along the drive, I wouldn't have raised an eyebrow.

"I wonder what the disposition of the land will be," Harold said.

"I don't know." If Erin was dead and Luther found guilty as an accomplice to murder, or worse, the land might be sold. "It's a terrible shame."

"I wonder why Janks settled on developing this particular plot of ground."

"Because Luther convinced him he could get it. The

development plan was enormous. It's hard to find a piece of property large enough for such an ambitious project."

"Maybe." Harold stopped in front of the house. The divided steps curved gracefully up to the front door, which was at the second-story level. "My question is this—in today's economy, what kind of sense does it make to think of developing a huge subdivision and shopping complex? Most folks are worried about surviving, not consuming."

"Good point, Harold." Which begged the question of why Janks had been so hot to develop the Carlisle land. What was his real role in the whole scheme?

Harold pointed to the house. "You had your picture made here in high school in the drama club."

"You weren't in my class. How did you know that?"

"Millie had an old high school annual at the café showing folks your school pictures. All of you thespians were lined up on the steps."

"This place was so beautiful then." My words seemed to invoke the spirits of the past. A wind whipped out of the south and one of the shutters banged.

Harold opened his car door and came around to assist me out. "Let's get this done," he said. "I want to satisfy your curiosity and then tuck you into bed. Graf and I aren't best buds, but I don't want him pissed at me because I helped your trot all over the county after being beaten."

"Maybe you should just chain me in the yard like some prize-hunting dog that you men control," I grumbled as I got out of the car. But I was happy for his supportive hand under my elbow.

"Now that's an amusing image." Harold was still chuckling as he assisted me up the steps.

The front door was locked, but we had a clear view though the sidelights flanking the stout mahogany. I paused for a moment before I saw the dead potted plant.

Without a second's hesitation I picked it up and hurled it through the glass. After the shards finished falling, I reached in and unlocked the door.

"Very subtle," Harold said, but he followed me inside.

The furnishings were dark shadows in the corners of the room, but the elegance still lingered. Had I not come home to Dahlia House, she would have had the same feel of loneliness and neglect. It was probably silly to personify a house, but I couldn't help myself. This had once been a home, a place of both laughter and tears. And perhaps murder.

Did the ghost of Lana Carlisle still walk the hallways, hoping that someone would eventually avenge her murder?

Wind whistled through the open front door and it slammed with a bang. I almost jumped into Harold's arms.

"A little edgy, aren't you, Sarah Booth?" he teased.

"It's been a hard couple of weeks." I managed a dry tone. "Let's check the kitchen."

Power had been shut off to the house for quite a while, so I was unprepared for the smell of decay that slammed into my nostrils when I pushed open the kitchen door.

"Some animal must have died in here," Harold said, walking briskly to the back door and opening it. A little more light illuminated the room, but the day was slipping away from us.

The foul odor came from the sink, and I went there and opened a cabinet. Instead of a dead creature, there was rotted food in a garbage can. "No one lives here. Why is there food?" The packaging was relatively new.

The thud that came made us both jump.

Without debating the issue, we ran to the staircase. To my surprise, Harold drew a small pistol from the waistband of his pants. It was sleek and sophisticated, just like him.

"When did you start carrying a gun?" I asked him.

"When you started calling me to haul you around," he said. "You forget, Sarah Booth, I've been in the hospital emergency room more than once to visit you and Tinkie. If bullets are going to fly, I want to be launching my share of them."

No point arguing that theory, because I agreed with it. I only wished that I'd brought a gun, too.

At the next floor, we moved cautiously. We had no way of knowing if someone was hiding in the house or trying to lure us into a trap.

"We should separate," I told Harold at the top of the stairs. "I'll go right."

"Not on your life." He snatched my arm and held it firmly. "You stay behind me." He didn't give me a chance to argue but moved down the hallway in the lead, the gun extended and me behind him like a shadow.

The house was deathly still. I'd begun to wonder if we'd imagined the thud when I heard something again. It sounded like furniture bumping against a wall. Or someone thumping down stairs.

Lana Carlisle had fallen to her death—the stairs were ten feet from where Harold and I stood. I couldn't resist glancing backward to see if some vestige of the past had presented itself. I had that kind of sick and twisted mind.

The staircase was empty, and the thud came from down the hallway.

"I couldn't convince you to stay here, could I?" Harold asked.

"Nope." I was on him like white on rice.

"Then stay behind me."

Holding the gun extended, Harold advanced with me at his back. The thud came from a room to the left. The door was closed, and I could see that a hasp and lock had been added. A serious lock.

"What the hell." Harold brought the butt of the gun down on the lock, but it held solid.

Another bumping noise came from inside the room.

"Someone's in there," I whispered.

"I could shoot the lock off," he offered.

Instead, I lifted my foot and smashed it into the door as hard as I could. The wood held, but the screws used to bolt the lock into the wood loosened. Harold kicked it this time, and the screws loosened more.

"One, two, three . . ." We both kicked at the same time and the screws gave with a tired screech.

The door flew open, and in the dim light I saw a figure tied on the floor, honey-gold hair catching the dying rays of light.

"Erin!" I rushed over and snatched a piece of duct tape from her mouth.

"Help me." Her voice was dangerously weak.

I tore at the knotted ropes that tied her hands and feet. Harold had his cell phone in hand. "Send an ambulance to the Carlisle plantation," he said. "Immediately. And get in touch with the sheriff. We need him here."

27

By the time Doc concluded his examination of Erin, Coleman still hadn't arrived from the dumpsite of Jimmy Janks's body. As ER nurses rushed to carry out Doc's bidding, I gently questioned Erin.

She was sure of only one thing—that her abductors were a male-female team. They'd worn ski masks and taken care to protect their identities. With help from Cece, who called in a few favors at the newspaper, I was able to get my hands on photos of Jimmy Janks and Bonnie Louise McRae to show to Erin.

She couldn't identify either. Nor could she implicate her brother, Luther, in the sequence of events that led to her abduction.

"I'd agreed to meet that newspaper reporter, Cece Dee Falcon, at the studio." She put a hand over her face. "It was stupid so late at night, but she had details on what

Janks and Luther intended to do with my family land. I was furious they'd gone so far. I got to the studio before Ms. Falcon and went inside to wait. I'd barely cleared the front door when I was struck on the head. When I came to, I was trussed up and the man and woman pushed me into the back of the vehicle."

"Did you ever see Cece?"

"Yes." She sipped the water I held for her. "We drove through the parking lot and I saw her lying there, bloody and beaten. I was afraid she was dead."

"You can't identify either of them?"

"They concealed their faces. They gave me some kind of injection in the vehicle, but before I passed out, I heard their voices. I don't know them."

In the hours of her incarceration, she'd been kept blindfolded and restrained. Her captors had fed her and allowed her to use the bathroom, but they hadn't spoken to her.

"Did they ever say why you'd been abducted?" I asked.

She shook her head. "They never spoke in my presence. Not a single word. That was one of the hardest things about it. There were times when I thought I'd disappeared into a place where I'd never talk with anyone again. And when I finally got the blindfold off I realized that I was back in my family home." She shuddered. "It was hellish."

For Erin, the Carlisle plantation held more bad memories than good. It must have been awful to awaken there and realize she was a captive in the place where she believed her parents had been murdered—and to realize that she'd been abandoned in a locked room on a derelict plantation.

"When was the last time your captor showed up?"

She thought about it, the toll of her ordeal showing clearly in her pale complexion. "Maybe midmorning."

"Today?" That was impossible.

"That's right."

"Are you sure?"

"Positive. Why?"

I looked at Harold, who was leaning against the back wall of the emergency room. "It couldn't be Jimmy Janks, then," I said. "He was dead this morning."

She pushed her thick hair out of her eye. "I'm not sorry he's dead."

"You're certain Luther wasn't your abductor?" Harold asked.

"No. It wasn't Luther, though I don't doubt he was involved in it. But I know the sound of his footsteps, the way he moves around that old house. I grew up listening to him sneaking in and out of his room. I can say one hundred percent that it wasn't Luther."

Then who the hell was it? I didn't have to ask the question aloud, because Harold was thinking exactly the same thing. His eyebrows had risen almost to his hairline.

"Let's check on Oscar," I told Harold. We were only a few corridors away from the private room where he'd been taken, and I wanted to speak with him alone.

We left Erin to the tender mercies of the lab techs and nurses as they began the process of collecting bloods and fluids for the battery of tests Doc had ordered.

"There's another accomplice in this," Harold said once we were alone in the hallway.

"It could still be Luther. A lot of time has passed since Erin shared space with her brother. If he was involved in hurting her, she might have subconsciously blocked it out." I was an authority on the power of subconscious blocking.

We stopped talking when we paused at Oscar's door. All of the patients had been moved to private rooms, and I'd heard Luann and Regina would be discharged in a matter of hours.

Remembering my sage advice to Tinkie, I tapped lightly and waited for an invitation to enter. Lord knows, I'd been scarred and battered enough for one case—I didn't need to see a personal encounter between Oscar and Tinkie.

"Come in," Tinkie called, and there was such life and pleasure in her voice that I wanted to clap and dance.

"Sarah Booth! Harold!" Tinkie came around the bed and hurled herself at us. She stood on tiptoe to kiss my cheek. "You're amazing. You're the most generous person alive. I thank you and Oscar thanks you."

Glancing over the top of her head, I saw the reason for her effusive thanks. Oscar gave me a weak smile. "Sarah Booth," he said in a thin, hollow voice, "I hear we're finally blood relatives."

I went to the bed, dragging Tinkie with me. She'd latched on with surprising strength. "Damn it, Oscar, you scared us half to death."

"I kept being drawn to this bright light," he said. "There was a beautiful tunnel, and people kept calling my name. I wanted to go—there was this really sexy red-head—"

"He's lying like a rug," Tinkie cut in. "More likely it was a straight drop down a black hole to a fiery lake."

Harold laughed, and I pointed my finger at Oscar. "That is not funny. We've spent more than a week thinking you wouldn't last another ten minutes."

His gaze locked on Tinkie, and his smile widened. "I never considered leaving voluntarily," he said. "Not even when I was so tired, I didn't think I could hold on another minute. I felt Tinkie there, standing at my bed, willing me to stay beside her."

Now that was amazing and creepy. "The only time she left you, Oscar, was when we tricked her into eating and sleeping."

"I know. She was outside the window looking into the room, but her spirit was beside me, touching my face, talking to me, telling me to hold on." He reached up and put a trembling hand on my arm. "I'm sorry for your loss, Sarah Booth."

"Thank you, Oscar."

"Your blood saved my life. And Gordon's. Doc said he's improving, too."

"I'm glad I could help." I meant every syllable of it. "Let's talk about the case." I couldn't keep the focus on my loss; I was still too raw.

"Have you found Bonnie Louise yet?" Tinkie asked.

She hid it well, but the glint of fury was there in the corner of her eye. Woe be unto Bonnie Louise if Tinkie got to her before Coleman could safely lock her up.

"She's disappeared from the face of the earth," I said. It wasn't the total truth, but I didn't want my friend going to prison for murder. "Coleman may know more when he finally gets back. He's at Goodman's Brake with the coroner."

"Before you leave the hospital, stop by and see Gordon," Tinkie suggested.

I wondered if that was a hint that Oscar was tiring. "Good idea."

"Sarah Booth, could I speak with you in the hall?" she asked.

"You two girls take a walk. Us boys will have a little gossip." Harold waved us into the hall.

I'd barely cleared the door when Tinkie jumped me.

Her arms went around me and squeezed so hard that I gasped.

"Oh, dear, I forgot you were hurt," she said. "I mean, your face looks like something from a cartoon, but your clothes cover up the other bruises."

"Thanks." I hugged her again, even if it hurt.

"What you said to me, about getting Oscar into a room and making him want to stay, it was the perfect thing." Her blue eyes were clear and untroubled. "Even with the cure that Doc cooked up, Oscar was almost gone. It was what you suggested that made him come back."

I had to laugh. "I doubt that, Tink. He came back to spend the rest of his life with you. You just offered a bit of dessert before dinner."

She inhaled and sighed. "I'm so tired, I could drop, but now that he's out of danger, I'm ready to help with the case."

"I think we're done. Once Coleman finds Bonnie Louise, that'll be the end of it. Luther's in jail already. Janks, whatever role he played, is dead. It's just a matter of dotting the i's and crossing the t's."

"Maybe I'll just go home and work to unsnarl Janks's financial backing. As best I can tell, he has one investor. One very wealthy man with his funding offshore."

"Perfect idea."

"I'll stop by and get Chablis."

I shook my head. "I'll bring her home to you. Sweetie will want to ride with me. You go on and I'll drop her by a little later. We can have a drink together."

"You're on."

I was about to signal Harold to leave with me when my cell phone rang. Expecting Coleman, I was surprised to see a strange number show up on the caller I.D.

"Sarah Booth, it's Peyton."

"Where have you been? Coleman has been looking everywhere for you. Have you seen Bonnie Louise?" It seemed like Peyton had been absent for the resolution of the most important aspects of the case. "Oscar and Gordon are recovering. Luther's in jail." I tried to give him the most important updates.

"Ah, it's difficult to talk. I need your help."

There was something strained in his voice. "Is something wrong?"

"Very much so. I think I'm going to be killed."

No wonder Peyton had vanished—he'd been taken captive. "Is Bonnie there with you now?"

"Absolutely. Could you meet me?"

"Where are you?" I started to signal Harold, but I couldn't risk involving Tinkie. "Shall I bring Coleman?"

"That would not be smart. You and I can work this out better than anyone else. Delicate situation, you know. Balancing is difficult."

If I was correct in reading between the lines, Peyton was implying that Bonnie was unstable. Not exactly breaking news.

"Has Bonnie hurt you?" I asked.

"Not yet. Can you meet us? It's literally a matter of life and death."

"Where?"

"The old Henderson cotton gin."

That was way off the beaten path, long abandoned, and a creepy place at high noon. It was night outside, and the old gin afforded hundreds of places for Bonnie Louise to hide and ambush me in the dark.

"How about the strip mall where Janks's office is?" I wanted a more public place.

"I'm not in a position to bargain," Peyton said, his voice rising. "If you don't meet me . . ."

"I'll be there." What choice did I have? It was possible that somehow I could get the drop on Bonnie. I had to.

"Come alone, Sarah Booth. If you try to bring the sheriff or anyone else, my life will be forfeit."

Well that was as clear as it could be. "Got it."

Tinkie was staring at me when I closed my phone.

"You look like someone walked over your grave."

Her words brought back the image that Madame Tomeeka had planted in my brain—raw dirt in the Delaney family cemetery. Death and loss. To go involved risk, but I intended to take every precaution I could.

"That was Peyton Fidellas. He wants me to meet him," I explained.

"Where?" Tinkie was nobody's fool.

"He's found something interesting."

"Where?" She wasn't going to let it go, that much was clear.

"He's in trouble."

She lifted her chin in that way that let me know she was about to enter the dead zone of stubbornness. "Where are you meeting him? And don't try lying. I'll know."

"At the old Henderson cotton gin out on County Road Eight." While I might be foolhardy enough to go, I wasn't a complete moron. Someone had to know where I was.

"Have you lost your mind?" Hot spots of pink jumped into her cheeks. "That's a set up for you to be killed."

"I have to go, Tinkie. Bonnie Louise is holding Peyton hostage. If I don't show, she'll kill him." I spoke softly, trying to calm her as much as possible. "And I have to go now. I can't wait. Peyton implied that Bonnie is losing it."

"Why does she want to see you?" Tinkie asked. "Why not Coleman or Luther? Why you?"

"I thought about this earlier, and I think the viciousness of the attack on me is motivated by her misbegotten idea that people have stopped her from having happiness. I mean, look what she did to Oscar, because she thought he took her family farm away. She's disturbed, so she finds a person to blame for the events in her life. Then she decides to make them pay, and she's willing to do whatever is necessary to extract what she sees as justice. She sucked Janks into this with greed, and then when he became an encumbrance, she killed him."

"Do you hear what you're saying?" Tinkie's face had gone from angry to pale. "She's willing to do 'whatever is necessary.' Still, why has she fixated on you?"

I hated to say it aloud, but I did. "Coleman. She fell hard for Coleman, and I think she realized that . . ."

"He's still in love with you."

I looked beyond her, down the hall to a couple of nurses who pushed a pill cart. I wanted to deny her statement, but I couldn't. Coleman still loved me. Despite everything that had happened.

Tinkie's arm went around my waist and she pulled me close. "Do what you have to do, Sarah Booth. Just be careful. Bonnie Louise is unhinged."

"I know."

"Promise me you'll take a gun."

The problem was that I didn't have time to go home and get one. But Harold had one, which I suspected he'd left in his car. A car that I needed to get to the old cotton gin.

"Can you get Harold's keys?" I asked her.

"Not a problem."

Before I could even react, she went into the hospital room. "Sarah Booth left her purse in your car and she needs it." Her voice shifted to a whisper. "Feminine products, you know."

I was appalled and impressed. No Southern man in his

right mind would question the euphemistic "feminine products." In this instance, it happened to be a gun. Just another example of what might be termed deadly PMS—percussive metal syndrome.

Tinkie returned to the hallway with the keys. She dangled them, then snatched them back. "Promise me you won't get hurt."

"I promise." That was easy. I had no intention of deliberately getting injured. Been there, done that, had the bruises to prove it.

"Call me as soon as you have Bonnie under control."

I agreed to those terms, too. "I have to get moving."

"I hope I'm making the right decision. If something happens to you, I'll never forgive myself."

"This is my choice, Tinkie. Give me about half an hour, then call Coleman and tell him where I went. If I can't handle Bonnie by then, I'm going to need the cavalry."

"I've got you covered."

I hurried down the hallway. Harold would be pissed when he discovered that I'd taken his car. And his gun. And driven off into danger without him. But Peyton's instructions had been clear—I was to come alone. And in the darkest, ugliest corner of my mind, I realized that I wanted a tête-à-tête with Bonnie Louise—without witnesses.

She'd done the unthinkable to me. And before Coleman or anyone else could stop me, I intended to hurt her. At least a little.

28

Mega-gins, huge complexes that separate the cotton fibers from the seedpods and press them into bales with speed and efficiency, now dominate the industry. The old, smaller community cotton engines are relics. Once, the local gin had been the heart of an area, the place where farmers gathered as the machine removed the sticky seeds and readied the cotton for shipment. Ruins of rusted tin and silent machinery, the dilapidated gins still dot the rural landscape, a reminder of a way of life that's slipped behind the curtain of time.

The old Henderson gin was about twenty miles out of town on County Road Eight, a lonely two-lane bereft of a center line because two cars seldom passed.

Even as far back as high school, the Henderson gin had been unused, at least for cotton. The building and grounds had become a favorite parking place for teens. I'd spent my share of crisp autumn nights there, intoxicated by the forbidden acts of sipping whiskey and kissing handsome boys. And giggling. My goodness, we'd giggled a lot in those days of fumbling kisses and dreams of a future we'd only seen in magazines or movies.

Someone would turn on a car radio, and we'd dance in the shadow of the old building under a clear night sky where the black velvet darkness wasn't interrupted by a single incandescent light. Couple by couple, kids would drift away, seeking solitude and those delicious private whispers and kisses.

Thinking of those nights, I keenly felt the loss of such innocence. Those had been the days when a kiss—or lack thereof—had meant jubilation or crushing defeat.

My aunt Loulane had been a straitlaced mentor in such situations. Proper young ladies didn't kiss passionately at abandoned cotton gins. Such things could lead to over-stimulation of the Delaney womb, which would only yield a lifetime of woe and irrational conduct—or worse, a Fallopian malfunction or the uncorrectable horrors of the tilted womb.

Delaney foremothers prone to uncontrolled necking had suffered tragic consequences in the past.

To make her point, Aunt Loulane would whisper the name of Aunt Cilla, whose proclivities for sexual conquests made her the scandal of the family. But she wasn't alone. There were other antecedents with lustful ways and what Aunt Loulane considered "insatiable and inappropriate appetites." She counted them off like a strange rosary to warn me of falling off the straight and narrow. Aunt Loulane's admonitions—and scare tactics—had stood me in good stead through my teen years. I owed her a lot. But not even following the rules had kept pain and loss from my door.

By the time I pulled Harold's sporty red car into the parking area of the old gin, I'd let go of the past, at least a little. What pained me now was the loss of my future. My child. Given my druthers, I would be in Dahlia House with Graf. We would be together, so we could begin the process of grieving and healing.

Graf had been told about the baby. As I sat in the car, I dialed his cell phone. It went straight to voice mail, which was exactly what I'd hoped.

"Graf, I'm wrapping up this case. Please don't worry. I'm fine. *Physically*, I'm fine. I'll meet you at Dahlia House as soon as you can get here. I . . . need you."

I hung up before I was tempted to erase it. Admitting that I needed anyone was worse than torture. But I did need Graf. I couldn't wait to deck Bonnie Louise and deliver her to the Sunflower County jail so that I could return to my life and my fiancé. We had to help each other through our loss.

Harold's gun was tucked beneath the front seat of the car, and I got it. It was small and sleek, the kind with a clip instead of a cylinder for bullets. A spy gun. The feel of it in my hand gave me a jolt of confidence.

Because it belonged to Harold, I trusted that it was clean, loaded, and in peak operating condition. That was Harold's M.O. He was always prepared, which accounted for the fully charged high-beam flashlight in the glove box.

Gun in one hand and flashlight in the other, I crossed the gravel-pocked ground to the slightly open door of the gin. Drinking and necking no longer seemed to be teenage occupations. At least not here. The place had an air of eerie abandonment, as if no living human had visited in years.

As I stepped inside the building, a roost of mourning doves blew out of the rafters, the cackling noise and fan of frantic feathers almost stopping my heart. Old Leatherface couldn't have given as near fatal a start.

Once my heart rate calmed, I moved forward. My footsteps sounded loud in the quiet, and I tried to conjure up memories of close dancing with a high school beau, but those carefree days were out of my reach. I was alert for a killer, a woman warped by a desire for revenge. My body was tensed for Bonnie Louise to pop out of a dark corner like some demented—and deadly—jack-in-the-box.

Yet the gin seemed strangely empty.

Even as I'd driven there, I'd had the sense that I was being played. How or why, I didn't know. Why had Peyton called me? Or a better way of phrasing it was why had Bonnie Louise *allowed* him to call anyone, and most especially me? It was possible that her ultimate goal was to abduct me and hold me hostage in an effort to work out some kind of deal with Coleman. Had she known him at all, she would have deduced he wasn't the bargaining type.

But where was Bonnie? The gin was empty, as far as I could tell. I shone the flashlight beam around the interior. Shadows stretched and jumped causing adrenaline to flood my body to the point I thought I might be able to lift a car.

The place was empty.

A loud, tearing sound made me whirl, gun at the ready, until I realized a gust of wind had caught one of the old tin panels. Rusted nails screamed a complaint. Nothing else.

"Peyton!" My voice reverberated. I didn't anticipate an answer, so I wasn't surprised when there was only silence.

Why had Peyton—or Bonnie—brought me to this place? What had been accomplished?

That Oscar had been left alone? Was Bonnie Louise so far gone that she thought she'd attack Oscar in the hospital and finish the job she'd started?

That prompted me to pat my cell phone in my pocket. I could call Dewayne Dattilo and get him to provide some kind of security for Oscar's room. If Bonnie was so nuts she meant to kill Oscar no matter what, it might be best to have someone watch over him.

Reception in the tin building was nonexistent. I'd place the call when I returned to the car.

Which would be in about three minutes.

I'd made it to the end of the gin and found only dust, rust, and shadows. My time had been wasted.

As I eased toward the front door, something wet struck me in the top of the head. I sighed. Just my luck to walk under a dove with gastrointestinal issues. Lovely conclusion to a horrible day.

The bird poo oozed down my temple, and I wiped it away. Harold surely had a towel or hanky or cloth in his car. He was always prepared.

Another drop plopped on my hand. I swung the light to look. Dark, sticky, red. Not bird poop. Blood.

I swung the light instinctively, the dread of what I would see already building. Instead of Peyton, though, it was the petite figure of Bonnie Louise that hung from the rafter, swinging gently as if a faint breeze moved her.

Blood coated both hands, and as I moved the light along her arms, I saw the long, open slices on each wrist that indicated she'd wanted to die. Just to make sure, she'd stepped off the second-floor landing with a rope around her neck. She was nothing if not determined. And she was definitely dead.

I didn't scream or run. I was frozen by the sight as my

brain processed the scene. And the implications. If Bonnie had killed herself, where was Peyton?

Not even Bonnie Louise could be a kidnapper *and* dead.

I had to get out of that gin and fast. My sense that I was being played had been all too true—but not in the way I'd imagined. Several images leaped forward in my head—Bonnie's clothes and shoes in a drawer in her desk, Peyton's sly manipulation of information to put Bonnie in the worst light. Bonnie had never abducted Peyton. The exact opposite was true, which was why neither Cece nor Erin could identify Janks or Bonnie as their abductors. It had been Peyton all along.

"Hello, Sarah Booth."

Peyton's voice came from the doorway and I turned to face him, the flashlight and gun trained at the exit. There was no one there. I shifted the light left and right until the beam caught him emerging from the shadows near the right side of the door. It was possible he'd been there all along, watching me explore the old gin. Or he could have just stepped inside.

"Why?" My question needed no explanation. Peyton would understand.

"Have you ever had someone take something from you, Sarah Booth? Something more valuable than gold?"

That was the wrong question to ask me. The growl came out of my gut, clawing up my chest. He'd taken something from me. Something that dissolved my fear and made me think only of lashing out.

The flashlight beam showed me that he held a gun. As much as I ached to rip his throat out, I controlled myself.

"What was stolen from you, Peyton?" As far as I knew, Peyton had no history with Oscar. Fidellas was not a Sunflower County name. Peyton had no connection to the Carlisle land, or at least none that I had unearthed.

"Have you ever heard of D-79?" He didn't wait for me to answer. "Broad spectrum insecticide now used in almost all commercial agricultural endeavors. I created it. And Austin Janks stole my formula and took it to DeFoe, got paid a hefty sum for it, and then stole it from them and resold it again. He earned a fortune off my genius."

"Austin Janks is dead." Peyton was crazier than I thought. "He was killed in a break-in at DeFoe's South American plant years ago. Besides, that has nothing to do with the people of Sunflower County."

Peyton's laughter rang out, bouncing off the tin walls. "You miss the point of my whole scheme. Austin Janks is very much alive. Who do you think backed Jimmy's development ventures? It was his father, and he did it off the money he earned from the formula he stole from me. Such a clever man. But now he'll have to live with the fact that his son died because of his greed. He stole from me so I took from him."

"You hurt a lot of people to get back at one man."

"But ultimately, it'll be worth it. I'll be a wealthy man, thanks to Bonnie's research. Or I should say the research that Bonnie conducted along with Austin Janks."

"What are you talking about?"

"She was brilliant. She's worked years on a type of cotton that would yield two harvests. She had it, too. She was all ready to give the seed to local farmers. Give it away! To benefit the farmers. The only way I kept her mouth shut was to contaminate the weevils' feed with mold and make her believe that her cotton was responsible for a potential epidemic."

Not even I had gauged the depth of madness at work

in Sunflower County, and I'd greatly underestimated Bonnie Louise's real character. "You've known all along that Oscar and the others had been exposed to mold?" I'd wanted to beat Bonnie Louise when I thought she was responsible for the loss of my child. I wanted to kill Peyton. My finger felt the trigger of Harold's gun. One good shot and I'd take him out.

"Not even I understood the genetic changes the mold would produce in the weevils—or that they'd carry the deadly mold on their backs," Peyton said. "I was just lucky there. Seems like luck is on my side these days. Too bad for you."

"Your luck has run out." He was in my sights, and I would kill him if I had to.

The first shot whizzed by my cheek, missing by only a fraction of an inch. As I darted for cover, I fired at him blindly, twice, aiming at his body because Coleman had once told me that torso mass was easier to hit than a head.

Crouched behind an old piece of machinery, I tried to pinpoint his position with the light. He was nowhere to be found. Peyton obviously knew the gin far better than I did.

"At last, someone who fights back," Peyton said. In the darkness, his tone was amused. "You're a real bonus, Sarah Booth. When I conceived of my plan to settle an old score, I never figured on you, but you're the perfect ending to a well-plotted crime. Beaucoup will kill you and then take her own life. It's a little out of order, but I don't think the local law will deduce that. Especially not when I'm alive to tell them exactly how it happened."

I'd been so eager to finger Bonnie Louise as the culprit that I'd made a terrible miscalculation. So had Coleman. We'd all followed behind Peyton Fidellas like lemmings.

Exposing myself as little as possible, I swung the flashlight beam across the building until I found him again tucked behind a conveyor belt. There was a slight stain of red on his left arm. I'd winged him with one of my shots but done no real damage—unless I could keep him talking until he bled to death. Not likely.

"Why do you hate Oscar so much?" I asked.

His laughter grated on me. "Collateral damage, Sarah Booth. That's where you went off the track. You assumed Oscar was the target. Someone had to get sick from exposure to the mold, but I didn't care who it was. I'd planned on it being Jimmy Janks. Death by mold would be more satisfying than the gunshot I had to resort to."

My brain was working hard to process the new facts. Peyton had engineered the weevils, the mold, everything. And he'd set it up so that Bonnie Louise would take the blame. Now Bonnie would also take the blame for my death—assuming Peyton could actually kill me this time.

I had him in my flashlight beam, but he also had a good shot at me, because I held the light. It was a stand-off. "You should have killed me in that cotton field, Peyton. You'd already abducted Bonnie, and you took her shoes out of her desk and wore them to throw Coleman off."

"Another rash assumption, Sarah Booth. But let me say I had no idea you were pregnant. A misfortune. Then again, you would be dead otherwise."

The idea that he could be so cavalier about my miscarriage steadied my hand holding the gun. My finger tightened on the trigger. I had it within my power to kill him. He might get a shot off at me—but I might get him first.

The things that I wanted to say—before I pulled the trigger—were lodged in my throat. I couldn't speak of the loss of a child to this creature. I thought of Atticus Finch in *To Kill a Mockingbird*. There was a scene where a rabid dog had to be shot. Atticus, a man who abhorred violence, did what had to be done to protect his children.

It was too late to protect my child, but I could prevent a madman from harming others.

"Take the shot," he said, taunting me, stepping out into the open.

Perhaps I'd never forgive myself for killing a person, but it was a risk I was willing to take.

The blow came from the dark shadows beside me and felt like it snapped the bone in my arm. The gun jerked down, discharging harmlessly into the dirt floor, and fell from my useless fingers.

Peyton's laughter rang eerily off the metal walls of the building, and I swung the flashlight around to spotlight a blond woman, tall, slender, and composed.

Sonja Kessler lifted the bat she held. "You're a hard one to kill, Ms. Delaney," she said. "But this time, I won't miss."

She lifted the bat a fraction to give herself more leverage. In a second she'd swing the weapon and I had no doubt she meant to strike me in the head. She was framed in the beam of my light, and I was unable to move. My arm was useless, the hand hanging at an odd angle.

Just as she started the downswing, there was an explosion. Sonja spun as if a giant hand had twisted her. She cried out, a noise that sounded like cloth ripping.

"No!" Peyton's cry came from the other end of the building. I swung the light to show him rushing toward me, his gun pointed.

I had no idea what had happened. In the darkness, everything was a jumble, and I was totally unprepared for the next assault. Someone—not Peyton—hit me in the midriff, knocking me backward. The weight of a body fell across mine.

I caught a whiff of something exotic and sensual—Tinkie's perfume. Another shot rang out, and Peyton grunted. Then, in the darkness, there was the sound of someone tumbling into some of the equipment.

It took a moment for me to regain my breath.

"Don't move," Tinkie ordered.

My arm was killing me, but I had no intention of moving. "What are you doing here?" I asked.

"Saving your ass," she said sweetly. "You can thank me at any time."

"Thank you, Tinkie." I let the pain roll over me. "You're crushing the life out of me, not to mention my arm. I think she snapped the bone."

"Well, I haven't slept in a week. What's your point?"

"I think I'm going to faint." It was amazing, but the darkness of the building was not nearly as dense as the black that was moving in from the center of my brain.

"Don't you dare," Tinkie said. "Not after Coleman and I rushed out here to save you. The least you can do is stay awake and thank him."

"I'm not feeling all that chipper," I told her.

"Hang on, Sarah Booth." Coleman's voice came from the fringes of the darkness. "We'll have you out of here in two shakes of a lamb's tail."

I pondered the fact that to my knowledge there wasn't a single sheep in Sunflower County. Not that sheep couldn't live here. No ordinances against sheep existed. Somehow, though, sheep had chosen other locations.

Strong arms slipped under me and in the distance there were sirens. In my mind, the patrol cars were driven by sheep. The place where I'd drifted to was strange and wondrous and I had no desire to leave it. While I wasn't unconscious, I'd shifted to an alternate reality.

I opened my eyes to the familiar high-intensity light and acoustic tile ceiling of the emergency room. It was a view I knew too well. I was flat on my back on an exam table.

In the corner of the room, Doc worked on something, his back to me. Even as blurry as my reality was, I could tell by the stoop of his shoulders that he was exhausted.

"She's awake," Tinkie said. Her face came into focus. "Good thing you were asleep when Doc set your arm. It was awful, Sarah Booth. He had to pull and twist and the bone—"

"Sarah Booth!" Graf appeared on the other side of the table. His fingers brushed a strand of my hair away from my face. "Doc says you're fine. It was a compound fracture, but it should heal quickly." He tapped the cast for effect. "Cece picked the purple paisley wrap."

I noted my new fashion statement with some trepidation, but my concern was on the two people who'd tried to kill me. Twice. "Peyton? Where is he?"

"Down the hall, handcuffed to a bed." Graf spoke carefully. "He said you shot him, but he's going to be just fine."

Graf's gaze held mine. I nodded. "I did shoot him. I would have killed him if I'd been a better shot."

"Coleman will make sure he has his day in court," Graf said. He touched the corner of my eye and I realized I was crying. "You gave him a flesh wound, Sarah Booth, but I'm glad you didn't kill him. Let the justice system take care of him."

"Sonja? What about her? She's the one who hit me with the bat."

Tinkie answered. "She's in critical condition. Coleman shot her in the chest. A rib punctured her lung." She blinked back her own tears. "Nothing can ever make up for what she did, but I managed to get a few licks in before Coleman pulled me off her."

Another voice came from the foot of the bed. "Dahling, we're going to have to stop meeting this way." Cece, her face still bandaged, patted my foot. "I checked with Doc, and there's no possible way they could incorporate any type of plastic surgery into a broken arm. I thought maybe some silicone somewhere, but he said no." She tightened her grip on my foot. "But I did try for you. My new nose is going to be . . . perfection."

"Millie has come and gone," Graf said. He held up a stack of magazines. *The Globe. The Star. The National Enquirer*—Millie's favorites. "She left these for you to read while you heal."

Graf wiped my face with a cool cloth. "Coleman needs to speak with you. He's waiting in the hall. Are you up to it?"

"Yes. I have to tell him what I found out."

Tinkie kissed one cheek and Cece the other. Graf kissed my lips softly, giving me a promise that made my eyes burn with unshed tears.

They left the room, Doc stopping by to give me a thumbs up before he, too, exited. Coleman stepped up to the exam table and we were alone.

"So we have the illegitimate heir to the Carlisle plantation and a scientist in cahoots to frame Bonnie Louise McRae for this mess," I said. "Peyton meant to kill me and lay that at Bonnie's feet, too."

"Thank goodness he wasn't successful," Coleman said. His hand hesitated at my face, but then he brushed it gently across my cheek. "With Tinkie's help, we tracked the financial backing for Janks Development. It came from his father, who'd assumed the name of Jon Unger. He faked his death in South America, stole the formula, and reinvented himself as Unger."

"And Sonja? She must have flown to Jackson after I left her place in Chicago. She was in a hurry to get somewhere, but I never dreamed it was Mississippi."

"She's not talking."

I held out my hand and he gave me his so that I could pull myself into a sitting position. The room spun for a moment, but then it righted. My broken arm pulsed with a red devil pain that made me inhale.

"Maybe you should lie back down," Coleman suggested.

I shook my head. "I want to talk to Peyton."

"He won't talk to anyone," Coleman said.

"It really isn't about conversation." I eased to my feet. Even that gentle movement made my arm scream. I wasn't in a mood to take no for an answer.

29

The compromise I worked out with Coleman involved riding to Peyton's room in a wheelchair. As Coleman pushed me into the hallway, Graf stepped behind the chair and took his place. Coleman yielded the position without hesitation.

"He's in room 312," Coleman said as he fell back beside Tinkie, Cece, and Doc.

He wouldn't come with me. He had legal standards to uphold; I had blood in my eye. It was a testament to the bonds of friendship that Tinkie, Cece, Coleman, and Doc made no effort to halt me.

Graf pushed me down the hallway until we came to an open door. Oscar shuffled forward. He looked like hell, but he was on his own feet.

"Thank you, Sarah Booth." His voice cracked and he

cleared his throat. "I've thought all morning what to say to you. The only thing I've come up with is 'thank you.'"

"Not necessary, Oscar." Seeing him standing was enough for me. "Thank Doc. He's the one who figured it out."

He motioned down the hallway. "Regina and Luann went home and Gordon is next door. You should say hello to him. Looks like the worst is over. Fidellas and Kessler are under arrest . . ." His voice drifted into silence.

"Tinkie loves you more than you'll ever know," I told him.

"And the same applies to you." He shifted from foot to foot before he stepped forward and patted Graf's shoulder. "Take good care of her, Graf, she's a rare breed."

"I plan to do just that." Graf set the chair in motion but I waved him to a halt at Gordon's room. Now that Gordon was able to speak, he might be able to resolve one tiny part of the mystery. Graf tapped at the door and we entered.

The deputy was propped up on pillows in the bed. He looked like warmed over hell, but he greeted me with a wave.

"Gordon, do you remember when Lana Carlisle died?" I asked.

"It's funny. I can count on my hands the number of times I ever saw my father commit an act of kindness. That was one. I was out of the house by then, but I remember one night he was talking about it on the front porch."

"How do you mean an act of kindness?"

"Lana Carlisle had cancer. Ovarian. She was facing a long, difficult death. She got her ducks in order and killed herself. She fell down the stairs so it would look like an accident. She didn't want her kids to have to live with a suicide."

Of all the explanations, I'd never have guessed. But it made sense, in a strange way. Her visits back to West Point, the purchase of a cemetery plot. For years she'd yearned for her home, and once she knew she was dying, she made the arrangements to see that she would rest there for eternity.

"And Gregory?"

"The way he cheated on Lana, no one would've believed his love for her. In his own way, though, he did. That was one screwed-up family, no doubt about it. I remember the talk that Gregory had killed Lana or that Luther had killed them both, but I think in the end, Gregory took his own life."

If Gordon hadn't been comatose, he could have resolved at least this element, and perhaps I wouldn't have been so willing to believe that Luther was one of the primary criminals. As it stood, both Luther and Erin were pawns in a dangerous game.

Luther's greed had been his undoing and had nearly cost him his sister's life.

"Thank you, Gordon."

"I'm the one who owes you thanks, Sarah Booth. Especially you, but Tinkie, too. I'm glad you're home. Zinnia isn't the same without you."

His words moved me, but before I let my softer side take over, there was something I needed to finish. Graf maneuvered me out of the room and we traveled in silence down to Room 312. He halted the chair at the door. "Sarah Booth, I'll take care of this."

"I have to do this myself." I awkwardly pushed myself out of the chair. My arm throbbed, a bass note complimented by the tremolo of my other injuries. I didn't have a gun or a bat, but I'd work with what I could find.

"I'll be right outside the door."

"Keep everyone else out." I pushed open the door and stepped into the room where Peyton lay in bed, both arms conveniently handcuffed to the bed railing. I closed the door.

"I don't have anything to say to you." His tone was so cheerful, I fought the rage that washed over me. Three people were dead. Oscar, Gordon and two realtors had almost died. I'd suffered a personal loss he'd never understand.

"Talking isn't what I had in mind." I kept my voice as dead calm as a cotton field in August. I moved up beside the bed. "I want you to clearly understand how much I want to hurt you. I have this fantasy of you screaming."

The first doubt flickered across his face. "Where's the sheriff?"

"In another wing of the hospital. He's detained. Like Doc and the nursing staff and everyone else. For all practical purposes, it's just the two of us, Peyton."

He looked out the window and I walked around the bed and closed the blinds. The hospital wasn't totally modernized, and an old air-conditioning unit cranked out cool air. I flipped it to high so the fan rattled loudly.

When I faced him again, he wasn't so self-assured.

"What are you going to do?" he asked.

I accepted then that I didn't know. I'd followed my gut need to come here and hurt him, but my taste for blood had waned. Hurting Peyton wouldn't undo anything. It wouldn't even give me satisfaction. What really mattered was that my friends and fiancé stood behind me if that's what it took to help me heal. That was the important thing to remember. I started toward the door.

"Defeated so easily?" he asked.

I gave him one last look. "No, actually, victorious. I'm not capable of the things I ought to do. And in the long run, that's the real victory."

I left the door open as I settled into the wheelchair that Graf held. His arms came around me and the stubble of his beard tickled my cheek. "For what it's worth, I'm glad you couldn't hurt him."

"Yeah, me too." But I felt as if I'd fallen deep into a hole with no ladder to climb out.

Graf spoke softly in my ear. "He'll spend the rest of his life in prison. He'll suffer more there than with any physical harm you could deal him."

Graf's confidence was the sunlight at the top of the hole. I turned my face up to it and closed my eyes, hoping that it would be enough.

Dahlia House settled around me. I crept out of bed and with Sweetie Pie as my companion walked across the dew-soaked grass to the pasture where Reveler and Miss Scrapiron grazed.

The night was soft and drenched in the sadness of wisteria. Inside, Graf slept. We'd talked until the early morning hours, and he'd held me while I cried. Now, I was alone with the past and the sense of loss that was as familiar as my own reflection.

A clear soprano cut the night sky. "Ah, sweet mystery of life, at last I've found thee; ah, I know at last the secret of it all." Jitty came across the yard in a beautiful gown.

I leaned against the fence railing and enjoyed the spectacle. I'd never known that Jitty had an operatic voice, but then she was quite the chameleon.

When she finished the Victor Herbert lyrics, I applauded gently. "The version I remember is Madeline Kahn in *Young Frankenstein*."

"That would be the thing you remembered," she sniffed. "Try Jeanette MacDonald in a little movie called *Sweethearts*."

Jitty did resemble the chestnut-haired songbird. Still, I wasn't certain how opera had become part of my evening.

I waved a hand toward Dahlia House. "Graf is exhausted."

"He won't hear me. No one hears me but you, Missy. And even you don't listen."

"I've had sort of a rough day," I warned her. "I don't mind a musical serenade, but I don't want a lecture." To be honest, I'd dreaded confronting Jitty. She was the only person who could fully appreciate what had happened, and she would be as wounded as I was. That was an additional burden of grief I simply couldn't shoulder.

"Take a walk," she said.

Jitty was prone to strolling through the dewy grass in ball gowns, wigs, and glass slippers, so I fell into step beside her. I wasn't surprised when she aimed toward the family cemetery. Somehow, I'd known this night would end there.

The old wrought-iron gate creaked as I swung it open. My parents lay buried in the center of the plot, side by side, their tombstones plain. When they'd died, the fashion for grave markers had been simplicity. All of the details for their burial had fallen on Aunt Loulane, a woman overwhelmed with a grieving twelve-year-old.

"I should replace these stones," I said. "Something more representative of—"

"They serve a purpose."

I couldn't argue with that. "I like the older ones, the

flutes and angels and ivy columns. They tell something about the person."

Jitty, with a columned stone topped with ivy, a lute, *and* an angel, was buried beside my great-great-grandmother Alice. Friends in life, survivors of the nation's most tragic war, they'd been laid to rest side-by-side as the partners they'd been.

"Why are we here?" I asked.

"This is just a place, Sarah Booth."

"That's where you're wrong," I told her. "This is a destiny."

Her laugh was soft and warm. "Your mama would shake you 'til your teeth rattled for such foolishness."

At last, she made me smile. "Death and taxes—the only certainties."

"There's this moment. There's this land and these dogs and those horses. And that man asleep in your bed in that house."

"And in a next few seconds, it could all disappear." I ran my hand across the top of the smooth stone on my mother's grave. I would have a new one done. One that symbolized who my parents were. And Aunt Loulane, too. She'd gone for the simplistic approach when she'd preordered her own marker.

"Would you really want to know when it will end?" Jitty asked. "Madame Tomeeka gets a glimpse sometimes, but she doesn't know. And even that is TMI." She held up a hand like a sassy character in a TV commercial. "You don't want to know the time line of your life."

"I had everything. For a couple of months . . ."

Awareness dawned in Jitty's eyes. "I see now what ails you. Once before in your life, you had ever'thing. You had it all, love and safety and joy. Then your parents died, and you lost it. Since then, you've been tryin' to pull all of that back into your life. Then you had it again, until that Peyton Fidellas took it. But Doc says you're fine and healthy. No lingerin' ill effects. It's all still there, Sarah Booth."

"And what do I do to protect it?"

"The gettin' and the havin' are two very different positions to hold." She nodded. "Requires a different skill-set."

I sighed. She'd hit the nail on the head. "So what do I do? Every decision I make in the future could be the one that destroys it. Like when I decided to go with Peyton . . ."

"Self-doubt isn't the bed partner you want." Jitty's face had gone stern. "You took every precaution. You did your job to help Oscar. Ain't no profit in beatin' yourself up for the actions of a vile man."

She was right. Jitty was most often right. But the doubt still gnawed at me. "If I'd only—"

The live oak that shaded the cemetery whipped in a sudden wind. The branches rattled, throwing wild moon shadows over the tombs. "You keep that up and you'll surely lose everything." Jitty was stern. "I came out here to make a point." She held up a hand and took an operatic stance, her pure voice floating on the night. "All the longing, striving, seeking, waiting, yearning . . ." She stopped and walked closer to me, her gown and hair a pale shimmer in the moonlight. "For 'tis love, and love alone, the world is seeking," she sang on. And then she spoke. " 'Tis the answer, Sarah Booth. Now get in that house and stoke the fires of love. Because of you, Tinkie has a man to hug up on. Because of you, she has the life she almost lost."

I felt the wetness on my cheeks, but I wasn't crying. The pain was simply leaking out. "Thank you, Jitty. I'd expected you to be angry with me. I mean, you've waited so long for a Delaney heir."

She shook her head and indicated we should amble homeward. "I hate to see you suffer, Sarah Booth. But I have faith. In you and in the future."

I realized that she'd grown transparent. I could see Dahlia House through her beautiful gown. "Don't leave," I requested.

"Oh, you don't want me around." Her chuckle was soft and slightly wicked.

"What?"

And then I heard Graf calling me. He came out the back door, a flashlight in his hand. "Sarah Booth!"

"I'm here," I answered. My feet skimmed the wet grass as I moved from a walk to a jog. The jarring sent shock waves up my arm and ribs, but Graf flicked on the back door light and I could see him, silhouetted against the house that I'd grown up in and loved. Sweetie ran forward, baying a greeting.

"I woke up and you were gone. What are you doing outside?" He came down the steps and softly brushed my hair from my face.

I'd worried him, and it was good to be the focus of his concern. "I couldn't sleep. I went out to the cemetery."

His arm came gently around me. "Come inside, Sarah Booth. I'll make you some cocoa laced with a little Kahlúa." His body was warm against mine. "Remember when you were little and your parents read you to sleep. I'll read that script Federico sent to you."

I nodded, taking comfort from his strength. "That sounds like a plan."

Read on for an excerpt from

BONE APPÉTIT—

the next Sarah Booth Delaney mystery from
Carolyn Haines,
available in hardcover from Minotaur Books!

1

Spring smote the Delta and fled before the onslaught of
May heat. A thick haze of warmth hangs over the fields and
the rivers, blanketing the land and the cotton bursting from
the ground, green and vibrant. Hope is alive here, where
farming is still a way of life.

To my shame, hope has died in me. The loss of my child,
my potential son or daughter, has done something to me,
and I'm afraid it can't be repaired. While the cotton is growing and my partner's husband, Oscar, and Deputy Gordon
Walters have both fully recovered from the "plague" that
nearly killed them, I have not fared so well. At least not
emotionally. Doc says my body is healing fine. No permanent internal injuries, and my broken arm is all but mended.
There should be no ill effects.

So what's wrong with my heart?

Dahlia House, my family home, echoes with loneliness.

The familiar rooms are too big and empty in a way I never noticed. Perhaps this malaise of melancholy is hormone induced, as Cece Dee Falcon, my transgender friend who is an authority on the tricky role of endocrine chemistry, tells me. She assures me that my body will balance itself and that time will buffer this loss.

I wish I could trust her words. There are no known Delaney genes for moping, yet I can't seem to stop. Songwriter Jesse Winchester, says it best, it takes "nothing to pity yourself—but it's dangerous fun."

Unable to endure the shadows of Dahlia House, I've taken myself outdoors into the heat laden with the smell of summer. The scent of this sun-warmed land—the taste of it—is imprinted on my DNA. These fields have been my solace through so many losses, but I find no comfort here now. I walk to the oak grove behind the Delaney family cemetery—the place I saw my dead mother in a dream or vision or visit from the spirit world. She assured me I would recover from this miscarriage. I hope she'll return today to guide me to that path, but I know she won't. She's warned me about lingering in the past, and she won't facilitate my melancholy.

"You're damn right, she won't!"

Jitty, the resident haint of Dahlia House, has found me. Jitty has the tracking abilities of a Parchman prison bloodhound and the fashion sense of Jackie Kennedy or, on some days, Carrie Bradshaw. Therefore I'm stunned by her white apron and chef's hat. Jitty does not "do" domestic, despite the fact she was my great-great-grandmother Alice's nanny and best friend. What she does do is tap into my private thoughts—a habit I find more than annoying.

"Don't badger me, Jitty, I'm not in the mood," I warned her.

"Pull it together, Sarah Booth. Tinkie will be here any

minute to pick you up. You're packed and ready, so quit waffling. This trip will be good for you, and the Richmonds have spared no expense. Tinkie and Oscar are tryin' to bust you lose from the tar baby of grief. 'Course, instead of lettin' go, you keep pokin' in another appendage. Soon enough you won't be able to let loose."

"I'm not going to Greenwood."

"Says who?"

"Says me." My fingers brushed against the rough bark of an oak tree, igniting a tickle of childhood sensation, just a split second of the past. I don't want a vacation or a stay in a luxury boutique hotel. What I want is to time travel, to go back to a place where my parents are alive and I'm the protected and beloved child.

Jitty is having none of that. "Wrong. Tinkie has gone to a lot of trouble to plan this trip for you. From what I've seen, you can sure benefit from some cookin' classes. Girl, that handsome Graf Milieu is gonna wanna eat sometimes. Even movie stars got to feed the gullet on occasion."

"Then he can cook." My tone was reasonable, cloaking the deep sense of loneliness brought on by the mention of Graf's name. He was my man, and I needed him beside me even though my logical brain knew he could not walk out on a movie. "At the moment, Graf is building his film career, and he doesn't care if I cook or not. Eating at Millie's Café makes me happy. She's a better cook than I'll ever be."

Jitty eyed me. "*I* would be happy—if you'd eat. You go up there and stir the food around on your plate. You look like an abused greyhound."

"Nothing like a compliment to make a girl feel better." That she was right only made me more morose. I did look unhealthy. My skin was waxen, and I'd given up shirts that showed my protruding collarbone. I didn't wear grief well.

"You want some compliments? Then go down to Greenwood and relax with Tinkie. Take your mind off things here. Have some laughs." Her expression became sly. "You can kill two birds with one stone."

"What two birds?"

"One, get away from here and start to heal your heart, and two, let your business partner take care of you. She wants to do that, Sarah Booth. It's selfish not to let her." Tinkie and I co-owned Delaney Detective Agency, but she was so much more than half owner. She was my closest friend.

She'd planned a vacation getaway for us to the nearby town of Greenwood and the famous Viking Cooking School. While it was a ruse to pull me away from Dahlia House and my depression, it was also, as Jitty pointed out, a chance for Tinkie to care for me. Jitty was right, but the lethargy that tugged at my heart left me unable to move.

"Sarah Booth, only time can help you get by this, and pinin' away here, alone, is only prolongin' it."

Another point on Jitty's scorecard. I pushed away from the old oak. I had to fight this depression. I couldn't give in to it. The Delaneys were fighters, not quitters. "Okay."

The smile that spread across her face carried enough wattage to light up Dahlia House. "That's my girl." She fell into step beside me as we walked past the old cemetery shaded by cedars and toward the house. "Now focus your cookin' lessons on manly foods. None a' that froufrou stuff that don't satisfy. And remember, don't ever eat nothin' pink and foamy. Those are words to live by."

I stopped in my tracks. "Pink and foamy? Like what?"

"Like cherries or strawberries mixed with cottage cheese. Or none a' that pink mousse stuff." She shuddered. "Nothing crème-filled that's pink. Just take my advice and stay away from it."

I'd never known Jitty to have an anti-pink obsession. "There's more to this story."

"And I'd tell it, but your ride to vacationland is here."

Sure enough, I heard the crunch of tires on the shell drive. Though the house blocked my view, I knew my coach and driver had arrived in the form of a brand-new Cadillac with Tinkie behind the wheel.

"Have fun." Jitty swept off the chef's hat as she faded into oblivion—a trick I was determined to learn if I ever got stuck between Earth and the Great Beyond.

"Sarah Booth! Sarah Booth!" Tinkie's little fists beat at the front door as she called my name.

"I'm in the backyard," I yelled. I put my ass into gear and trotted around the corner of the house to meet my friend.

"Your chariot awaits," she said, waving at the brand-new tomato red Caddy Oscar had given her as a gift.

"Let me grab my bags."

A silver bowl of green apples centered the marble registration desk of the Alluvian Hotel. I sampled some iced peach tea in the lobby as Tinkie checked us in. Although I wasn't P.I.-ing, I did deduce that the Alluvian had a great dental plan—the hotel staff all smiled, displaying handsome teeth.

The lobby was quiet, a reflection of the noon hour, and cool, a tribute to man's ability to air-condition. A bar and restaurant branched off one side of the lobby, and a series of lounging areas were on the other side. Peeking into a room, I could imagine folks gathered around the grand piano in a far corner.

Across the street was the famed Viking Cooking School. Delta ladies entered and exited with shopping bags full of kitchen spices and the latest in equipment and gadgets.

Tinkie and I were scheduled to take classes at the school in a matter of hours.

"Ready?" she asked. A bellman loaded our bags on a cart.

"Absolutely."

Tinkie offered separate rooms, but I'd opted to share one. After all, the point was to battle the loneliness, not give in to the desire to hide in the dark. The bellman took our luggage to the top floor, where a chilled bottle of champagne and a pitcher of orange juice awaited us in a room that gave a view of downtown Greenwood.

"The hotel staff thinks of everything, don't they?" Tinkie said, popping the cork with proficiency.

She mixed mimosas in crystal champagne flutes. Indeed, the hotel supplied a polished touch. She kicked off her shoes and climbed into one of the double beds. "So, we have our first class this afternoon. It's party appetizers. When we get home, Sarah Booth, let's have a party. We can show off our new entertaining skills."

"You assume I'll acquire some." The mimosa was delicious, and I settled onto my bed. The tension in my shoulders lessened.

"Oh, we'll both be prepared to dazzle guests when we finish this course."

From the hallway came a loud thumping and banging. Tinkie and I both started to our feet. What sounded like a scuffle ensued, and someone pounded on the door of our room. Before we could react, the door flew open and two beautiful young women tumbled in. They were almost buried in luggage, which they unceremoniously dumped to the floor.

"Who put us in the same room?" the brunette growled.

"I'm going straight to the desk." The blonde picked up a huge suitcase and tossed it into the hall where it slammed against something—or someone.

Tinkie calmly put down her drink and picked up the telephone. She punched in the number for the front desk. "Yes, this is Mrs. Oscar Richmond. We have intruders in our room. Please come immediately." She hung up with a smile.

Both young women finally realized they had an audience. They stood, luggage up to their thighs, and stared at us.

"Who the hell are you?" the brunette asked.

"Tinkie Bellcase Richmond." She hoisted her drink as if in a toast. "Don't bother with your name. You won't be staying long enough for me to give a damn." She settled back onto the bed. Tinkie had taken an instant dislike to the women, which was unusual for her.

The brunette rose to the challenge. "Wanna bet? We'll have those beds stripped and you out on your ass before the flies can settle on you."

The blonde, petite and wide-eyed, put a restraining hand on the brunette. "Calm down, Karrie."

Karrie shook her off. "Don't touch me, you country-fried hick. If this old bat wants a fight, I'll give it to her." Karrie, whoever she was, had seriously misjudged Tinkie. While my partner was short, she could kick ass like a Spartan.

Tinkie slid to her feet. She was a good ten inches shorter than Karrie, but she was undaunted. Tinkie and her eight-ounce dustmop dog, Chablis, had more courage and spunk than a busload of gang members. "Who, exactly, are you calling an old bat?" she asked, advancing.

I snapped to, aware that for the last three minutes I hadn't been depressed at all. "Hold on, Tink," I said. I fell in beside her. If there was going to be a hair-pulling, Tinkie and I were going in together.

The blonde stepped between Karrie and Tinkie. "Stop it. We obviously have the wrong room." She pushed Karrie's bags toward the door. "Let's go to the desk and get this straight. I want another roommate, anyway."

Karrie wasn't ready to back down. She glared at Tinkie. "Do you have a daughter in the contest? You're too old to cut the competition."

"I may have a few years on you, honey, but genetics tell all," Tinkie said. "Your bone structure gives it away—some combination of Snopes and Wicked Witch of the West."

"What contest?" I couldn't help myself. I felt like my earlier wish had been partially answered and I'd fallen backward in time to high school. I'd actually been aiming for grammar school, but time travel is hard to predict.

"The Miss Viking beauty contest and spokesperson competition," the blonde answered with a world-weary roll of her eyes. "The finalists are here this week for the cook-off and the runway talent contests. The winner gets a $200,000 contract to serve as Viking spokesperson and travel the world, not to mention scholarships and potential endorsements of food products worth millions."

"Fascinating," Tinkie said.

"I'm Crystal Belle Wadell." The blonde made it clear the rhyming of her name caused her much grief. "That's Karrie Kompton." She pointed at the brunette. "She's already way ahead in the Bitch on Wheels category and she's about to win the Most PMS-ing title."

"I see," Tinkie said in a droll tone that told me Crystal Belle had amused her.

"Ladies, you obviously have the wrong room. Best to take this up with the desk." I'd enjoyed the fireworks, but now I was done with it.

And just in time, two hotel staffers appeared in the doorway. In a matter of moments, Karrie and Crystal were assisted down the hallway. A door slammed and loud complaints blasted from both women as the hotel staff did their best to resolve the roommate issue. From what I overheard, the lodging decisions had specifically been made at the request of the contest manager—someone with a wide streak of sadism or who'd perhaps grown weary of the spectacular bitchiness of Karrie Kompton. I felt a brief second of pity for Crystal Belle.

"Surely all the contestants can't be that awful," Tinkie said, somewhat echoing my thoughts.

"Might be worth catching the talent competition if it's being held locally."

Tinkie's face lit up. "Excellent idea. I'll check at the desk for tickets or information. For now, let's have a facial. The spa across the street has this to-die-for facial. Then we're on to appetizer school at four o'clock."

She babbled happily about beauty products I'd never heard of as we refilled our glasses with mimosas and ambled across the street for a full beauty treatment.

2

Even I, a non-cook, was dazzled by the Viking Cooking School. I donned my apron and stood surrounded by state-of-the-art appliances that actually had me thinking of whipping up a batch of . . . well, nothing specific came to mind, but I wanted to create some magnificent edible concoction. Such is the power of fancy tools. I couldn't help but wonder if the same would apply if someone put a really nice drill into my hands. Would the urge to "do" carpentry come with the tool?

"Earth to Sarah Booth! Earth to Sarah Booth!" Tinkie tugged at my sleeve. "What in the world are you thinking?"

"About carpentry," I admitted.

She shook her head. "Don't even try to explain." Her smile told me that whatever my mental deficiencies, I looked more relaxed. She gave me a big hug. "Let's make those appetizers."

I'd never considered appetizers had a history, so it was interesting to learn the Athenians introduced the first hors d'oeuvre buffet. Even more fascinating was the concept that appetizers are meant to *whet* the appetite. I'd always assumed they were designed to keep guests from chowing down like porkers at the main course.

Tinkie, of course, was a scholar in this field. We chopped, blended, whirred, and designed our Bouche Cream Cheese Prosciutto into elegant scoops nestled in crystal star-shaped holders and garnished with cross-cut cherry tomatoes. We then turned our hands to Miniature Quiches as light and delicate as the flowers they resembled. During the process I watched Tinkie with pleasure. She loved to cook—as long as it wasn't part of her job description. She cooked for pleasure, not necessity, and her parents and Oscar provided her a life that allowed such an attitude. Tinkie had married well.

To my surprise, the class was a total delight. When we finished, Tinkie and I headed back to the Alluvian and a revitalizing cocktail. The hotel bar was jammed with beautiful young women, and we found a table in the corner and sat back to watch the interaction.

Karrie held court at the bar, surrounded by a half dozen well-dressed men who did everything except chew her martini olive for her. Beauty is a powerful weapon, and those men had been mortally gaffed. They hung on Karrie's looks, flirtations, and expressed whims.

A dark-haired woman, half in shadows, sitting alone in the farthest corner of the bar, caught my attention. Black eyebrows over china blue eyes, delicate cheekbones, and full lips—she looked like a movie star.

"Who's that?" Tinkie asked.

I shook my head. "Never saw her before, but she is striking."

"She's got a burn on for Karrie Kompton." Tinkie, too, had observed the way the dark stranger's gaze drilled holes in Karrie's back.

"Somehow, I can understand that." We clinked our glasses in a toast.

"Think she's part of the beauty pageant thing?" Tinkie asked.

"Yeah, I'd say so. The other women seem to know her, but I wonder why no one is sitting with her."

"Maybe she has cooties," Tinkie said.

"And I thought we'd been time-warped back to high school. Now I see we've regressed all the way to second grade, where classmates are infested with that legendary parasite."

"Seriously," Tinkie said. "I've been watching the interaction. The other girls act like they're afraid of our Dark Stranger."

I signaled the barkeep for another round of cosmopolitans. Despite Jitty's admonitions, we were drinking pink in honor of Cece Dee Falcon, who would join us as soon as she finished a deadline at the *Zinnia Dispatch*, where she was society editor and chief investigative reporter. It was an unusual combination of journalistic work, but then all the best crimes in the Mississippi Delta involved high society. She had the background knowledge on debutants and debuts, soirées, socials, engagements (broken and otherwise), marriages (those that held and those that didn't), and other information crucial to a good juicy story when a crime spree broke out amongst the landed gentry.

Cece had also been a part of the landed gentry until she went to Sweden and had the part of her that bore the name Cecil permanently excised. Her family had disowned her, but Cece carved out a new life for herself from the ruins of her old one. She had strength I could only envy.

The bartender brought our drinks, and Tinkie motioned him closer. "Who's that woman in the corner?" she asked.

"Hedy," he said without hesitation. "Really nice gal, unlike some of the other contestants." He glared at Karrie's back. "Some of these girls think the whole world spins in an orbit around them."

Before he could collect our empties, a bouquet of white roses as wide as the doorway waddled into the room on two human legs.

"Karrie Kompton?" a rough, low voice said from the midst of the flowers.

"For me?" Karrie squealed with the best sorority girl abandon I'd heard in years. "Oh, look, everybody, someone sent me flowers."

While the bartender rushed over to help the deliveryman put the flowers in a safe place, Karrie snatched the card and ripped it open. Her face flushed with pleasure, and she tapped her glass with a cigarette lighter to make everyone hush.

"Everyone! Shut! Up! I want to read my card." She cleared her throat. "'A gift for the fairest princess in the land. Knock 'em dead.'" She fluttered the note and squealed again. "It's signed, 'Your secret admirer.' Isn't that just the best? A secret admirer. It's so . . . romantic."

The deliveryman produced a giant box and handed it to Karrie. "This is also for you." He stood a moment and when it became clear she had no intention of tipping him, he gave her a disgusted look and left.

One thing about Karrie Kompton: She knew how to play a moment to the hilt. She held out the box, shook it lightly, and then very carefully untied the pink organdy ribbon that adorned an ornate, foil-stamped, fuchsia box. Chocolates were my guess.

When she lifted the lid, instead of a squeal, she sighed

with pleasure. "Look at this. I've never seen chocolates like this before. They're so big and dark and expensive looking."

The girls and male admirers all leaned in to examine the box. Even after eating a dozen or more appetizers, I couldn't stop my mouth from watering. Chocolate was definitely my weakness, and Karrie had the ability to make others want what she had, even a box of candies. I waited for her to pass them around to her friends. Instead, she picked one out and held it up for all to see.

"It's like a chocolate shell," she declared, turning it this way and that. "And stamped onto the top is an exact replica of the crown I'm going to win. These had to have been handmade just for me."

"Eat the damn thing or put it down," Crystal Belle Wadell finally said. "You aren't going to share, so just eat it and shut up about it. Brook, Janet, Gretchen—let's go find out about our schedules."

The four young women stood.

"Jealous because I have a secret admirer?" Karrie taunted. Her laughter danced around the room. "I'll bet this is a gift from one of the judges."

The audacity of her statement made Tinkie's eyes widen. "What an instigator she is," Tinkie whispered. "I'm surprised one of the other contestants hasn't whipped her ass."

"The night is still young." I sipped my drink as Karrie teased the other contestants with her flowers and candy. She had a genuine talent for torment, and everybody in the bar, including Tinkie and me, couldn't stop watching. Whatever Karrie lacked in kindness, or even basic human decency, she made up in spades with the ability to mesmerize an audience.

Two women stepped into the bar, one a bit older than me and the other obviously one of the contestants. Pale and elfin, she had an ethereal quality. When she turned around, I checked to see if she sported fairy wings. Whoever she was, she was lovely. And the older woman was attractive, too. The possibility that they were sisters crossed my mind.

"Amanda, let's order something in the room," the older one said.

"I want to stay here, Mother."

My relationship questions were answered. Mother and daughter. If I were a beauty contestant, I'd want my mother with me for moral support. Hey, given my druthers, I'd have my mom around for all occasions.

Karrie reclaimed the floor as she eased the candy to her mouth. She did it slowly, playing to her audience. She placed her perfect white teeth on the delicacy, and then she slowly bit the candy in half.

To my utter horror, the half she still held in her hand began to move. Hairy legs protruded, and the back half of a giant cockroach fell onto the bar and began crawling crazily around. Headless, it had no sense of direction.

Karrie froze. She stared at the half-a-roach, which wouldn't accept its own death. The most intriguing expression passed across her face, and then she spat chocolate and roach all over the bar.

Shouts, shrieks, and screams of laughter erupted. Pandemonium ruled. Tinkie and I stood on our chairs for a better view of a fistfight between several of the contestants. Women shoved and trampled one another to get away from Karrie. Ingeniously, Tinkie clicked photos of the mayhem with her cell phone.

Someone pushed the candy to the floor, and in the melee, people stepped on the chocolates, freeing more roaches that had survived being dipped in chocolate and were understandably pissed off. The area around Karrie was an expanding disaster.

"Holy Christmas." Tinkie was having a blast. "Can you believe that? Someone sent her chocolate-covered roaches. That is too creepy." And then she burst out laughing. Karrie didn't generate a lot of sympathy. At least not from Tinkie. Or me. I was enjoying the spectacle as much as she was.

I looked over to see Hedy's reaction. She was gone. As were the mother-daughter duo. The roaches sent a lot of people scurrying, but a team of Alluvian staff arrived to work damage control.

"How hard would it be to chocolate-coat a roach?" I asked. "Maybe just heat a little chocolate—"

"You wouldn't even have to do that. There's a product that hardens instantly on cold surfaces. Someone froze those roaches—like fishermen do catalpa worms—then coated them in chocolate and got them over here before they thawed enough to eat their way out of the shells."

"Someone really doesn't like Karrie Kompton." My smile was painfully wide.

"We'll have to remember this. The day might come when we want to make our own chocolate delivery." Tinkie loved mischief.

We raised our glasses and drained them. "Thank you, Tinkie. This was exactly what I needed."

We'd just ordered another round when Tinkie's cell phone rang. Cece had been delayed at the newspaper and would come the next evening for sure. When Tinkie relayed the roach episode, Cece wanted Tinkie's photos for the newspaper.

Tinkie held the phone so we could share it. "Cece wants to hire us to cover the beauty contest until she gets here."

For some reason, that appealed to me. "Sure."

"We're on," Tinkie agreed into the phone.